# BOCAGE

### Charles Birmingham

The Cider Circle Press — Laguna Beach, CA

ISBN: 978-0-692-16520-1

Library of Congress Control Number: 2018915142

*Bocage* | Charles Birmingham

Available Formats: eBook | Paperback distribution

# DEDICATION

To Jane, my occasional copy editor and eternal beacon. Thank you for finally reading the last chapter and *Allez les Bleus* 2018!

# Table of Contents

# PREFACE

These early interviews may never see the light of day because they tell a crazy story that may ultimately be understood and appreciated only in the narrow circle of the initiated. They will describe my improbable and minor role in one of the greatest crusades in history along with the individual stories of the brave men and women who seized a moment in time 75 years ago to save the world through sheer force of will.

I am privileged to have been one of them, albeit as a reluctant conscript at first. It must be said, however, that the threat that we confronted then remains largely unabated now.

Our gains against the evil that is hidden in the folds of time, space, motion and matter came at great loss to which I will attest in my story. But as someone very close to me, who will be at my side in the fight ahead, once told me, *the darkest times create the brightest moments.*

# I. GHOSTS

# MONTGOMERY INTERVIEW I

It was a dark night, which is a statement, because I live in the land of dark nights in the middle of cornfields and cow pastures in Northern France, in the Bocage, among the celebrated and, at one time, deadly hedgerows of Normandy, jogging distance from the D-Day invasion beaches.

The darkness in the Bocage that cloaks the looming and ubiquitous hedgerows for which this part of France is known is a like a black hole whose gravitational pull has captured for eternity the roar of the men who fought and died here over half a century ago. You can hear them in the fusillades of wind and rain that come and go on almost a daily basis in Normandy.

I was buzzed that evening by the high-test, homemade Calvados from the bottomless bottle offered to me before, during and after dinner with Madame Broc and her husband. Monsieur Broc was at it again with his creepy stories about the Nazi ghosts who still roamed the countryside and could often be seen standing just outside his gate.

Everyone here knew, but no one spoke of it, he said with a wild look on his pickled face.

For crying out loud, I had my own ghost to deal with, but I would soon learn that Monsieur Broc was not a total nut job. Finally, Madame Broc put an end to his inebriated babbling with a not-so-subtle kick to his ankle.

Fortunately, I made it home that night, although to be honest, I don't remember how. I live just a couple of kilometers away from the Broc's separated by fields of new wheat and rape seed.

I drove from our front gate hidden in an ancient stone wall along an ageless country lane down our long driveway flanked by its honor guard of winter lime trees and spotted the light on in our house. I didn't bother to go back to shut the gate.

When I see that light in the window, I have a micro-millisecond of hope that she would come to the door to greet me with a beautiful smile that could light the darkest night and banish its demons. I would even have enjoyed being scolded for drinking too much.

But now she never came.

I trudged from my Peugeot 308 across the gravel driveway to the front door. I dragged my feet like a child to accentuate the crunching sound of my footsteps. By the time I reached the front door, I had created an ankle-deep berm of gravel. I entered an empty house.

There was still some Gigondas left in the pantry from the night before when I polished off a boat load of oysters from Asnelles, so I grabbed a glass and finished the bottle. I sat in our dining room dominated by a large oak table and heavy wooden ceiling beams of the same dark oak staring at my reflection in the now opaque front window. I didn't have the energy to light the old wood burning stove.

The house that Jane and I bought almost a decade ago was an 18th century cottage built with stone from the Caen quarries, the same cream-colored stone used by many of the great European castles and cathedrals. It was attached at a right angle to a barn made of the same stone that was twice the size of the cottage. You can still see the old hayloft, which is now the window of a guest bedroom.

We slept, that is I sleep alone now, above the kitchen on the cottage side under the exposed wooden eves of the finished attic. The window next to my bed looks out on Madame Jardin's pasture next door now occupied by a few chubby sheep huddling against a stone wall.

From the same vantage point, one can also see a formal English garden roughly the size of an Olympic swimming pool. We bought the house from a famous landscape architect who once flew palm trees hanging from helicopters to the Riviera for Jagger. There are no palm trees in our garden, but it is brimming with castle hedges, wild and cultivated roses of all colors, which were then in full bloom that evening in July, and my prized cider apple trees just beginning to bud in what we call the cider circle. We tried our hand at making cider and an apple-based liqueur called *pommeau*, but we laughed every time we did because we could barely drink the rotgut we produced.

The ancient stone wall protected us on one side of the garden while on the other side of the garden a large six-meter-tall *fuck-off* hedge shielded us from our neighbors on Chemin de Breholliere. I will come back in due course to the part the garden plays in this story.

It had all been a tidy life for us to be sure in a warm house wrapped in a lush garden protected by a large stone wall along an obscure country lane sheltered by towering hedgerows. *Was,* that is.

We loved Normandy and the house. It was unlike anything that we had ever known back in the States. We called it our alternate reality.

Our place is about ten minutes outside of Bayeux, a prosperous town known for its historic tapestry. Yup, you guys are men of the world and have clearly done your homework – very good.

The Bayeux tapestry is in fact not a tapestry but a 271 foot long medieval embroidery that depicts the Norman Conquest of England in 1066, remarkable as a work of art and important as a source for 11th-century history. And, yes, you are right again, a tapestry is generally woven on a loom and an embroidery is done stitch by stitch like the Bayeux "tapestry" itself.

We are also a few minutes from Arromanches where we buy our baguettes in the morning.  Yes, right again.  Arromanches is the home of the artificial harbor built by the Allies soon after D-Day and which they used for 10 months to land over 2.5 million men, 500,000 vehicles, and 4 million tons of supplies. Winston Churchill had conceived of the idea as early as 1917, and they called it Port Winston.

We were within walking distance of Gold
Beach, one of the five landing beaches on D-
Day or *Le Choc,* as the French liked to call it.
Juno and Sword beaches are to the East, while
Omaha and Utah sit to the West. Omaha Beach
and the American Cemetery there are barely a
20-minute drive from the house.

We were living most of the year in
Normandy because I am a history buff, and
Jane always had a natural affinity to France
and spoke the language like a native. I can fool
the natives for about ten seconds because I
have a pretty good accent, but they catch on to
me quickly.

I was still trying to figure out then whether
I could love it without Jane because she and I
had been inseparable since we met in
Philadelphia. She had been stepping down as a
principal in the ballet company there to teach
and I was nearing the end of my eight-year run
as a cornerback with the Skins.

We met for the first time in a deli on Locust
Street in Philly the afternoon before one of my
away games against the Eagles. Although she
liked to give me shit that I was more interested
in the fact that Pete Rose was at the table next

to us than I was in her. There was probably some truth in that.

Jane refused to believe that the short, blonde guy with mutton chop sideburns, who was trying to pick her up that day, could play in the pros. But I did and, as slow and as small as I was compared to what they put on the field today, no opponent took me lightly.  I made up for my size with intensity and made captain of the defense my last five years on the team.

Fortunately, I got out with my knees and noggin intact and found a place called Silicon Valley at a time when any chump with an idea and some hutzpah could make his mark. I still have a hand in an investment or two there.

But the sad fact that I have been nibbling at in this interview so far is that Jane is gone. Not gone in the sense of going to the village to buy a baguette gone. Jane is over a cliff gone. Dead and gone. "Done gone," as the country music writers liked to say when we lived in Nashville.

She went over a 60-meter cliff on the English Channel – Cap Manvieux named for our village. She loved to jog to the Cap every morning. That day it was barely dawn, and I would like to think that if it happened there, it was an accident and that it was quick and painless. There had been a huge landslide that buried her running path from the Cap to the rocky beach below or that is what they say.

Jane and I had often joked about going over the cliff together as our answer to long term care. But this was no joke. I knew Jane too well to believe for a moment that this was deliberate on her part, and she was too clever and agile for it to be an accident. So, what was it? What had really happened?

She did not leave a note if it had been deliberate. Jane wasn't the most sentimental person that I had ever known but, hell, she would have left me a note if she knew what she was about to do -- even if it were simply to remind me to take the trash out to the gate on Friday morning.

All that was found was a bloody running shoe. It had been high tide that morning, so the prevailing wisdom was that she had been washed into the English Channel rather than buried under the slide. She could possibly wash up on the beach here in several weeks, I was told, or be found wrapped around a sounding buoy near Calais or Le Havre.

The French Gendarmerie searched the area. I told them about the older man who lived in a little camper near the cliff who might know something. Jane had always said that he was polite although his exceptionally large dog was not.  It bit her the first time that they had encountered each other. A small nip but it left an ugly bruise. There had been no sign of him or his camper or the mutt when the authorities had searched the area.

I hired a private detective, actually two, but only one has stuck. The first person that I turned to was my friend Roddy in London who is a former MI6 spook.  He offered to help me find someone but steered me clear of the posh club of desk chair gumshoes in Westminster, as he described them, who would soak me for thousands of Euros, all for naught.

I took it upon myself first to hire a ne'er-do-well Brit, who was recommended by our commune's mayor because he had done this kind of work in the U.K. He arrived for our first meeting with his wife from Baltimore (an heiress I was told) and his two unruly toddlers who ground chocolate croissants into my veranda floor with their trainers. He was fashion forward in a uniquely British way and sported a shock of dyed blonde hair that was every bit as big as his sense of self-importance.

The Brit also said that he did gardening, so what the hell, I hired him for that too. A week later he accidently cut the electrical cord that powered our electric hedge clippers while he was using them. He survived but with bad burns on his hands, so I let him go with my best wishes for a speedy recovery. What a dick: him for being a dick and me for hiring him.

Roddy then put me on to a Tunisian by the name of Mondher, who had grown up in Marseilles but had spent that last 15 years in Normandy. Mondher had done some contract work for Roddy's former colleagues and came highly recommended.

Roddy said that Mondher had a multitude of connections in France including a sinister group of friends who for a price could find anyone or anything. The main advantage to using them was that very often they were the ones who had made off with the missing item or person in the first place.

However, this was not the case with Jane, although Mondher quickly offered a theory of the case that rang true. Apparently, there had recently been a rash of shootings and fatal car accidents up and down the Normandy coast, along with a suspicious fire that had incinerated a large chateau in Crepon. The common thread seemed to be a witness that the authorities were trying to find – an older dude with a dog living nearby in a trailer with Dutch license plates.

Despite my honest efforts to find Jane on my own, I had become a marked man to the Gendarmes in Bayeux. The dearth of evidence and absence of facts were the ideal conditions for the local magistrate in Bayeux to schedule a hearing to ascertain how and why I had murdered my wife.

Our local magistrate was a plump and officious woman of about 45 with a wall eye that confused most of us at my preliminary hearing. You had to calibrate whether you were the target of Madame Leroyer's good eye, in which case she was addressing you, or her bad eye, in which case you were likely to mistakenly answer a question that had been intended for someone else.

Madame Leroyer had obviously never studied the investigative styles of Lieutenant Colombo or her own countryman, Inspector Magret, who through patience and deduction from cleverly oblique questioning always trapped the bad guy. After one or two preliminary softballs, she cut to the chase at the hearing, *so, Monsieur Montgomery, how were you involved in the harm that befell Madame Montgomery?*

Subtle, right?

Well,  I was fortunate that day because the hearing was set for 11:00 in the morning but got started late at roughly 11:15. It ended abruptly at Noon because one of the immutable laws of French life is the sanctity of the lunch hour. Noon is the hour when all business stops, and a two-hour lunch break begins. Madame Leroyer dismissed me and said, as she hurriedly organized her papers, that there would be a follow-up hearing.

They didn't book me; they didn't even take my passport. They would, however, trail me from time to time because I would occasionally see the Gendarmes' blue van barely concealed in a stand of trees at the end of Chemin du Village as I drove from my house into Bayeux or Arromanches.

Or they would occasionally pull up behind me if I took a longer trip on the N13 and hang on my tail for several kilometers. Perhaps they thought that the threat of a fender-bender would break me.

So back to that evening. I finally brushed my teeth to get rid of the increasingly stale taste of Gigondas and Calvados and thought about locking the front door but didn't. Fuck it. If a French Dick and Perry were heading down the driveway, then so be it.

From my bed in the attic, I could look through the sunken door then past the green wooden banister and make out the rough stonewall at the far end of the dungeon room in the house below. We used it as our living room.

We called it the dungeon room because it was a dark, sunken room next to our wood beamed dining room that had one small window in thick stone walls and black leather furniture. Jane hated the furniture; I loved it, although you would never have found this stuff in any self-respecting French dungeon.

Jane and I could navigate the steps from the attic easily in the pitch dark, as it was all muscle memory for us – dancer and jock -- four steps down to the attic door, right turn, eleven steps to the stone landing, left turn, and two steps to the dungeon room floor.

To sleep, perchance to dream. Sleep always came quickly to me as I am a borderline narcoleptic. It is a trait I had cultivated because my father was an Air Force sergeant whose family spent countless hours in waiting rooms for transport from one of his postings to another and because in my early years with the Skins, I roomed with a 300-pound defensive lineman who snored.

But I had not been much of a fan of my dreams lately. I slid the toggle switch to the off position on the little lamp next to the bed, which looked like a fake candle in a fake candle holder. The sliver of dungeon room disappeared from sight as everything went pitch black, on that dark night, in our dark house, in my dark world.

******

It was a pang of gas that woke me. A hint of apple flavored nausea. I looked at the clock and knew that I had to go downstairs and pee because I couldn't hold it for another four hours until the sun came up.

But I was lolled back to sleep as I always was having seen the hint of light from the kitchen reflecting against the rough stone of the dungeon room wall and having heard the faint scraping of a dining room chair. Fantastic, Jane's putting the coffee on. I sighed and felt good and dozed off.

Moments later, the nausea returned like a cascading wave, as I shot straight up in a cold sweat. My chest felt like a pulling offensive guard had speared it.

The light was on. Fuck me. Did I leave it on?

And then there was the voice. Was it a British accent? What the fuck? It is three in the morning in the French countryside, and I feel like puking my guts out, and there is a fucking British guy in my house?

And then there was another voice. American? My nausea was getting worse, and the shits were lurking just around the corner.

I got up on wobbly legs to face whatever it was, just as Jane had faced her last few moments alone. The morbid thought crossed my mind that I may be about to join her.

There was the scrape of the chair again on the stone tile of the dining room floor. I knelt and listened for a minute.

Then the adrenalin hit. Game time. Steeling myself for battle, I took a deep breath, clenched my sphincter to keep the diarrhea at bay and took the steps in stride – 4, 11, and 2. There was no fucking way people were going to fuck with me in our house.

I sensed movement as I turned the corner from the dungeon room to the dining room and let out a growl, ready for contact.

# MONTGOMERY INTERVIEW II

And there they were. Two of them. The first sat at the near end of our dining room table with a cocktail glass full of my Pommeau. He was slender and looked like David Niven. And he was sitting as if he were standing at attention.

The second was a stud with a lantern jaw who was built like a middle linebacker. He was stoking the fire in the wood burning stove at the far end of the table and was working on a super-sized bottle of my Coke Classic, which he held in one hand. The French neighbors love Coke Classic.

They were both dressed oddly like the French do here on D-Day when they put on period military costumes and traipse from one invasion beach celebration to the next in vintage jeeps and Red Cross trucks.

Before I could open my mouth for a war cry, David Niven said, *good evening, Charley or should I say good morning, I am Captain Richard Percival of the Green Howards Regiment attached to the Special Operations Executive, but they call me Bobby*. He said this with the practiced smirk of someone who knew that you were wondering why someone by the name of

Richard would call himself Bobby rather than Dick. This was the Brit.

Then the squarely built stud with a shock of blonde hair on his white walled flattop introduced himself as Babe Caffo with what seemed to me to be a Philly accent. He was as informal as Bobby was formal, *Mornin. I'm Babe Caffo, Army Rangers, 2 Battalion, and I am attached to Bobby,* he said grinning.

Then my gut gave way, 30 feet of large and small intestines ready to blow, and I covered the 10 feet of ground between me and the bathroom door just beyond Babe and the wood burning stove like I was closing on an opposing wideout.

It took a few minutes to purge and collect myself before rejoining the party with my uninvited guests. I walked back into the dining room more ceremoniously than I had left it with my bowels intact if not my dignity. I resigned myself to addressing head on whomever and whatever the hell it was sitting there drinking my booze and my Coke Classic.

Babe, who was a stud and must have been the inspiration for the GI Joe action figure, was packing a very large, holstered gun, a holster that was unlatched. He had made coffee and put a steaming cup of coffee on the dining room table for me. Between the roaring fire in the Godin stove and the coffee, it was kind of cozy.

Bobby, who stared at the wood burning stove radiating its warmth seemed lost in thought. I noticed that they had Rigoletto playing in the background on BBC Radio, *Bella Figlia del'Amore* to be exact, one of the great quartets in all of Opera. Bobby seemed to think so, or so it appeared, and I could not resist getting sucked into the mood however perverse the circumstances.

Except, who the fuck were these people?

I had not noticed earlier that Bobby and Babe looked like hell. Bobby's right arm was in a sling that I had not spotted because the sling itself was khaki green like Bobby's uniform. He also had one big honking bruise on his cheek.

The left side of Babe's face looked like he had been sprayed with shards of broken glass. He had tiny cuts everywhere and they were healing a gooey scarlet. On the right side of his head, he had a long, fresh scar that had created a swath of naked scalp through his wiry blond hair.

*You guys look like hell,* I said almost solicitously to the two strangers who had invaded my home. Bobby smiled and scowled at the same time. Nice trick.

Babe said, *well, that's what we are here to talk about.*

*Well then let's talk,* I said. *Is this a practical joke -- my friend Roddy in London? Kind of his style. Or are you really a couple of freaks who are going to chop me into small pieces and leave parts of me in local poubelles.*

*We are neither,* Bobby said, humorlessly, making real eye contact for the first time. *It's better than that,* Babe said with a wry smile. *We are Jedburghs,* Bobby then said. I knew about the heroic Jedburgh teams that had infiltrated France in the lead up to D-Day as an amateur historian of the Normandy invasion and WWII.

*You mean that you play them in the school pageant,* I said. *Or is this your shtick when an army of shit-faced Frenchmen drive around Normandy celebrating D-Day in fake American military uniforms?*

My sarcasm did not go over well. Bobby just sat there looking at me with a steely glare. Babe, who I was beginning to peg as an ally, looked at me with a strained half smile.

*Alright,* I said, *keep going. I do know a little something about the Jedburghs but tell me more.*

I really had no choice, did I?  What was I going to do -- run for it in sweatpants, a t-shirt and my bare feet in the middle of the night? Was I going to tell Madame Leroyer and the French police, the same French police who were sure that I pushed my wife off a cliff, that I had two armed interlopers in combat uniforms in my house, who claim to be something that had not existed for 70 years?

Yup, I didn't have many options. So, what the fuck? I listened as Bobby continued, *so, if you are indeed knowledgeable about our work, you may recall that 93 Jedburgh teams parachuted into France immediately before Operation Overlord, the invasion of Normandy, to work with the French resistance.*

*I am the commander of our team. Our executive officer is Leftenant Martragny of the Free French Army. I will come back to her in due course.*

*Sergeant Caffo,* nodding toward Babe, *is our radio operator. Do not let that mislead you, as he is an American Army Ranger, who is exceptionally gifted when it comes to finding ways to dispatch our enemies to their just deserts. We are Jedburgh team Hugo.*

*My background,* Bobby continued without waiting for a reaction, *is the British Special Operations Executive, and I have been in France off and on since 1940. My job has been to organize a way out of France for all manner of wild game -- the hunters of course the Gestapo, Milice and their friends. That is until the chaps at Bletchley Park got a hold of the three of us.* Bobby and Babe had a private moment of commiseration. It meant not a thing to me.

*And,* I said, *you two live to talk about it 70 years later. You are looking rather fit for someone pushing 100 years of age.*

Babe snorted genially and looked at Bobby. *Let's start there, Boss. The believable part.* I looked at Babe and said, *I sure as hell can't wait to hear the unbelievable part.*

*Coffee, I asked, as I lifted my cup.* Babe obligingly got up to fetch another cup. Nice guy. An awkward few minutes of mutual meditation ensued for Bobby and me until Babe returned with coffee and, as a bonus, three generous servings of my best Calvados.

Bobby picked up where he left off, *the day that we left 1944 to come here was the 20th of June. I will make the question of how that was possible as simple as I possibly can, as I am not a scientist nor mathematician. I was, in fact, comfortably ensconced as a classic's instructor at Oriel College, Oxford, before brother Adolph turned history on its ear.*

*So, we start with the subject of Alchemy,* Bobby said. I held my tongue.

*Many look at Alchemy as the province of reclusive, rather bohemian chaps carrying the remnants of lunch around in their beards or of Victor Hugo's maniacal archdeacon Frollo. But science owes much to them because Alchemists kept the spirit of experimentation alive for centuries with profound consequences that we are only just beginning to fathom.*

*Alchemy is as you may know most notably associated with the idea of turning base metals into gold – the transmutation of matter. But Alchemy also established the existence of gases, molecular theories of matter and discovered elements like zinc and sulfuric acid.  One alchemist on the hunt for the philosopher's stone in his urine actually discovered phosphorous.*

*Their focus on the transmutation of metals led to lesser known but infinitely more dangerous discoveries. The Paris of my time has been a hotbed of activity by the opposing forces to find the recipe for the most horrific of these discoveries.*

*I will come back to this point because it is the basis of our mission. Still with me,* Bobby said. Mission?  Here?  What the fuck.  I could only shrug.

*If you know your mythology, the god of Alchemy and Magic is Hermes. Well, there is a mysterious chap, who first appears in literature in roughly 200 BC -- Hermes Trismegistus, who is attributed with thousands of writings on alchemy and magic and who fancied himself as the God Hermes incarnate.*

*He seems to find a way to pop up throughout history in the strangest of places. He appears in the Qu'ran as the prophet Idris, the ancestor of Mohammed, who indulged in time and space travel and is said to have arrived in Egypt and India from outer space.*

*We see him also in Hindu mythology, the Mahabharata mentions the story of the King Raivata Kakudmi, who travels to heaven to meet the creator Brahma and is shocked to learn that many ages have passed when he returns to Earth.*

*The Buddhist Pāli Canons also mention time moving at different pace, in the Payasi Sutta, one of Buddha's chief disciples Kumara Kassapa explains to the skeptic Payasi that, 'In the Heaven of the Thirty Three Devas, time passes at a different pace, and people live much longer – a century is experienced as a single day.'*

If Bobby's earnest narrative was not getting me much closer to believing this shit, the Calvados had begun to do its work, and so I went with the flow.

*So, what does this have to do with you two,* I interjected perhaps somewhat abruptly. I could see that I had interrupted Bobby's train of thought. *If you are who you say you are, how the hell did you get here?*

*Fair question,* Bobby said. *Our scrum of chemists, physicists and mathematicians at Bletchley theorize that our universe is tantamount to a big, sponge-like sphere that is expanding at an accelerating rate. The physical laws of the universe seem to dictate that this sphere grows in quite an irregular fashion and thus the sponge grows faster in some areas than in others. And in point of fact, some kind of external resistance frequently turns this new growth back on itself in certain spots creating what our best minds call Time Dilations.*

*These Time  Dilations are like tunnels that are traversable in both directions, meaning that the forward end of the dilation – forward time – can lead back to the rear facing end of the dilation – the past and vice-versa. It requires the projection of something called "negative energy," to open a dilation in order to make travel in either direction possible. The projection is produced by very small quantities of certain types of exotic matter,  a discovery that is attributable to none other than Hermes Trismegistus, himself.*

*We have Alchemy to thank then for our ability to manipulate the principles of the physical universe and to exploit imperfections in the continuum of time, space and matter, as we have done to be your guests at this moment.*

Bobby paused to let this sink in and seemed to be organizing the next part of his lesson plan. I for one used the occasion to take my last sip of Calvados. Babe had long ago downed his in one chug. My kind of guy.

*Screwy story, huh,* said Babe in a solicitous sort of way. I could not have agreed more, but could not help but be impressed by how seriously Bobby seemed to take it all.

Somewhere in the back of my mind I suppose that I was hoping that this could indeed be true because it meant that I had some chance of getting through this night with these lunatics alive. It also did not escape me that there may be a way to use this information in my search for Jane.

At that instant dogs began to howl and whine in the walled yards sparsely arranged along our remote country lane from the direction of the old Norman Church that anchored our village. It was unusually loud. The dogs were terrified.

Babe was at the window in one motion, shoulder to the rough stone wall carefully peering through the front window -- hand on his holstered gun. Bobby was moving toward the door and, as he did, turned to me and said that they would make contact again soon to finish the discussion.

Babe was already out the door by a step or two, handgun now held high, looking around like he meant business in the faint light of a new dawn and said, *careful, Boss*. I caught up to Bobby who turned at the door when I grabbed him by his good arm.

*Why are you here, and why am I involved?*

Bobby looked me in the eye and said simply, *you have a personal stake in the outcome of our mission.* Babe nimbly backpedaled toward the door keeping his eyes on the driveway and added, *we are on the hunt, Bud.*

*Who the hell are you hunting,* I asked?

Bobby hit me with one of those earnest tractor beam stares of his and said -- *a butcher and  a demigod. And we need to find them before they find each other.*

That was it. Bobby marched up the driveway toward the fuck-off hedge on the far side of my property.

However, Babe lingered momentarily and said, *if I were you, Bud, I would lock my door from now on.* There was the flash of a broad grin, and then he too was gone into the remainder of that strange night.

# II. MONSTERS

# MONTGOMERY INTERVIEW III

The next few days were an agitated blur of normal activity mixed with the anticipation of another visit by my new best friends from 1944.

It was a distraction from my frustration and sorrow about Jane, but the feeling of loss, like I had been kicked in the gut, never completely left me.

I still didn't believe this shit -- it – them but had no better explanation.  In Northern France, it gets dark around 10:30 pm in late July, so over the next few days, I would make sure that I put the Coke Classic in the fridge and that my best Calvados was well hidden at about that time. I then waited expectantly in the dining room as day faded into night.

Would they come and knock at the door, I wondered? They sure as hell didn't bother with that formality last time. Or would they just ooze through the stone wall?

No one came.

On a foggy morning, about a week after their visit, I returned from my run over to the old German artillery batteries at Longues-sur-Mer to find a first-class SNCF ticket in my mailbox, Bayeux-Paris, *aller et retour*, for the next day along with a scribbled note – Le Portail de la Vierge, Notre Dame, 11h.

This was all very 007 of them, but I had nothing better to occupy myself at the moment, except perhaps steering clear of the Peeping Tom Gendarmes, who continued their occasional surveillance from the shrubbery just outside my gate. So, it was off to Paris the next morning.

It was an uneventful two-hour trip to Paris from Bayeux. I sat with a well-heeled French crowd from Bayeux and from further up the line toward Cherbourg.

There were of course the ever-present American tourists at this time of the year, who had been out to the invasion beaches, and a stocky blonde backpacker wearing a Paris St. Germain baseball cap, who seemed too big to be a Frenchman but looked European all the same.

It turned out to be a cool, rainy day in Paris, so I took a cab from Gare St. Lazare to Place Dauphine and had a café crème at *Le Rose de France* before walking the short distance to Notre Dame. The plaza that spreads out before Notre Dame is usually swarming with tourists at this time of the year.  Perhaps it was the weather, or perhaps I was just early enough, but the crowds weren't bad at all.

I found myself in the plaza at 11:00 am staring at the Southwest corner of the Cathedral of Notre Dame standing side by side with a large and gregarious pigeon. The two of us had staked out just about the same spot to study Le Portail de la Vierge, or translated, the Portal of the Virgin, which is the rightmost entrance of Notre Dame if you happen to be looking at it head on from the plaza.

I have to admit now that the thought did cross my mind that maybe he – it -- the pigeon was one of them. I looked to see if it was wired. The pigeon cocked its neck and looked up to check me out as well and perhaps concluding that I was a lunatic, beat a hasty retreat toward the Seine.

I waited a few more minutes and then saw Babe come around the Northwest corner of Notre Dame. He was dressed in civvies, khakis and a nondescript shirt and jacket. He surveyed the plaza, glanced at me, nodded and then casually kept moving toward the rear of the plaza along its perimeter near the taxi stand.

In short order, a couple emerged from the same direction and moved toward me casually. Just friends out for a stroll it would seem were they not making a beeline towards me. One was a tall, older man in a beat-up trench coat and the other was a striking young woman, almost as tall, in a fashionable suit and Fedora hat who looked like she had just stepped out of a Humphrey Bogart movie.

They might have simply passed as very fashionable Parisians, I thought then, rather than time traveling, Allied freedom fighters if indeed that is what they were.

As they strolled toward me, it was apparent that the young woman was very much on guard. She was evaluating me as they approached and anyone in close proximity to me on the plaza.

I noticed that she concealed a slight limp and like Bobby had one arm in a sling resting against a large leather bag that she had slung over the same shoulder. It was a cross between a briefcase and a stylish handbag.

*Magnificent isn't she*, he said in a deep, professorial baritone as he came within range, *the Portal of the Virgin. Hello, I am Professor Frederick Soddy of Oxford University by way of*

*Bletchley Park of course,* he said with a wry smile that reminded me of Bobby's self-absorbed sense of humor. We shook hands.

*And I am Marguerite Martragny,* his companion said softly, looking me up and down, with a cautious, somewhat serious expression. She was about eye to eye with me in heels and wore rose water, which reminded me of my grandmother.

She extended her good hand, and we shook hands rather formally. Partially hidden beneath the Fedora I now saw was a beautiful girl of barely 22 or 23 years of age. She could just as easily have passed as a French schoolgirl or a model from the fashion houses that bordered Place Vendome rather than a first leftenant in the Free French Army.

*It was installed in the period 1210-1220 A.D.,* Soddy forged ahead shaking me from my reverie, *somewhat after the Sainte-Anne portal. The Portal of the Last Judgment comes slightly later.*

*Le Portail de la Vierge traces the story of Mary, in the tradition of the 13th century Christian community. Mary's death, her ascent to Heaven and her coronation as Queen of Heaven are all depicted here. On the uppermost lintel is Mary on her deathbed surrounded by Jesus and the twelve apostles. Two angels at the head and feet of Mary raise her shroud and ascend into Paradise with her.*

I raised an eyebrow glancing toward Marguerite to see if she also felt like a child on a class trip and got a stern look in return.  OK then, I thought. I am clearly supposed to be paying attention.

*Then at the center of the tympanum, we find Mary in Heaven, sitting on the same throne as Jesus. She is crowned by an angel while Jesus blesses and gives her the scepter. She thus becomes Queen of Heaven, Regina Caeli, you know, before the whole heavenly court composed of angels, patriarchs, kings and prophets that we see installed in four successive arches.*

*A little lower, above the pier, we distinguish under a canopy representing the heavenly Jerusalem a large chest. It is the Ark of the Covenant, which contained the promise made by God to his people to save them. Mary is seen as the New Ark of the Covenant because he who saved mankind came from her.*

I said off-handedly to Soddy that I guess you are a Classics guy like Bobby or a theologian perhaps? Soddy replied, *no, I am a physicist and that is in large part why I am here, as he absent-mindedly rummaged in one of his raincoat pockets and then the other.*

He retrieved a pair of opera glasses and said, *Charley, my boy, please if you would be so kind, look at the rounded medallion on the left of the portail just before we get to where the central portail of the cathedral begins. A reptilian head should be your reference point.*

I took the opera glasses and looked for the medallion, fiddling with the angle of each lens and adjusting the diopter to get the focus right. It helped that it was an overcast day because the worn bas-relief features on the Cathedral's façade stood out more clearly in the gloom.

There it was -- the reptilian head. *OK, got it,* I said. *Lovely,* he said, *please go on and describe what you see.*

I said that I could also make out a winged figure, its right arm raised in a gesture of aggression like it was going to strike a blow in the next instant. Much of the medallion was filled with what looked like a cloud in a funnel shape or maybe it was something coming from an oddly shaped gourd. The reptilian head planted on a human torso was falling head-long out of the cloud, which was filled with what looked like six pointed stars.

*Nice job, my boy. Let's try one more, Charley, if you please. Opposite side of the same portal – more of an oval than circular medallion…frame of reference, a man with a shield and lance.* I scanned and shook my head. With some sense of satisfaction, I said, *got it.* Soddy asked me to describe what I saw.

*Well,* I said, *in the lower right-hand corner there is the man with a shield and lance protecting what appears to be a fortress from a horrible looking sheath of flames projecting from the top left-hand corner of the frame. Good,* I heard Soddy say. *Is there anything else,* he asked?

At the bottom left-hand corner which seemed more weather worn than the rest of the medallion, there seemed to be a seated figure, head bowed mournfully with what looked to be flaking flesh and a mutilated three fingered hand.

*What is this supposed to be,* I asked when I finished my description. Soddy nodded solemnly and in his deep baritone said, *we cannot afford to have history, this history, repeat itself* and with a slight hesitation, *at least not at our expense.*

*J'ai meur de faim!* Soddy bellowed suddenly turning on a dime to a new subject. He asked if there were a suitable bistro nearby where we could continue the conversation over lunch in some privacy. I said that in fact there was, and I knew the owner.

*Then we shall put ourselves in your good hands, Charley. Lead on, chap. Bobby will be joining.*

*How,* I said. Marguerite softly weighed in that Bobby had been nearby from the start. *He will rendezvous with us at your restaurant,* she said.

*Then follow me,* I said, and we walked toward the *Pont au Double* and the Left Bank of the Seine beyond.

# MONTGOMERY INTERVIEW IV

It was a 10-minute walk to *Rôtisserie du Beaujolais* at *Quai de la Tournelle*. The spot had a perfect view of the rear of Notre Dame and *Île de la Cité* across the Seine and had been our favorite restaurant in Paris for years. Jane and Madame Doucette, the co-proprietor, were best buds.

The professor did not shut up during the entire walk over and seemed to be enjoying his field trip to the 21st century. In spite, or perhaps because of, that he was growing on me. Marguerite answered one or two of my questions in a low, soft voice that accentuated her youth. Otherwise, she was not one for small talk. I wondered what she thought about today's Paris and for that matter what she thought about me.

The only rise that I got out of her was when we approached a strappingly large black guy with dreads working a book stall along the Seine. He turned and looked at me and then rushed toward me. Marguerite clutched that big leather bag of hers more tightly, her good hand disappearing into a fold.

The dude wore black jeans and an open black leather jacket with a violet-colored

V-neck t-shirt and a black flat brim ball cap worn backwards. The back of the hat on the front of his large head said *Bar Pinxto*. Great tapas place in LA, I thought. I had been there more than once.

He offered his fist, and we did a bump hug. At first, it was not clear why.  He said at the top of his voice, *this is Sick, Dude. I loved you. I was shorter than most of my friends at school and my dad had me watch you play. I didn't feel so much like a midget anymore. It made me feel good to see you pound on dudes twice your size.*

*I guess your condition was self-correcting,* I said, looking up at him.

I should have been flattered. In fact, I was. It was not the first time I had heard this. I had become iconic for what could be accomplished athletically despite being short and slow.

I laughed and asked the guy whether he was on vacation. He said no man, I am at the Sorbonne. French and economics.

I wished him well, and we moved on. I heard Soddy, who couldn't take his eyes off the stud, whisper, *Brilliant,* under his breath as we walked away. Marguerite relaxed. Sort of.

******

*We did a big loop in from Southampton and hit land near Vannes in Brittany in poor visibility bouncing 50, 100 feet at a time, up and down, as we skimmed above the cloud deck to remain hidden from German antiaircraft spotters until the last moment.  A bright quarter moon shimmered next to us in the broken clouds and was so large it could have been sitting next to us in the cockpit*

*They brought us in that night in a black-painted Lysander, used by the Moon Squadron to ferry special operations teams. The passenger section in the back was barely room enough for Babe and me and our ordinance. Babe refers to it as coitus in the clouds.*

Bobby continued his story, *as we approached the landing zone, the clouds broke as if upon command. We circled, doing the customary, evasive s-curves and finally picked up the radio signal. As the pulse of the signal quickened, we could see red lanterns that defined the four corners of our very small landing strip.*

*If one had any sense at all, this is when one said a quick prayer that it was indeed your side down there framing the drop zone.*

*The landing was uneventful, and we were met by Raoul and his boys. Raoul had been working the area for me since 1940. He was one of Villon's men, that is to say a communist, who had fought in Spain. Officially, Her Majesty's government does not trust them but, from my perch, he and his compatriots are cracking good fighting men – the best in the Macquis. We set out for Oradour-sur-Glane where our mission was centered and where we would rendezvous with Marguerite. The plan was to be there by dawn.*

*We picked up a new team of Macquis guides in the nearest village called Le Bas Dieulidou, who reported heavy Waffen SS activity crisscrossing our route to Oradour. We were forced to take a long detour via a Le Masferat to avoid the heaviest troop concentrations in our general path.*

*We came to a short rise topped by a hedgerow just outside of Le Masferat three hours later. From that vantage point, we could see the village about the length of a football pitch to the right across a grassy marsh. We saw no lights, nor did we see any movement.*

*We would have expected to see a light in a window here and there as the farming village came to life in the predawn. So, we moved forward with heightened caution.*

*We swung around the leeward end of the rise toward a lane that arced from left to right along the far side of the marsh through a rough stand of alder trees and brush that turned into an ancient, cultivated allee of huge willows. It was then that we heard the sound carried by the stiff breeze that swept the marsh grass in random patterns.*

*The sound came and went, and we stopped to assess what we were up against. It was moaning that sounded human but could not have been in its sheer amplitude. There was also a subdued cacophony of creaking and thudding.*

*Babe went ahead to scout the approach. After an uncomfortable delay, he flashed the all clear. As, we moved into the allee, the atmosphere turned oppressive as we moved into a zone seemingly devoid of oxygen. Within a minute my shoulder brushed a shoe attached to a human form swaying above me.*

*Then there was another, and we emerged from this garden of hanging bodies into a circular clearing in the allee anchored by an old stone fountain -- a gift from Cardinal Richelieu to the village's ancestors. We found Babe looking up as if he were admiring the Christmas decorations at Fortnum and Mason.*

*In the faint light that illuminated a heavy mist from the wetlands filling the enclosure of the clearing, our torches, which is to say flashlights, shone on the human forms that surrounded us,*

*hanging from the willow trees, scores of them --
men, women, boys and girls. Two nuns, hanging on
higher limbs with their necks askew seemed to be
staring intently at each other as if they were
engaged in a serious conversation as they limply
swung back and forth in the breeze.*

*Worse still on a lower branch where the lane led
from the clearing to the edge of the village there
were three little girls, my daughter Marion's age,
dressed for school, and arranged according to height
in a neat row on the same branch of a tree.
Someone's private joke, I would imagine.*

*So many hung in close array that it created a
thudding sound accentuated by the creaking and
moaning of willow branches that bore their terrible
burdens. This moaning was amplified by the
interplay of the breeze and a vapor escaping from
the corpses. It appeared that they had been there
since the prior afternoon.*

*I looked at Babe, and he was already counting
the toll. After a few minutes, we made our way into
the village along this lane of sorrow. More men,
women and children hung from balconies and from
the lamp posts of the village. In all we counted 99
souls in Le Masferat that morning.*

*We sent one of the Macquis to alert his
compatriots to come take down the bodies. We could*

*not stay, as much as we felt obliged to, and pressed
on for Oradour-sur-Glane.*

******

In time, I would know the rest of this story
and the sense of loss that is the constant
companion of the warrior. However, Soddy,
ever the bon vivant, suggested another bottle
of wine when Bobby took a breath in his
account of the saga of Le Masferat, and he got
no argument from me.

Bobby and Marguerite sat there shoulder to
shoulder in stoic silence. It was clear that there
was an unspoken and at least for now
impenetrable bond between the two.

Madame Doucette had given us a corner
table in the window with a view of the Seine,
isolated on so many different levels from the
happy, contemporary clientele that was
feasting on wild game, roasted chicken and the
best *pommes puree* in Paris.

After seating Soddy, Bobby, Marguerite and
me, Madame Doucette had come over to take
our apero order and noticed Bobby and
Marguerite's banged-up state. She does not
have much a poker face, Madame Doucette.
When Bobby glibly volunteered that all of it
was due to a minor auto accident, the tilt of an

eyebrow and the subtle change in pitch of Madame Doucette's expressive Gaelic nose signaled that she wasn't buying what Bobby was selling.

I studied my companions with fascination – the gregarious Soddy and his tweed blazer that carried a hint of mildew. In what place and time did he put that jacket on this morning, I wondered?

Then there was Bobby who had nicked himself shaving, trivial by comparison to the other insults visited upon his body. It struck me for the first time that if you removed his mustache and the air of command he projected, he was a very young man.

And of course, there was Marguerite, the schoolgirl leftenant, who had removed the fedora to reveal her peaches and cream complexion, brown eyes and dark hair composed in one of those WWII style hairdo's. I think that they called them Victory Curls. She had beautiful hands with long fingers, and I wondered whether she had once played the piano or still did.

Three of the fingers on the hand of her bad arm were black and blue where she had lost the fingernails. I could relate having been stepped on many times by opposing players and a few of my own teammates. Her battle scars contributed to an aura of quiet strength that stood in counterpoint to her youth.

I wondered whether they thought about escaping to our time – how easy life would be. Was it possible that they could actually meet themselves as 90-year old's here in Paris or in London or that they could check in on children or grandchildren?

They ate with gusto – big appetites. Perhaps it was a generational thing. Perhaps, if you were used to deprivation in war, you ate as well as you could when you could. Perhaps, as warriors, they approached every feast as if it were their last.

But I digress, and to break my reverie, Soddy said, *Charley, my boy, let's take a brief respite from Bobby and Marguerite's ordeal in the Limousin. I for one could use it whilst we talk about why we had you meet us at Notre Dame.*

*Works for me*, I said.

# MONTGOMERY INTERVIEW V

*If I am correct,* Soddy continued needing no further encouragement, *I believe that Bobby introduced you to a mysterious -- one might even say mystical figure called Hermes Trismegistus.*

*Well, we are in pursuit of an equally mysterious figure who is known only as Fulcanelli. He might be Hermes Trismegistus himself or a disciple. Like Hermes Trismegistus he appears to be an ageless chap who pops up here and there, in this century and that, often in the scientific literature of the day.*

*Fulcanelli made contact with a colleague of mine, a brilliant physicist by the name of Arnaud Barberel, along with another physicist Thierry Debruyn in 1937 at Barberel's laboratory at the Gas Board, a stone's throw from where we were today in Place Notre Dame. You may be interested to learn, Charley, that the Gas Board is, or should I say was, one of the leading research centers in France dedicated to radioactive materials.*

*Arnaud wrote to me with a verbatim account of the meeting. Fulcanelli told both men, 'You are on the brink of success, as indeed others are today. May I be allowed to utter a word of caution? The dark secret in alchemy is that there is a way of manipulating matter and energy to produce what modern scientists call a field of force.'*

'Certain geometrical arrangements of highly purified materials are enough to release nucleic forces without having recourse to either electricity or vacuum techniques, as Curie and Poincaré would have us believe are necessary. Indeed, such forces can be produced from a few grains of metal that are powerful enough to destroy whole cities and civilizations.'

'So, I warn you,' Fulcanelli went on to say, 'the liberation of nucleic power is easier than you think, and the radioactivity artificially produced can poison the atmosphere of our planet. I am telling you this for a fact that alchemists have known this for a very long time.'

'This field of force can also be harnessed by the experimenter to put him in a privileged position vis a vis the universe. From this position, he has access to the realities that are ordinarily hidden from us by time and space, matter and energy. This is what we call the Great Work. It is not simply the transmutation of metals of which we speak but the experimenter himself. It is an ancient secret that a few people rediscover each century.'

'The work upon which you and your colleagues are embarked is fraught with terrible dangers that threaten not only you, but the human race. Indeed, there might once have existed a civilization that *knew about atomic energy and was destroyed by its misuse and'* – his eyes seemed to focus on something invisible to us, Arnaud said, *'a few partial techniques survived.'*

Soddy continued, *Charley, Victor Hugo, had it right when he wrote in Notre-Dame de Paris or as we Anglophiles know it, the Hunchback of Notre Dame, that there are aspects to the structure of Notre Dame that have little apparent connection to the Bible.*

*In point of fact,* and here Soddy paused for effect, *these features are a journalistic chronicle of the history of hermetic science and of past civilizations that were hardly the primitives that we assume them to have been.*

*To digress, if I may,* Soddy added, *I was adjutant to General Sir James Willcocks and fought on the Ypres salient in Belgium from June 1917 to November 1918 with the 2nd Queen Victoria's Rajput Light Infantry. The Indians were bloody good fighters, and my counterpart in their ranks with whom I liaised for Willcocks was a young Hindu man and quite a renowned scholar in India.*

*So, you fought in the Great War,* I said obligingly and for no particularly good reason.

Soddy's eyes bored into me like a drill, and he replied, *let my silence speak to the adjectives that I would ascribe to that war or any other.*

Soddy continued with his story. *In the few precious moments of solace that we enjoyed together, my friend regaled me with Hindu lore, which seems to combine legend, history and religion.  One such legend held that about four million years ago, give or take a hundred thousand years or so, there  was a great civilization in which people were happier, taller and lived longer, a civilization that appears to have vanished without a trace.*

*Our science currently tells us that we homo sapiens evolved from our more primitive ancestors around 300,000 years ago and were hunter gathers until we domesticated animals and plants about 12,000 years ago. This science is based on fossil evidence.*

*How do we explain this discrepancy if it can be said to be one, and what does it have to do with Fulcanelli?* Soddy must have been reading my mind.

Soddy soldiered on, *in science, one abhors loose ends and coincidence. In his warning to us about Man's impending use of nucleic weapons, Fulcanelli may well have been describing the devastating forces and destruction wrought on that mysterious civilization in the Hindu Canons and at the same time so artfully depicted on the façade of Notre Dame.* This was creepy enough to make the hair on the back of my neck bristle. I said, *so that was in 1937? What does this have to do with us now? Nucleic, I mean Nuclear, weapons are a fact of life today in case you didn't already know.*

Soddy nodded agreement solemnly and then looked at his watch. *Well,* he said, *they were not a fact of life in 1937 and in the wrong hands, they could have changed the course of the conflict. Your lovely restaurant here might now be serving schnitzel or borscht instead!*

*So, what happened to Fulcanelli and your friends,* I asked. *Sadly, Arnaud and Thierry have disappeared,* Soddy continued. Soddy then turned to look at Bobby who shook his head as if to say yes. Soddy turned to me and said, *our friend Fulcanelli arrives at St. Lazare on the 4:15 train from Rouen today with the intent of finding those wrong hands of which we speak. That is why we are here.*

******

We left in a hurry delayed slightly by Madame Doucettte who gave me a hug and words of encouragement. Jane would be found safe and sound, she said.

We piled into two Citroen vans. Babe, Marguerite and a young couple that I had not seen before were in the first van. Bobby and I took the second van with two wiry Frenchmen with matching five o'clock shadows.

Babe's troop was to take the Rue du Rome entrance to Gare St. Lazare. We were to approach the station from the other side on Rue Amsterdam, where the station was still suffering the effects of a rebeautification project that had torn up the area around St. Lazare for as long as I could remember.

Paris Saint-Lazare is one of the six large terminus railway stations of Paris. It is the second busiest railway station in Paris, behind Gare du Nord, and handles 450,000 passengers each day. It's a monster with 27 platforms sorted into six destination groups in Northern France. I came into Lazare from Basse Normandie. I believe that Rouen is Haute Normandie but could be wrong.

Apart from its size, its major distinguishing feature is a new *Gallery* or high-end shopping mall – three levels of retail glory attached to the front of the station. I wonder what Monet and Manet, who had lived nearby and painted Lazare on many occasions (I wasn't a total jock and loved art history), would do with the clashing green and red of Starbucks and Burger King, *Chez* Whopper, anchoring one end of the upper Gallery side by side.

I did not see the other van dump our compatriots. Our group waited until the ever-present French Naval commandos patrolling the station sauntered by packing their huge M16's – fingers poised above their triggers. This group wore fatigues and small sit-on-top blue berets jauntily pulled to the right. I have always wondered how they keep the damn things on.

Bobby told me to stay put at the Rue Amsterdam entrance but, after Bobby and his team dissolved into the crowd, I moved into the station for a better look at what might be going down.

About 10 minutes later, as I approached platform 17 in a swarm of commuters going to and coming from trains, I picked up steady movement coming from the Gallery toward the same train platform, which seemed out of place in the milling crowd. Despite the crowd, I could make out a blue baseball cap moving purposefully toward Babe who was now looking the other way watching for the Rouen train. I moved forward for a better look.

Something clicked. Fuck me. I knew that dude with the ball cap. It was the tall blonde backpacker who had been on the train from Bayeux with me earlier that day. He was holding something close to his chest under his jacket.

I didn't know why, but something told me that this would not end well. I started to walk and then jog toward him dodging folks heading toward their trains who were oblivious to this totally whacked out situation.

I was picking up speed and then my feet fell out from under me as I stepped on a bed pillow that belonged to the family of a fat guy wearing an Ohio State sweatshirt. Tourists! What is it with their fucking pillows?

He shouted some profanity as I tumbled head over heels forward and in the direction of the dude with the ball cap. My momentum brought me back to my feet just as I cleared the swarm between him and me.

The backpacker glanced briefly in my direction but was distracted by shouting from the quai where the train from Haute

Normandie had just pulled in. He accelerated toward Babe and I toward him closing on him fast.

I didn't get a clean shot at the dude's knees, which would have disabled him, but I was able to spear him in his lower back. We both landed hard, and it knocked the wind out of me.

My first reaction was that I am too old for this shit, but the sight of a very large gun in his right hand was all I needed to get over it. His left arm was trapped under his body, and he was trying to use it to gain some leverage. He had managed to hold on to the butt of the gun despite the impact of my tackle and was trying to get a finger around the trigger.

I lunged over his back and sent my elbow into his gun-side shoulder. Hell, this guy was a brick, all muscle, and he was gaining control of the gun. I was losing ground, and he almost hoisted me off as he tried to roll out from under me.

Then the spiked heel of a woman's shoe came down hard on his right hand, creating a bony pulp where the big knuckle of his trigger finger had been. He grunted when I would have been crying like a baby.

At the same instant there was a soft metallic clang, a muffled pop and the smell of a firecracker. The backpacker's torso seemed to flop below me and then lay still.

I looked up to see Marguerite, hat drawn down over her beautiful face, who had discretely put a large hole in the backpacker's head using a gun with a silencer, a hole that was already oozing an ugly red-gray goop through the back of his Paris St. Germain cap.

She didn't miss a beat and returned the gun to her ever-present leather satchel as she continued to stroll toward St. Lazare's Metro station as if she didn't have a care in the world.

I felt myself being lifted by the neck of my shirt and jacket. Babe had me headed toward the door on Rue Amsterdam at a fast clip blending in with the swarm of Frenchmen exiting their trains.

We had just made it to the street when the French commandos coming from the far end of the station reached the spot where the backpacker had gone down.

******

It was a long, mostly silent, trip back to Bayeux for me, Babe and Bobby. Bobby made the command decision to get the hell out of town, and I rented a car at the Hertz place below the Louvre. We stayed as far away from Lazare as we could, so I took the long way around heading first in the direction of Orly Airport and then onto the Peripherique.

The guys seemed to waver between crestfallen and angry. About the only meaningful conversation that we had was an exchange between Babe and Bobby. Babe asked, *Boss, were we set up?* It took Bobby several minutes to respond.

With a deep groan, he said, *the targets were there of this, I am sure. The fracas on the quai and that with the backpacker suggests that our operational plan had been compromised in some way.*

They knew the backpacker in fact. He had been a Panzergrenadier in the 12th SS Panzer Division *Hitler Jugend,* an *SS-Obersturmführer* or the equivalent of a 1st Lieutenant. The *Hitler Jugend* were the most ruthless and fanatical of all opponents during the Allied effort to break out of the Normandy beachhead, and this dude had been the worst of the worst.

We stopped once outside of Caen on the way back to my place. Babe got his customary jug of Coke Classic, Bobby tea, and I got a screw capped bottle of Sancerre.  I wasn't upset, but my adrenalin was still over the top, so I had to drink something if I couldn't hit something.

We got back to the house in one piece despite a storm that swept in from Brittany with heavy wind and rain.  I was ready to turn in – no Calvados, no nightcap, no nothing. The other two agreed.

Babe took the dungeon room as a bunk, and Bobby took the role of lookout in a second-floor bedroom on the barn side of the house that had a sweeping view of my property. A lot of good it would do him in the dark, wind and rain that was now blowing sideways.

As we were getting ready to turn in, Babe turned to me in the Dungeon room  and put out his large paw with a smile. We  shook, and he slapped me on the shoulder. *I owe you one, Bud,* was all he said.

Bobby smiled – it wasn't that stuffy, smug shit that I had seen from him before, the good news.  The not so good news is that it  masked something important that he was not about to reveal  to me certainly not then. We all went our separate ways.  I hit the bathroom one last time and stared at my mirror image in the opaque bathroom window. It was pitch-black in the small patio beyond that separated the window from the imposing stone wall that bordered Madame Jardin's land. I needed a shave, I thought, as I surveyed my haggard reflection.

This had been the strangest fucking week of my life, but a good one, I thought. It wasn't just an OK kind of Good as in I'll make it to cocktail hour Good. I have had a bunch of them lately. Instead, it felt like a three-point win Good in which my interception set up the winning field goal.

I kept cycling through the questions that were rattling around in my head like loose marbles. Why me? Why them? What had been going on when the train reached the quai at St. Lazare? What was the *Hitler Jugend* dude doing on a train from Normandy to Lazare in first class sitting a couple of rows behind me?

But the biggest question of them all reverted to what Bobby had told me that first night just as they were leaving. What was my personal stake in all of this?

It would be some time before this question was answered and it would be then that I would also learn how closely my fate was intertwined with the figure in the great coat with a battered left hand that looked like a claw, who was at that moment malevolently staring back at me from the other side of the bathroom window, invisible in the opaque black void of the patio from which he slipped away like a feral animal as I turned out the bathroom light.

# III. HEROES

# MONTGOMERY INTERVIEW VI

The lifeless body dangled, head severed from the torso but for the bloody sheath of gristle that barely held the two pieces of the victim intact. The bottom limbs drooped limply, while its upper limbs splayed sideways in an agonistic pose.

The victim's face was contorted, front teeth and eyeballs protruding from its head as if it had peered beyond the eternal veil and been horrified by what it had seen.

This was in stark contrast to Beckham, the sleek gray cat with lime green eyes, which was at that moment trotting triumphantly down the driveway with the victim in its mouth, today a partially eviscerated field mouse.

I sat nursing a glass of Côtes du Rhône feeling sorry for myself while finishing the basket of oysters that Monsieur Boccanegro over in Asnelles had plucked from la Manche for me that morning. Mondher, my private eye, had come by to report that he had nothing to report about Jane, but he had a good head on his shoulders and a couple of leads worth pursuing.

I should simply admit, I suppose, that she is dead, but I am not ready for that. Yet I would rather search and keep the hope alive rather than bring this story – our story – to its bitter end.

I sat at the small café-like table that is nestled in an inlet of our gravel driveway between our kitchen window and my disheveled kitchen garden. Beckham jumped onto the concrete pier anchoring the working pump of an ancient well directly across from me completing an isosceles triangle with the main door to the house and the wood beamed dining room beyond, which had recently been commandeered by two Jeds.

Beckham took a bow and casually dropped his prey, which glanced off the peer onto the gravel driveway below. Unfazed, he preened, ignoring his prize for the moment, licked his paws, never looking me squarely in the eye.

Whether this reflected a bond between us, ritual or instinct, he knew that I knew that this oft repeated performance fascinated me. Beckham would typically stay just long enough to achieve the intended effect.

Such was the stuff of daily life in the Bocage, among the ancient hedgerows of the

Norman countryside.  Or perhaps such was not
the stuff of real life, really.

My adventure the week before in Paris with
the merry band from 1944 made me wonder if
the life that I had known was real at all, or
rather little more than a happy illusion made
possible by the elemental battle between good
and evil, strength and weakness, which
provided the real energy in the universe.

I wondered about Beckham's occasional
companion, Diamanté, whom I had not seen in
quite some time. She was a dainty female,
black and white, named by our neighbors for
the diamond shaped patch of white on her
forehead. Unlike Beckham, Diamanté was
more social and actively sought to engage me.

Her modus operandi was a bit different, as I
had discovered to my occasional surprise. One
night I awoke in the vaulted bedroom above
the kitchen aware that a spectral presence sat
patiently in the open window, eyes boring into
me. Jane was in London setting a recently
uncovered Balanchine ballet on the dancers at
the Royal Ballet, which is just as well, as
Diamanté treated her as a rival.

Diamanté held a small, petrified turtle dove
in her mouth that night, wings still flapping

away. This was not the first time that she had paid tribute to me with small gifts like the remnants of a frog, the ubiquitous field mouse or a swath of feathers recently removed from its owner.

I graciously accepted the flapping gift that had been dropped behind the nightstand next to the bedroom window, given it a bit of water, checked its working parts and helped it make its escape through a small window on the barn side of the house facing the old Norman church.

My walk down memory lane with Beckham and Diamanté was abruptly interrupted by a call from Roddy in London shouting as he always did into his phone because he distrusted mobiles.

*How are you, my friend? It was good to hear your voice, and I am bloody well ready to roustabout with you this week coming,* Roddy said. *Anythin's better than chaperoning this blubbery bugger who has been preordained a new master of self-help or should one say self-absorption by Oprah's book club.*

*We have one more engagement, a reading with the old bags at the Parliamentary Women's Club today, and then I plan to deposit 'Il Doctore' in a cab forthwith and dispatch him to Heathrow. Can't come soon enough, bloody hell, he shouted even louder than before.*

Roddy and I had been blood brothers for nearly 25 years – ex-jocks, battle-tested gladiators in our respective arenas. Jane and his wife Ophelia had been colleagues at the Royal Ballet. Ophelia died several years ago of a brain tumor launching a period in which I drug Roddy out of more pubs than I could ever count.

Roddy is a former rugby player and star for the British National team for almost a decade. And he was also a mean drunk if provoked. He is a giant of a man with a face that has had just about every possible bone broken or fractured at one time or another during his playing career. He has long, always disheveled hair, and the effect is that of a Saxon or Danish warrior straight out of a Bernard Cornwell novel. His looks belied the fact that he is also one of London's most successful literary agents.

He was also a former spook, whose daughter Victoria, or Rory as we called her, had gone on to follow in her father's footsteps joining MI6 as a field agent, although the proud father made a great show of never confirming it but, in his gushing denial, always did. He would not have had it any other way.

*Fancy a jog on Tuesday, Roddy bellowed. Shall we 'faire un rendezvous' at the communal pissoir? I take it that you mean the Diana Memorial, Roddy, I asked.*

*Yes, at that fucking abomination.*

During Roddy's playing days, he and Ophelia were a glam couple and charter members of the Sloane Rangers, who had been chums of Princess Di. He was a committed Monarchist until it came to how Di had been treated by the Royals and then he became Guy Fawkes ready to put a keg of gunpowder "under the old broad's arse" as he liked to say for how Diana had been treated. He thought the Diana Memorial in Hyde Park to be wretchedly ugly and unbefitting Diana's beauty. The subject always set him off.

*I'm on Ryan from Dinard Monday afternoon and then at the Belgravia, I said. Let's say 8:00 a.m. sharp. I will be coming from the direction of the Albert Gate as usual.*

*I have a favor to ask, Roddy, I said. Name it, Old Boy, he shouted back. Can you do some digging with your former colleagues? I would like a little information about a group of Second World War fighters, who were connected to the Special Operations Executive. They were called Jedburgh Team Hugo. I would imagine that you have something in your archives.*

*I will see what I can do! Mardi, mon ami, over and out,* shouted Roddy into his portable as I held mine six inches from my ear to avoid a punctured eardrum.

As we signed off, Beckham, who had been captivated by the noise coming from my hand, took his final bow and gracefully slipped down from the pier surrounding the ancient water pump, swooping up his victim in one seamless motion and darting through the castle hedge to Madame Jardin's field beyond.

******

Roddy and I met as planned on Tuesday morning and did our tour of Hyde Park. There was still no small amount of competitive drive left in both of us, and we pushed the pace to see who would give in first. Each of us was determined to drive the other into the ground or die trying. It was always the battle of American Football versus British Team Rugby.

London was the city that Jane and I loved most, and Hyde Park was its epicenter for me, while Jane's orbit took her to the rarified atmosphere of Covent Garden and performance at the apex of the dance world. Although Roddy, as he did with me, seemed to bring out the wild Jane in the otherwise quiet and introspective ballerina, and some of our best times were spent with Roddy and Ophelia partying our way through their encyclopedia of favorite people and places in London.

In the same way that homing pigeons have a mineral deposit in their brains that reads the magnetic field of the earth to guide them reliably home, my lode stone always seems to bring me back to Hyde Park. This place has a primal attraction for me. As a Saxon-Welsh mutt, my instincts tell me that my tribe came from this spot and that one day I will return here for all time.

On that day, Hyde Park was lush – oaks, chestnuts and maples in full dress uniform. Scores of goslings and other hatchlings were enjoying their first balmy summer, the Horse Guards were drilling new recruits in the paddock across from the Serpentine and dogs off-leash were chasing squirrels and each other joyfully.

Roddy said nothing about my request at first, but I could tell that he had something on his mind. So, I was hopeful that he might have an answer to my query.

As we jogged, he began where I thought that he would and asked why I had inquired about this particular subject. I told him that I had my reasons but could not get into details right then. He simply nodded.

He then said, *Buddy Boy, there is no formal record of Jedburgh Team Hugo but in the Sub Rosa culture of which I was once a part, there is a record of everything. So, this got my juices flowing as you Americans like so crassly to say.*

*One would think, wouldn't one that one takes the list of 93 World War II era Jedburgh teams and works through the alphabet to Hugo. Nyet, Nada, Non. No trace. Kept coming up with 92.*

*But if you are willing to travel to the ninth ring of hell and happen to be a crafty bugger, much is possible. I still have access to the inner reaches of MI6 because I still do an occasional odd job.*

*Interestingly, I was intercepted in my quest by a scrum of sniveling administrators, one of whom I launched in the service when he was barely a snot-nosed schoolboy. They seemed very curious about my search for the non-existent and not just a little perturbed. Brilliant. This served only to confirm the existence of that which I sought.*

*One scrap leading to another as they often do, I found a reference to a numerical code of the kind that was associated with provisioning the Jeds for which there was no cross-reference to a team name. The odd man out if you will. This number matched one found on another scrap that referred to a storied spot in west-central France called Oradour-sur-Glane.*

*On 10 June 1944, an SS massacre killed 642 people in a 24-hour period in the village and its environs -- men, women and all too many children. It was an ugly day to be sure.*

*At the bottom of the list of deceased that was compiled at that time, there was a rough notation – J80J2-08=10644-3=Term. The first number was this provisioning number for a particular Jedburgh team for which I could find no match among the 92, almost certainly pointing to Jedburgh Team Hugo as the odd man out. The full notation in the service's shorthand means three people lost in action or, viewed another way, what we believe to have been Jedburgh Team Hugo ceased to exist on 10 June 1944.*

We were pushing each other hard as we got to our finish line at the boathouse on the

Serpentine, and my lungs were burning.  I gasped for air and, as he finished, I proceeded to vomit into the Serpentine.

Roddy bent over and put a hand on my back and said, *buck up, chum. My dearest Rory is in a tizzy to talk Redskins football with you and would be grateful for the pleasure of your company at Cubitts. Treize heure sharp, and she is brutally punctilious about these things, so do be on time. Bon appétit.*

# MONTGOMERY INTERVIEW VII

I did buck up. I didn't puke on the puffins in the Serpentine because he beat me. I puked because I was back to square one in a situation where I was having a hard time getting a fix on where square one was. Fuck it.

These people from my grandfather's generation had barged into my life. More than that they had dominated it for the last month. And for that matter, I actually liked those fuckers whoever or whatever they were.

So, if you are following this, you too are questioning the math. Bobby said that they had left 1944 on 20 June 1944. Jedburgh Team Hugo was history, that is kaput,  according to Roddy, on 10 June 1944.

So, are my compatriots imposters? Are they ghosts? Are they lunatics? Worst yet, was the tableau at St. Lazare just a hallucination caused by my failing liver from the liquor I had consumed since losing Jane?

Did Roddy get it wrong? He never does with this kind of thing though. Or if I were an optimist, which it is hard to be these days, was the so-called time dilation thing doing a loopty-loop so that you can die and come back and die again in whatever generation suits you?

Shit, and I am channeling Jane here, because this is the first thing that would have occurred to her, would a good meal eaten in the 21st century have any nutritional value when one returns to the 1940's?  This bit of obsessive detail reminded me of Jane's nuttiness and made me smile for an instant because it felt as if she were nearby.

Though it makes you think about the nature of reality.  Do our lives proceed apace in measured time in an orderly way according to the laws of nature? This is what we have always been conditioned to believe.

But what if the laws of nature dictated that time was a circular function, one that was as disorderly as the growth of time dilations, in which the events of the past and present feed on each other and are influenced by people traveling from the past to steal information from the present and those of us in the present going back to screw with the past. Are we nothing more than prisoners of this circular function, one which corrupts itself?

And for some unexplained reason, Jedburgh Team Hugo had given me some hope. I don't know why, but they did. It was like how I felt playing for the freshman football team in high school. We sucked, but when we put that uniform on, we went out there every week believing that we were going to cream the opposing team.

The Jeds connected me to something heroic and victorious and to the slim, irrational hope that my as yet unexplained personal stake in all of this had something to do with Jane.

******

The morning had turned from one in which a warm sun made the Serpentine glisten like a reservoir of diamonds to an overcast and increasingly brisk afternoon. So much for global warming, although I jest because I worry that one day a verdant place like Normandy will become a tropical desert. No more four seasons in a day, just one sultry season forever.

I was hungry and looking forward to some grotty pub food at Thomas Cubitts, a tony gastropub on Elizabeth Street at the edge of Belgravia where Roddy now lived. I also looked forward to seeing Rory. I reckoned that I hadn't seen her since she graduated from Penn.

She had graduated Magna Cum Laude and as a Rhodes Scholar.  Some of my best times with Roddy were visiting Philly to see Rory compete in the Pentathlon at the Penn Relays.

Elizabeth Street always reminds me of the main drag in a quaint Victorian village rather than a city street in a bustling metropolis. Cubitts was a gathering place for the young royals, expats, rock stars and media types who lived in the area, which made for some great people watching on the outside patio.

I didn't see Rory sitting on the patio as I approached so I ducked inside as a fleeting rain shower swept down Elizabeth Street. I heard a hearty *Hail to the Redskins* in a born to the manor British accent over the loud chatter in Cubitts and spotted her standing at a table in the rear next to a window that ran along the side of the main dining room facing Ebury Mews, an alley that intersected Elizabeth Street.

Rory is tall. Got that from Roddy.  She is thin and all legs.  Got that from Ophelia.

She wore a sky-blue running suit opened at the collar and trainers. When we hugged, I could have been holding onto the upper torso of a Navy Seal.

She was breathtaking with chiseled features, green eyes and auburn hair cut boyishly short. The haircut reminded me of the early Beatles.

Did I say that she was breathtaking? Hard to believe that this had once been the little tomboy that Roddy and I would flip a coin to carry on our shoulders in Hyde Park to handicap our races around the Serpentine.

*Thank you for coming, Charley Dear, at such very short notice,* she said. *I am flattered that you asked,* I said. *I suppose that you caught wind of the project that I gave Roddy, or did you really want to talk Redskins football?*

She smirked, dimples jumping to attention, green eyes boring into me, but she did not take the bait. I sat looking at Elizabeth Street, shoulder to the window on Ebury Mews. Rory sat to my right facing the Mews at a table that I noticed was set for three. She had ordered a Hendricks and tonic, and I joined her in one.

We spent a few minutes catching up during which I lied telling her that I had kicked Roddy's ass that morning at the Serpentine. Several minutes later, I caught her looking over my shoulder toward the back entrance of the restaurant on Ebury Mews.

I turned hoping to see Roddy, and I'll be damned if it wasn't Marguerite coming in the side door. As she approached us, she gave a smiling Rory a kiss on both cheeks as the French do and me a light hug. Just a hug? Better than a salute, I suppose. What did I have to do to graduate to *un double bis*?

So, imagine this. I found myself at that moment in the presence of two beautiful, Amazonian warrior princesses. One was probably 22 (or 92 depending on how you counted) and the other was barely pushing 26.

One operated at the blunt end of MI6, the other was a living breathing member of the Free French Army of 1944, who carried an arsenal around with her in that ever-present leather handbag. I wondered if Rory had any lethal toys stashed away in the London Marathon knapsack draped over her chair.

Makes ya think – I mean their ages. I once met a guy at the Normandy American Cemetery above Omaha Beach from Greenville, South Carolina, who was visiting with his son and daughter-in-law to attend a D-Day ceremony. He was a mellow guy whose passion these days was singing in the choir at his Unitarian church. Damned though if he didn't fly 37 missions over Europe as a B-17 pilot during WWII. He was 21 when he made Captain. His bombardier was 18.

Marguerite had changed her hair. It was pulled backed severely in the front and worn in a way that looks like a fan in the back – another WWII do, but I don't know what it is called. The way she wore her hair drew your eye to her big brown eyes and the peaches and cream complexion of her full cheeks. She wore a simple dress and sweater, which would have worked for her in any century.

When Marguerite took the third seat, I turned to look at Rory who seemed to be getting a kick out of my reaction as I must have looked cross-eyed with bafflement, like someone who had just taken a bullet between the eyes.

I thought, well this is going to be one hell of an interesting lunch. What a fucking understatement that would turn out to be.

We dispatched the preliminaries with our waiter and then I said, pleasantly enough, *can I assume that we are here to enjoy a wonderful lunch together and to get to the bottom of the situation?* At this, both Marguerite and Rory deadpanned in unison as if they had rehearsed this move together.

I took the bull by the horns and added, *my two questions are these – is Jedburgh Team Hugo real or are you –* I stopped short of saying 'fucking with me.' They got the drift. Also, I added, *why me of all people?*

Rory was quick to say, *both fair questions at this juncture, Charley Dear.* So, Rory is involved in this somehow, I thought. Marguerite added with a voice like a soft breeze, *might I start with some background.*

Did I have a choice, I thought to myself? *Please*, I said, but not before ordering another Hendricks and tonic.

Marguerite began. *My family placed enormous value on education and the arts. My father in fact had designed sets as a young man at La Scala and Opera Garnier. My aunt performed with Ballet Russe and was a protégé of Diaghilev's before she fell in love with a suave French artillery officer and settled down in the Limousin.*

*So, at least in ballet, we have something in common, don't we,* I offered somewhat abruptly. Marguerite and Rory's eyes met for a split second, but Marguerite did not skip a beat.

Smooth, I thought. Had I said something out of school?

*So, my brother Frederic and I were fortunate to live a privileged life thanks to Maman and Papa, who wanted us to see the world beyond Villiers Bocage in lower Normandy where we grew up. Indeed, Papa had my career in opera completely mapped out for me.* At this, Marguerite smiled sweetly, for the moment a loving daughter rather than a lethal army leftenant.

*I can vouch for the fact that Marguerite has a beautiful voice,* Rory cooed. *'Love if you must but do it for fun,'* Rory sang slightly off-key.

I thought that I recognized the tune until Marguerite responded by softly trilling in perfect pitch a few bars of the actual melody from *Cosi Fan Tutti* (you can't hang around Covent Garden without seeing a little opera, even an ex-jock). This brief glimpse of unexpected humor in the young warrior princesses warmed the atmosphere at our table. I must have been staring at that point and when Marguerite noticed she looked down at her hands folded on the table.

I was fascinated by the electricity between Rory and Marguerite. The rapport between them was all the more striking because there was none between Marguerite and me.

Rory picked up on the vibe and saved the moment by saying, *but we digress, Charley Dear.* Marguerite took a deep breath and continued with the story as if she were giving an after-action report.

*Freddy and I shared a small flat in Paris near the Metro at Rue du Bac. He was a medical student, and I took voice lessons at the Académie de France. Freddy was in love and his fiancée, Vanessa, and I were like sisters. She studied to become a pharmicienne.*

*When les Bosch invaded France in 1940 and moved on Paris, we made a pact that we would not stand passively by and let them have their way with our country or us. There were rumors that the free French, as we began to call ourselves then, were going to regroup in Toulouse, so we set out for Toulouse -- Freddy, Vanessa and an army friend of Freddy's by the name of André. We left Paris on the 12th of June 1940, 48 hours before the Germans took control of the city.*

*The mass exodus from Paris was chaotic and humiliating, and we felt like lambs being led to the slaughter. We and thousands of our countrymen streamed southward threatened both by our own* army, which was in a fast and disorderly retreat, and by the German artillery and aircraft that constantly harassed the fleeing refugees with deadly results.

We made it to the outskirts of Blois a few days later and came under attack from a squadron of their fighter bombers, causing absolute panic. We watched as a beautiful young girl barely 16 was crushed in the confusion by a fleeing French army truck.

Freddy and André carried her carefully to an ancient orchard of apple and cherry trees. There was very little that we could really do for her, but Vanessa and I managed to buy a small quantity of injectable lidocaïne from a passing medic to help take the edge off her pain.

Freddy told André to see us safely to Toulouse. He would follow later. I did not want to leave him, but Vanessa was becoming increasingly emotional, and I took charge of her for Freddy's sake. They were bringing other wounded under the broad canopy of the orchard, and it was like my older brother to take charge, as he did. We agreed to rendezvous in Toulouse within the week.

We managed to get a ride on the running boards of a milk truck and a few kilometers to the south came to a low, wooded ridge and looked back to see *the leafy green orchard in the distance surrounded by people who at that distance looked like stick figures.*

*We then heard the rhythmic grinding of engines from Bosch aircraft nearby and in the blink of an eye saw the canopy of the orchard disappear in a fireball. The concussion of that massive explosion even at such a distance was like a hard slap to the face. Vanessa and I harbored no illusions about Freddy's fate.*

*We turned to look ahead and held each other tightly. From that moment on our lives came to reflect the simple principle that death for us in the crusade against les Bosch would be as random in its timing as it would be certain to come.*

At that Marguerite stopped, took a deep breath, and looked down at her hands again. Rory reached out solicitously to grab her wrist.

Two things occurred to me at that moment. First, no wonder that Marguerite is anything but bubbly even if she looks like a young schoolgirl without a care in the world. What the hell had I been expecting?

It also occurred to me that given the recurring subject matter with these people, there had to be a better way to do story time with the Jeds than over a meal.

As we ordered an after-lunch coffee a bit later, Marguerite pushed on with the story, *we did arrive in Toulouse a week later and made arrangements to cross the border via the Pyrenees. Spain is technically neutral but fascist all the same. The Gestapo work very closely with their border patrols.*

*We hid near St. Girons on the French side of the Pyrenees for a week and then set out. The terrain was not for the faint of heart and the constant rain during the pitch-black nights made the steep and narrow passes all the more dangerous.*

*The three of us were joined by an RAF flyer and a senior officer in the French First Army who were being shepherded by an MI9 agent. The MI9 man had managed against all odds to get them through a series of safe houses from Dunkirk to Toulouse with the Gestapo close on their heels. That MI9 agent was Bobby.*

*We eventually arrived in Spain and were transported first to San Sebastian and then a full 10 days after we had left St. Girons, we presented ourselves to the British Consulate in Bilbao. The RAF flyer was dispatched immediately to Gibraltar in the boot of a consular car. Bobby, Vanessa, the French officer, and I boarded a fishing trawler two days later for the short trip to Southampton.*

*André decided to stay with Françoise, the brave woman whose compatriots guided us through the mountains. They make a wonderful team in more ways than one and are still active in the Pyrenees Ariégeoises. Cher Vanessa  is now a nurse with LeClerc's 2nd Army.*

Rory was eager to add at this point that Bobby and the French officer recruited Marguerite on the spot. Bobby liked to say they had seen something in Marguerite that would wreak havoc on the enemy.

Having seen Marguerite pop a guy in the back of the head without the slightest hesitation, I gave that decision a mental two thumbs up.

*Marguerite is also modest to a fault,* Rory went on, *but we do not have time today to learn about how she earned the first of her elegant scars as a decoy for the group during their holiday in the Pyrenees.*

I looked for the scar in question but saw only the relatively new bumps and bruises that I had first seen a couple of weeks before. They seem to be healing nicely. I was a gentleman and did not ask for more information on the location of the scar nor dwell on when and how Rory and Marguerite might have compared scars.

I pressed forward with the question of the moment, somewhat impatient with where the background story was leading us if anywhere at all. *So,* I asked again, *is Jedburgh Team Hugo real? What happened on the 10th of June 1944?*

Marguerite answered unperturbed by my pushiness. *The mission to Oradour sur Glane represented our first mission for Bletchley and our last as Jeds according to their plan for us.*

At this Rory added, *Oradour was a bloody cock-up, and the team walked into an ambush by the SS between le Masferat and Oradour due, we believe, to a traitor among the Macquis, who seems to hang on with us like a bad cold. Our goal had been the capture of a key figure in the planning for a nucleic detonation by the Germans.*

*As with le Masferat, there was a little that we could do for the villagers at Oradour sur Glane once we managed to get within range,* Marguerite added, *although Bobby and Babe were able to divert two dozen school children returning from another village before German reinforcements moved into the area.*

*I was to rendezvous with the Macquis when Bobby and Babe flew in on the Lysander because I know that area well. Much of my family is there, and I had some familiarity with the target. His name is Philippe Delain, a member of the Brotherhood of Heliopolis, disciples of Fulcanelli.*

*In truth, Delain is my uncle. He and my aunt, the dancer in the Ballet Russe, are loving and generous people. Soon after I left to study in Paris, they adopted a young girl who had barely learned to walk. The origins of the girl are unclear but apparently her parents had been swept up by the Germans along with dozens of others and executed as retribution for a raid on a German railway depot. Word is, they had nothing to do with it.*

*My aunt and uncle adored the girl. My aunt, herself a former prima ballerina, dreamt that one day their young daughter would perform on the stage at the Palais Garnier as one herself.*

*Fulcanelli had taken Delain in as a student at 16, and he is perhaps Fulcanelli's most brilliant protégé. As such, he is keeper of the keys, that is to say the two remaining but mysterious factors that are necessary for our enemies to complete their work on the nucleic weapon that Frederick, that is Professor Soddy, described to us and that you saw chronicled on the face of Notre Dame. The weapon is very real, and we believe nearly ready.*

*Who the hell has it…had it…whatever,* I said, eliciting little amusement from Rory? What the fuck, let's stay in the moment, I thought.

*We think that Fulcanelli may have been turned by the Gestapo but requires the two factors that are not in his possession and the means to activate them that we believe are in Delain's possession. Our mission was to snatch Delain before the SS found him, but he slipped through our fingers when the SS moved into Oradour in force.*

*Whose side is Delain on,* I asked? Marguerite replied, *we think that he is neutral at best, but Fulcanelli now has something of great importance to Delain and is using it as leverage to obtain the missing factors.*

*What is it,* I asked, *and for that matter what business is it of mine?* At this point, Rory and Marguerite drew closer and Rory whispered, *Charley, Fulcanelli has taken Delain's adopted daughter hostage, his prima ballerina and Marguerite's cousin. She is the one thing other than his wife that he holds most dear in the universe.*  At this Rory hesitated…*and she is your Jane.*

In all of my days of smash mouth football I had never had a kick in the head like this. Rory watched me, sympathy writ large on her face.

Even Marguerite's hard shell seemed to crack just a little bit. My head was spinning.

And then all hell broke loose.

******

My memory of what happened next is a jumble of images, twisted still further, I suspect, by the morphine drip that came later, an amalgam of real events and perhaps a few things percolating upwards from my subconscious, moving in slow motion, changing in order and relationship, one to the other, swirling like that gelatinous goop in a lava lamp.

Nausea ebbs and flows with the changing imagery. The memory of it makes me feel like the morning after a romp through Covent Garden with Roddy soon after Ophelia's funeral when we mixed designer Bourbon with gin and tonics and a few Tequila shots.

I remember that, as I struggled for a response to Rory's revelation about Jane, gripping the rounded edge of our table, there was the screech of tires as a London cab came to a stop opposite the restaurant's front door on Elizabeth Street. The car had come from the direction of Victoria Station.

Both Marguerite and Rory reacted instantly drawing a bead on the cab that sat astride the center line of the street. I saw at least four guys emerge from the cab directly opposite the front door. They looked familiar and in a split second, I knew why. They were to a man, big, blonde Adonises, clones of the backpacker we had left to die on the floor of Gare St. Lazare.

From over my shoulder on Ebury Mews moving rapidly toward the cab was the young couple that I had seen enter the first car with Babe in our caravan to St. Lazare. They had machine guns at the ready. Everyone seemed to have machine guns and then both sides let loose with them.

The sound of gunfire and the terrified screaming of patrons was deafening as everyone seemed to be firing at everyone else. The front door of Cubitts disintegrated in a rain of bullets along with the plate glass window behind the patio that fronted the restaurant on Elizabeth Street.

Marguerite and Rory, who had indeed been packing a machine pistol into which she snapped a large magazine, were both moving toward the front door trying to get a clean shot while pushing Cubitts' patrons out of the line of fire.

Chaos reigned. Patrons were screaming bloody murder and those who didn't hit the floor were hit with flying glass and worse. Our waitress went down hard, propelled backwards against the bar. She lay there -- with a look of shock on her face and a gaping hole in her chest that spurted blood in time with her still beating heart.

I for one stood there like a fool at first mesmerized by the intense action. That is until it occurred to me that I wasn't watching fucking HBO.

A shower of bullets hit a nearby wooden beam and a large block of wood came flying off to hit me in the head. It hurt like hell but otherwise brought me to my senses.

I remember moving toward my right and the front of the place to help a young, pregnant girl who had collapsed on a top of a table. She had not been hit, and I managed to get her back behind the heavy oak bar despite slipping in the copious puddle of blood on the floor surrounding the waitress whose heartbeat no more.

The pregnant girl asked about her husband. I remembered the dude from earlier, so I got up to look for him while dodging bullets and debris. He was unconscious when I found him at the window and, as I grabbed him by the collar, I saw standing across the street through the shattered window a tall, spectral figure wearing a trench coat and fedora. One of his arms hung limply at his side, and he appeared to have a claw for a hand.

Next to him stood a figure that could best be described as a Carnaby Street dandy. Both stood apart from the general mayhem in front of them until the stylishly dressed dandy, a young good-looking guy, walked over to the young woman from our team who with her companion had come from Ebury Mews to return fire. She was flailing on the ground in agony and the dandy stood above her, said something I could not hear, and smiled as he shot her twice in the head.

I got the pregnant woman's husband, who was beginning to regain consciousness, back behind the bar as well and rushed forward again to the front window. Something hit me in the thigh like a jackhammer stunning me momentarily as I saw another German dude take aim at Marguerite. I grabbed a baseball size piece of brick that had been chipped from the front of the place and threw my best breaking fastball high and tight. It managed to knock the gunman off stride so that he missed the shot.

Then came the point when both sides started screaming and moving away from the cab. My last memory was of a flash and the ragged and rapidly expanding area of blood on Rory's face and track suit as she body checked me to the ground.

# IV. BRAVE HORATIUS

# MONTGOMERY INTERVIEW VIII

It was a variety of things that gently pulled me back from the spongy, queasy netherworld in which I had been trapped.

The first of them was the brisk aroma of ozone carried on the breeze from a Spring shower. A window near my bed must have been open a crack. It made me feel like a school kid waking up on a rainy Saturday morning, a leisurely day of endless possibilities.

I did not seem to be able to open my eyes at first. It was as if they had been epoxied shut. I was beginning to regain some sensation – toes, the hamstring that always seemed to ache in bad weather. But lifting my upper body was still a work in progress as if I were trying to jettison two 300-pound defensive lineman, one sitting on each shoulder.

I recall running my fingertips up and down what felt like a galvanized steel pipe that I eventually came to realize was part of the bed frame. I would tap the bed frame…---…. SOS and Morse Code were probably the only meaningful things that I retained from my 18 months as a Cub Scout. I was a bad Cub Scout. All that I wanted to do at that age was play football and chase Girl Scouts.

At the same time, I noticed that my blanket itched like hell. It was like one of those old army blankets that I got when I was a kid away at Camp Yokomiko. The camp was on my dad's Air Force base where the camp mess had some of the best cooks in the world. This fleeting association with food made my stomach growl.

But there was also a recurring dream that kept me tethered to my unconscious state. I was in a dark place like a cave with Jane, sitting next to her shoulder to shoulder. We were high school versions of ourselves both of us aching to say how much we loved each other, but we could not get the words out. Much as we tried, an unseen force prevented our doing what we both yearned to do.

It was a recurring dream because we, I, since it was my dream, came back to the same scene and tried to chip away at the barrier between us, to trick the unseen force into letting us say what we needed to say, but to no avail because the dream ended the same way every time. Jane finally left to go home each time to relationships unknown to me, to people more important than I and whom she loved more.

Jane would always end the dream by saying, 'The darkest times create the brightest moments.' And as much as I wanted to believe that and hold onto her, she would be taken away from me. Sartre could not have created a more awful hell than to be taunted by an unseen force in this way.

Eventually the voices that had orbited around me became more distinct – familiar voices, but I didn't know why. One such voice was always associated with an intense hit of Aqua Velva.

It made my nostrils itch, but I could do nothing about it. Aqua Velva was the aromatherapy of my dad's generation, and whoever it was near me must have been swimming in it.

Then it all came together suddenly, as if my consciousness could finally be brought into focus like adjusting the lens of a camera. The thing that finally did the trick was the rattle of approaching carts and the aroma of food. They were rolling breakfast down the hallway and, as they drew closer, I could smell the bacon, and my desire for bacon and eggs finally overwhelmed my stupor.

I lifted my 1,000-pound head and rolled onto an elbow. *Good morning, Bud. It's about time you decided to rejoin us,* said Babe who gripped my arm with his meaty paw as he loomed over me smiling.

They came in with a good English breakfast and just the proximity to sausage and bacon began to clear my head and lift my spirits. As I wolfed it down, I noticed how sore my jaw and my left leg were.

*Where am I Babe? You are in a military hospital a couple of hours from London, Bud,* he replied. *We thought it was safer here.*

I felt that there was something strangely primitive about my surroundings. Then I seized on the old telephone with the frayed chord next to my bed and pointed.

*Do all military hospitals have these antique telephones? They do in 1944, Bud,* Babe replied.

*So, you are saying that I am not only not in London, I am not even in the same century?*

*Roger that,* Babe smiled.

My synapses were beginning to reassemble my memory from torn scraps. The image of a handful of blonde dudes packing heat came into focus. I began to sweat. Jane!

*Where is Jane, Babe?* At this, Babe went stone faced.

I sat there trying to put two coherent thoughts together. I had nothing but a fragmented set of images. Jane. She saved me. Threw me to the ground. Could she be here too? Then someone else appeared to me. A beautiful girl with hair like a Beatle. *Rory!*

Babe put his hand firmly on my shoulder and looked at me glumly. *What happened to her, to them,* I growled as I swept the tray off the table in front of me and tried to spring out of bed. Babe kept me pinned to the bed with one tree trunk-like arm. The hospital staff came rushing into the room, and Babe waved them off.

*Calm down. I will let Marguerite fill you in when we see her, Bud. You need to regain your strength. You're a stud, Pal, and saved a lot of people in that shit storm,* Babe said.

I again growled at the top of my lungs, *but she saved me…Rory…I remember…I want to know what happened…Was Jane there?*

*Bud, I can have them give you a little shot with some happy juice in it or you can calm down on your own. Then I will give you the low down.*

*Rory…*I said again. *She'll pull through, but barely*, he said. *Does Roddy know*, I said as I tried to reign in my anger? *Yup*, Babe replied glumly.

*Ok, Ok, Babe. Start talking.*

*Our guys were losing ground against those Hitler Youth shitheads, and Rory left you to help Marguerite and her squad regroup.*

*You started pulling the wounded behind the bar and were grazed by a bullet and hobbled by some shrapnel. You looked like you had been through a war when we found you.*

Judging from the smirk on Babe's face, that was intended as a bit of gallows humor, but I ignored it.

*You remembering any of this? Not really*, I said. *Just scraps.*

But then I stopped Babe with a wave of my hand. I said, *I remember blood streaming down my face, Babe. I remember the smell of the blood more than the blood itself. I think that I was moving toward the front window of Cubitts, and there was this dude – tall and thin in a topcoat. One of his hands looked like it had been through a meat grinder.*

This made an impression on Babe, and he looked at me grimly.

*I got closer and there was Jane lying at his feet on the sidewalk,* I continued, *no wait, was it Rory?*

*It looked like the man in the trench coat or someone next to him playfully kicked her head to one side as if to get a better angle for the shot before delivering the coup de grace. But then he turned the gun on me, or am I imagining that?*

*You got a big piece of a front tire in the kiester, Bud. The Krauts had turned the cab into a giant Molotov cocktail and had Rory not had you moving away from the blast and had the building next door to Cubitts not taken the brunt of the explosion, you would have looked like that piece of crispy sausage lying on the floor.*

*The chunk of tire put you in a coma and the shards of metal from the bumper took a real fucking toll on Rory. You also had a neat little bullet wound in the leg. Patching up the wound was relatively easy, but we had to wait for you to find your way back to us from the coma. You've been here six weeks.*

*So, who was that guy? You are going to get to know him a lot better, Bud,* Babe replied.

*And what about Jane. Was she there? Why do I think that she was?* It was cold sweat time for me, and I was shivering like hell. *She wasn't there,* Babe replied, but I didn't find this reassuring.

*And who is Fulcanelli and who the fuck is Jane's uncle or father, or whatever,* I asked. These images and words were pouring into and out of the piece of rotted cantaloupe that had once been my brain so fast that I was losing control, descending back into delirium.

Babe sat on the bed next to me as an orderly, the one drenched in Acqua Velva, pushed me back and put a cold compress on my head. Babe said, *the man in the trench coat wants you out of the way, so that he is the only game in town when it comes to grabbing what he wants the most. And that is Jane.*

*We have to get your ass out of here, Bud. We need to find both of them or everything that we have been working toward will be lost.*

******

We spent the next couple of days talking about why a ballerina and an aging jock who were perfectly content with their self-indulgent lives had been caught up in this shit. It was slow going and Babe was exceedingly patient. It was hard enough for me to piece together a coherent set of thoughts let alone voice them.

Along toward the third day, I was asked to report to the head of the psychiatric division who had requested to see me. My left ear was ringing, something that still bugs me to this day, and I was working through my other aches and pains as I had been conditioned to do with the Skins as the toll on my body mounted toward the end of every football season.

I couldn't shake the feeling that I had let down Marguerite and Rory, the kid that I had carried on my shoulders as I raced her dad around the Serpentine in London, about whom Babe was still tight-lipped. I obsessed about what that meant.

For this reason, Babe thought it would be a good idea for me to get myself 'shrunk' as he liked to say. I was not given the choice to say no.

As chance would have it, the head shrink was a Brit who just happened to own the estate where the Army hospital was located, he was the 5th Marquis of Lansdowne, which I understand is a big deal, better than being a count or a duke. His name was Arthur Fitzmaurice and damned if he didn't tell you to call him Bertie. What is it with these Brits and their nicknames?

Bertie was running late so I hung out with his orderly in the anteroom of his office as he was listening to an address from Winston Churchill, who was wrapping things up with a poem that my high school football coach used to recite to us:

> *Then out spake brave Horatius,*
>
> *The Captain of the Gate:*
>
> *To every man upon this earth*
>
> *Death cometh soon or late.*
>
> *And how can man die better*
>
> *Than facing fearful odds,*
>
> *For the ashes of his fathers,*
>
> *And the temples of his gods.*

It was surreal, no doubt about it. This was the real thing rather than a coach's pep talk. Bertie came sauntering in at that moment and announced himself by repeating the last two lines of the verse, head held imperiously high, as he looked down on me across the bow of a prominent nose.

He brought me into his massive office boasting all of the appurtenances of a rich man's man-cave, at least one in the 1940's. There were oak polished floors covered with a massive oriental rug, plush leather furniture, two of the four walls lined with books, another wall with an ornamental portrait of someone who shared Bertie's prominent schnoz and finally double doors looking out toward a garden dominated by lilac trees in bloom.

He was a fastidious sort who adjusted the position of the tea pot and cups on the tray that someone had placed on his large mahogany desk. Once satisfied that all was in order, he offered me a cup with a therapeutic shot of Calvados, which I gladly accepted.

Tucked in among the bookshelves on one wall was a gun case with rifles and a few handguns including an imposing German luger. I stopped to admire them, and Bertie joined me. *They are my pride and joy,* he said pointing to three rifles of one particular type. *Behold, the Brown Bess,* he proclaimed.

I smiled obligingly, as the Calvados warmed my tongue and disposition, and he continued. *She is a muzzle-loading, smoothbore 75 caliber flintlock musket used in the era of the expansion of our Empire, and she has acquired symbolic importance for us at least as significant as her intrinsic physical beauty. Bess is a symbol of the history of the British people and their dominion over nations large and small. She served our armies well from 1722 until 1838.*

*Indeed, most of you chaps in the American colonies were required by law to own arms and ammunition for militia duty. She was a common firearm in use by both sides in the American War of Independence.*

*How did it…she…get her name,* I asked, as the Calvados loosened my tongue? He pounced on the answer like the know-it-all kid in fifth grade whom no one liked. *One hypothesis is that the 'Brown Bess' was named after Elizabeth I of England, but this lacks support,* Bertie said.

And then Bertie launched into a stream of perfect German, ending in the recognizable words "braun buss." *In my view old chap, the name is more likely the offshoot of the German words 'braun buss,' meaning either strong gun or brown gun depending on one's posture toward the German etymology. Before all, King George I, who never spoke English and commissioned its use, was German.*

Made sense to me, although I made a mental note to look up the word etymology. They were beautiful guns. I didn't know much about guns, but I was learning quickly thanks to the ever-increasing number of people who were pointing them at me and my friends.

I asked whether they could be fired, and Bertie offered that most had their bores blocked. The Luger and one Brown Bess were still in good working order, however.

He pulled a Brown Bess out and let me hold it. *These are strictly off-limits old Chap, and I have the only key*, he added, as he held up the strange little gold colored key that he had just taken from a pocket in his crisp khaki uniform and used to open the cabinet.

My lesson in historic firearms ended abruptly, and Bertie directed me toward a plush leather chair and finally inquired about how I was doing. I shared my experience with him in a more coherent way than I had been able to do with Babe at first. Bertie seemed particularly interested in my degree of recall.

*Charles or is it Charley*, Bertie didn't wait for me to answer. *We have the means to help you with tools and techniques that range from mild hypnosis to new and exciting forms of Narcosynthesis pioneered by our prodigal cousins in Deutschland. Much of my research in Berlin was on the use of cocktails of pentothal and pervitin, which create a much deeper hypnotic experience, which can itself be induced and reversed with but a single word when necessary to great effect in behalf of the patient.*

*So, you studied in Germany,* I asked. *Yes,* Bertie replied. *I was a fellow at Humboldt University before the National Socialists went off the beam.* He seemed to double clutch at that point and abruptly changed the subject to his job and the work of the hospital in which we found ourselves.

*Fortunately,* he said, *our front-line forces now have a program in place to address battle shock cases better than they had done at first. It is not uncommon for a regiment to see 100 new cases a day, many of them from the raw replacements who seemed to collapse within 48 hours of arrival on the front line.*

*It is a psychoneurosis, not lack of character, My Boy, although with notable exceptions our boys are not on the same plain as the disciplined, battle-hardened German fighting man. The medical breakthroughs of which I speak have done wonders for the worst of the shock cases, which are sent to us as a last resort.*

Bertie stopped and thought for a moment, *Charley* he said, *would you like to meet a few of our boys? There is a young man, in particular, a difficult case, young Kimbrell, Edward Kimbrell, an American.*

*Physical exercise is such a key part of the regimen to return them to full health and, inasmuch as I hear that you are a renowned athlete in your own right, would you consent to a football match? I* asked, *An American football game, you mean?*

*Quite,* Bertie responded enthusiastically! *I will make arrangements forthwith, Charley. Thank you for your gracious offer.*

There had not been an offer although anything that I could do to help a fellow American was  fine by me. Bertie dispatched me soon thereafter with his best regards. I am not sure how much Bertie did to help me with my own psychoneurosis that day, which I am sure was abundant, but I felt a hell of a lot better just getting out of there.

# MONTGOMERY INTERVIEW IX

That evening, Babe nicked a bottle of Old Bushmill's from somewhere, and we wandered out to a grassy ledge overlooking the Lansdowne House estate and its sprawling city of Nissen huts that spread down the long gentle slope of a hill to a large stream at its base.

Backs to an ancient stone trough that might have once been used with livestock but that now collected rainwater and sludge, we lounged on the ground amid a tribe of British Bluebells that were competing with overgrown grass. We looked down the long hill to what appeared to be a Roman temple on an island dividing the stream into two channels.

The lush farmland beyond, which stretched to the horizon, was blanketed in haze. The cool evening air smelled like the sea, which was not all that far off in the distance.

Some of the Nissen huts looked to be as large as a warehouse but most were roughly the size of barracks. They all had concrete floors, flush toilets, clean water and coal burning stoves.

Here the real work of the wartime General Hospital was done with thousands of G.I.'s who had made it through a system of collecting stations, clearing stations and field hospitals in France and now were lucky enough to be out of harm's way and receiving care from medical personnel in a hospital as complete as any that could be found stateside.

We talked about what an odd duck Bertie seemed to be as we let the scene pour over us and the Bushmill's do its work. I then asked Babe whether he had ever thought about chucking it all and using one of the time dilations to get the hell out of Dodge (I had to explain that metaphor to him) to set up shop in the relative safety of the 21st[th] century.

*It would be desertion, Bud. They asked us that same question before they approved us for the mission,* Babe said. I asked whether he had ever been tempted on one of his trips forward, as he and his compatriots liked to describe their excursions into the future, to look up the Caffo's in the telephone book, to snoop on a child or grandchild.

*Well, maybe they picked us because we weren't that sentimental,* he said. *There will be no children or grandchildren living in something that resembles the world that we know if we fuck this up, Bud.*

*But we know the outcome, Babe,* I said. *Why can't you use your knowledge of what will happen to your advantage.* I was thinking about the Falaise Gap, which the Allies inexplicably failed to close when they were breaking out of Normandy in August of 1944. Closing the Gap would have trapped and permanently crippled the German army in France probably ended the war six months sooner.

*This is what worries the top brass and ISA,* Babe added. *They call it the Confounding Principle. In simple terms for us dogfaces, knowing the future in detail won't necessarily lead to better results if you used this information to reengineer some prior detail of the past.*

*There are too many random confounding factors associated with any change that could then take what appears to have been a step toward the desired result and turn it into something very different. Maybe something a lot worse.*

*In other words, a little bit of unplanned chaos is just as important to a good result as the plan itself, or so the Eggheads say. So, there is a lot of resistance to cheating, that is using the known future as a game plan to finagle a better result today. Although, whatever we accomplish in the fight against these jokers that changes the outcome for the better — well that's fair game.*

*And besides, no one wants to find out the hard way what happens to the history that we know if the other side actually does set off this nucleic bomb.*

*Although it wouldn't surprise me if the Nazis were a little less fussy about the ethics of using time dilations to win the war. The fracas at Cubitts made clear that they know how to exploit them and aren't going to be fussy about doing so,* I said in turn.

I handed the Bushmill's back to Babe with a perplexed smile. *ISA?* I asked.

Babe hesitated but responded by saying that Soddy spilled the beans once after a hard night at the pub that there is a group of Americans, actually German physicists, who had been relocated to America, working at Princeton who were pulling the scientific strings on the time dilation angle and therefore the work of Jed Team Hugo.

I finally got around to the question that had been bugging me for a while. *Babe, we are here well after D-Day. When do we go after Jane and rendezvous with Bobby and Marguerite?* Babe handed the almost empty bottle back to me with a self-conscious smile and, as if talking to no one in particular said, *93 days ago. And we leave in a week.*

I took another hit as I looked pie-eyed at Babe. A response was pointless.

A few minutes later, Babe said, *Bud, when my number's up, I would like you do one thing for me that is cheating, I suppose. Look up the Caffo's on Snyder Avenue in Philly and stop by to say hello. Promise?*

I wondered if Babe had been handicapping the life expectancy of the people around me including his own. I would have.

*Roger that, Babe.*

# MONTGOMERY INTERVIEW X

Babe and I dragged our asses out of bed the next morning and managed to show up more or less on time for football, each of us leading one of the teams in a pick-up game. The Marquis had tipped the guys off to the fact that I was a pro football player, but I feigned modesty when they wanted to know who I played for. That would have been a hard one to explain.

They had carved out a baseball diamond and football field in a secluded part of the Nissen hut complex bordered on one side by the stream at the bottom of the long hill at Lansdowne, on another by a lower scrubby hill and on the remaining two sides by makeshift warehouses. For a bunch of banged up dudes, the G.I.'s who showed up played one hell of a spirited game.

The prized patient that the Bertie had clued us into was a fellow by the name of Eddie Kimbrell from Nashville, TN. He seemed pretty normal to me and was probably the best athlete of the bunch. He played wideout on my side while I played the gimpy QB.

The bullet that had hit me in the thigh was fortunately a ricochet and had lost some of its kinetic energy by the time it found me. I got another break because it went through soft tissue and exited, nicking the muscle only slightly.

In spite of my lack of mobility, my side won thanks in large part to Eddie. And when all was said and done, we made a beeline to a wooden cask of warm ale provided by Uncle Sam and Uncle George and shot the shit for a while. After a few chugs of the strong ale, it didn't matter how warm it was.

Eddie hung back but the ever-gregarious Babe took a mug over and started to chat him up. After a while, I joined them in mid-conversation.

*...His legs were blown off clear up to his pelvis, Sir. Damned if he didn't stay conscious and when I got to him raised what was left of himself up on his elbows and told me not to waste my time with him. 'Go help the others,' he said.*

*He lived another six minutes, conscious the whole time, Sir. I might could'a done more, Sir, but I just don't...*and then Eddie just trailed off as he stared into space, unable to conjure another word, a prisoner of his terrible memories.

Bertie had clued me in to this part of the story. Eddie was talking about the fate of the commanding surgeon of his medical unit. What Eddie had not told Babe or at least I don't think he had by the time I joined them was that his best friend, a fellow Army corpsman, had also been killed in the same barrage.

One minute he and the commanding surgeon were standing next to Eddie, and the next minute the barrage hit killing viciously and at random. When the dust settled, they found Eddie cradling his friend's decapitated head, still strapped into its helmet, about 20 yards way from the commanding surgeon or what was left of him.

I suppose that this is why the frontline soldier liked to say that if your number's up, it's up, and if it isn't you'll come through no matter what.

Babe and I liked the guy and yeah, he was here with the shock cases, billeted in a padded cell with steel doors, but what the fuck would we have done under similar circumstances?

******

Babe owed me a night at the pub after the thrashing his football team had taken that morning. On our way down to the pub in a nearby village called Ashford, we saw a crowd at the big French doors in the south wing of the main building. If there was someone there rather than in one of the many Nissen huts on this sprawling estate, that someone must be a VIP, we thought. So, we went over to take a gander.

We wedged our way into the room, or should I say that Babe used his broad shoulders to run interference for me through a crowd of doctors, nurses and other personnel that seemed transfixed by the scene before them.

There we found Jack and Jack, a sight that to this day both haunts and nourishes me. In the same large bed sat both Jacks -- propped up by large pillows against an impressively carved oak headboard that looked like a Norman wedding gift.

The first Jack was a scrawny, tow-headed kid with a shock of red hair sticking straight up through a small gap in his head bandage. He looked like he was 16 but, what the hell, everyone fighting our fight over here looks like he's 16. He was eating a large bowl of ice cream and savoring every spoonful.

His face was badly bruised, and he wore a gauze bandage around his head with bloody bumps that made it look like a crown of thorns. The rest of his body was swathed in thick bandages and was indistinguishable from the bed linens. He seemed to breathe and move with some difficulty.

The other Jack was a Springer Spaniel sporting the same crown of thorns who was merrily eating a bowl of offal. He would take one large slurp of his treat and look lovingly at the other Jack, slurp, adoration, slurp, loyalty, slurp, love.

He looked like shit too. Spaniel-Jack's beautiful black and white markings were desecrated by bruised and treated areas that were an awful purple and yellow.

I noticed a banner draped haphazardly over the large armoire near the bed and asked the orderly next to me what it was. He said, *it's the 13th Lancashire's, Sir, or what's left of them. A Parachute Battalion, Sir. The two of them parachuted into Normandy on D-Day with the 13th, the Spaniel is a Paradog.*

Apparently, tow-headed Jack had been assigned to a battalion of engineers that had removed several booby traps set by the 12th SS Division, the *Hitler Jugend*, who were chewing our guys up in the blood-soaked wheat fields between Gold Beach, one of the British landing zones, and Caen.

These Paradogs parachuted into action with their masters. The Allies had found that the dogs' slim bodies were an advantage during test jumps and that they could use parachutes that had actually been designed to carry bicycles. Paradogs were specially trained to get used to wartime conditions, like aircraft propellers and loud noises.

Getting them to jump out of an airplane was often a different matter, but Spaniel-Jack was a legend who excelled in his training. For him and his fellow Paradogs, the training regimen was *jump, land, eat* and Jack, the Paradog, happily allowed himself to be thrown out of the airplane or leapt without coaxing.

Jack was also trained to identify the smell of explosives and assigned to finding booby traps. The Jacks were among a handful of survivors in a company of nearly 100 that was ambushed by the Germans, who detonated the huge cache of their own ordnance that Jack and his team had been trying to defuse. The Germans, as they often did, allowed our guys to advance past their abandoned positions and then by means of an intricate network of tunnels worked back to ambush them from the rear.

Tow-headed Jack had drug two of his wounded comrades to relative safety behind a large hedgerow under heavy enemy fire before going back to find Spaniel-Jack, who continued to sight the explosive booby trap as he was trained to do in spite of the fracas surrounding him.

It was a massive blast that caught the Jacks a split second before they could make it to cover over the berm of the hedgerow, a blast which ironically also wiped out most of the Germans who had set the trap in the first place.

This was the stuff of a Silver Star or Victoria Cross. Where was Life or Look Magazine when you needed them?

Someone within ear shot was heard to say that Ernie Pyle had been in the village just a week or so earlier, and he loved dogs. What a hell of a story this would have been for him to tell the folks back home, that same someone said.

The crowd waxed and waned while Jack and Jack enjoyed their snacks and each other seemingly oblivious to the attention that they were getting. Having dispatched his offal,

Spaniel-Jack shimmied with some difficulty closer to his comrade to lick the residue of the ice cream out of his bowl.

The medical staff, whom I had gotten to know pretty well, stood there with fake smiles laying like thin gauze over their stone faces, as this tableau unfolded before us.

We got the hell out of there. Babe was fighting the same suppressed sadness that the medical staff struggled to conceal, as did I, amidst my own feelings of guilt and loss when it came to Rory and Jane. Without a word Babe nudged me firmly back in the direction of the French doors just as the subdued chatter of the crowd gave way to the old English ballad 'John Peel,' which the onlookers joined as one to hum in Tow-headed Jack's honor because he hailed from John Peel's Cumbria just a *wee shy* south of the Scottish border.

We heard later that Jack and Jack died in each other's arms before reveille the next morning.

******

We arrived in Ashford that evening just as a pea-soup fog blanketed the small village. It felt like a cross between heavy fog and light rain, and we could barely see our feet, or a handheld up to our faces.

The weak glow of lanterns atop each door in the village guided us toward a much larger lantern above a large wooden sign indicating that we had managed to find the pub. As we were approaching, we saw a figure escort two people to a waiting car, whose headlights illuminated a misty sphere in the fog around the people and the car. The effect was that of a Christmas scene in a snow globe after it had been shaken to set the snow afloat.

One of the silhouettes in the roiling mist looked vaguely familiar and it soon became apparent that it was Bertie of all people. A tall man in what appeared to be a trench coat waited to let another figure, a woman, I couldn't tell whether she was young or old, enter the car first. I could tell that she was blonde, very blonde, and the interplay of the light and mist made her hair glow like a lit torch, which was abruptly snuffed out as she and her companion disappeared quickly into the car.

After the car pulled off, we hailed Bertie with a shout. His silhouette made a beeline toward us until he materialized in the halo of the lamp above the pub door and said, *Gentlemen, how are you on this lovely summer evening. Brilliant English weather, isn't it?*

He was decked out in an African hunting hat à la Indiana Jones and a tweed jacket with knickerbockers and what looked to be riding or hunting boots. He was the true image of a landed country squire.

*Gentlemen, while I would enjoy immensely belting the grape with you, I have business to which I must attend back at the house. I do trust that you will understand,* he added.

Bertie struck me as a little fidgety but pleasant enough. And before we could say *gin and tonic,* he was disappearing into the fog. We both raised an eyebrow over Bertie's odd behavior and were curious about the identity of his guests. Babe said, *did you smell him. He must have had a hot date.* I said, *yup, his cologne smelled like Narcissus, Daffodils. Jane and I have a bunch in the garden in Normandy.*

We did belt the grape…tap the admiral…bend an elbow that evening in the atmospheric public house in Ashford. It was over the top rustic like something out of the Hobbit or Game of Thrones except that no one was disemboweling a fellow guest with a broad sword while we sat there.

We had ordered one for the road just as a young MP came rushing into the pub. *Please come with me, Sirs*, he said. *It's Kimbrell.* This sounded serious, so we ditched the last round.

When he got us outside, the MP told us that someone had broken into Bertie's gun case and taken a fully loaded Luger. That someone was believed to be Kimbrell. The MP also said that Bertie was nowhere to be found.

Somehow, the MP got us back to the house in his jeep through the dense fog, and we made a beeline to Bertie's office. Other MP's had reported that Kimbrell was headed toward the playing fields.

Babe told me to take a look in Bertie's office and to get a fix on his whereabouts. *I'll take Eddie*, Babe said, and he was out the French doors to the playing fields in double time.

And so, I did. Clearly, the Luger was gone, but they had overlooked the fact that one Brown Bess was also missing, and it was the working model.

The heavy wooden door of the gun case was unhinged at the bottom. This had pulled the tongue of the lock out of its recess suggesting that the double door of the gun case had been pried open at the hinge.

This did not look like a smash and grab by a deranged patient. Someone had been fastidious about doing as little permanent damage to the gun case as possible.

How did Eddie know which musket to steal, I asked myself? And why bother if he had the Luger? Had Bertie confided in his young patient…given him the same pompous lecture on historical firearms that he had with me? That seemed unlikely.

Two and two was not adding up to four for me. Until it did.

*Fuck me,* I said to myself. I immediately told the lead MP on the scene to cordon off the athletic field but to have his men stand back at some distance, and I got my ass out of there hoping to get to Babe in  time.

I ran toward the athletic fields like my life depended on it, although it was not mine  that did. It felt good to run even if I did a couple of headers over unseen obstacles in the fog. The run produced an encyclopedia of sensations that reflected where I had been shot, bashed, bruised and bloodied.

I screwed up and took the wrong turn down a lane of Nissen huts and realized that I was taking the long way around and would end up on the hillock to the north of the field. Any delay could be deadly, I thought.

The Nissen huts still had blackout shields on the single light bulb that hung at each door, which reflected light downward. The glare of the light and the swirling ground fog made my footing impossible to judge.

I was chanting, *don't fuck this up, don't fuck this up*, beneath my breath as I sprinted to the crest of the hillock from where I could finally see the outline of the athletic field. My first bit of good luck was that the fog had collected at the river and lifted for the most part from the playing fields. Next came the bad luck.

Babe and Eddie were on the field about 25 yards away, and Eddie was pointing the Brown Bess squarely at Babe's chest. Babe's hands were halfway up in the air, a football in one hand. Babe was a lefty like Stabler.

Eddie was ranting and raving but the guy talking was not the Eddie that I got to know on the football field. Babe was clearly trying to reason with Eddie.

Then the shot rang out.

But that son of a bitch was shooting at me. Not Eddie, Bertie. Had I not been moving toward the field at just that moment, he would have plugged me in the side of the head with the Luger.

Both Babe and Eddie turned, but Eddie swiveled to keep Babe squarely at bay, musket still pointed at his chest.

Then a madness set in with me. I had to get to Bertie at all costs. I saw a flash of movement about 20 feet to my right and charged. Enraged, I flew through the bramble and brush, bouncing off a tree trunk and managing to extend my arm just enough to get Bertie by the ankle as I tripped.

The fall knocked the Luger out of his hand, and I rolled him over. *The word, mother fucker, the trigger word that pulls him out of it, you asshole, now before it is too late,* I said as I got Bertie in a choke hold. I pounded his head against the ground. *The word.*

Reluctantly, he mumbled something, and I eased up to let him talk. I raised my other fist ready to pound his head again, *Horatius,* he said, gagging.

I grabbed the Luger and tossed it into the far brush and ran to the crest of the hill and shouted, *Horatius* and damned if Eddie didn't immediately look at the musket as if he was confused, and two heart beats later hand it to Babe. Babe tossed the football straight into the air taking the musket in hand and a deep breath. He wrapped his arm around Eddie's shoulders like someone embracing a comrade and they both walked toward me.

And then the second shot rang out.

Babe and Eddie hit the ground as a bullet buried itself in the dirt nearby. I swung around and returned to where I had left Bertie. I could still smell the sulfur of the gunpowder from the last round. And then there was yet another shot.

Bertie had managed to find the Luger, take one more crack at Eddie and Babe, and get as far as a small ceremonial garden with two ornate wooden benches. It was there that I found him. The 5th Marquis of Lansdowne was slumped over the arm of a bench with the Luger still in his hand and a gaping hole in his left temple.

# V. THE CLUSTER

# MONTGOMERY INTERVIEW XI

We left Lansdowne House a few days later at dusk as the painted Western sky changed from bright red to a battleship gray. Save for our truck slowly crunching down the long gravel driveway, a stillness held the place in its grip reducing the great house and the heroic battle that it fought between life and death to an idyllic scene worthy of a picture postcard.

It took them some time to peel away the various layers of the rotten onion that had once been the 5th Marquis of Lansdowne. Aesop once said, 'A man is known by the company he keeps,' and it was not helpful that Bertie had a close personal and philosophical tie to Edward, Duke of Windsor, an admirer of Hitler, whom the Nazis planned to install as the leader of Britain after a successful conquest. Bertie was also a frequent hunting companion of Sir Oswald Mosely, who led the British Black Shirts.

Despite his bravery as a young subaltern in the First World War, Bertie had been passed over for a battlefield command in the next, and his coterie of fascist friends played no small role in his fall from grace. It is unclear when and how Bertie had been recruited as a Nazi operative in the U.K., but there was no doubt that his marching orders at Lansdowne that night were to eliminate me and Babe. Eddie was the unwitting instrument of that plan.

We had our suspicions about his guests in Ashford that night, and I will come back to this in due course. Babe came through with only his pride damaged as he managed to give himself a black eye with the butt of the Brown Bess when he hit the dirt hard after the second shot. As to Eddie, the flawed hero, he has since returned to the Third Army as a corpsman and is rolling through France with Patton.

Who am I to call him flawed? What do I know about heroes, really? I am simply target practice for the next Nazi in line.

For my money, I think heroism is best measured by the enormity of the gap between a life and death challenge and where the Average Joe who confronts it falls on the Average Joe scale. Eddie, the reluctant hero, is the poster child for this principle, a good 'ole boy from Tennessee who just wanted to live and let live and help his comrades.

I wondered whether I could measure up when we caught up with the monster who had set the plots in motion at both Lansdowne and

London and who now threatened Jane. That said, I also wondered whether catching him was really going to be worth risking the lives of the people who had become my friends. But that was not my choice.

We passed through Ashford one last time as we left for France in the soft embrace of that balmy evening. I knew that we were heading to an airfield, but I didn't know where. Navigating was difficult because the British road signs had been covered with the insignia of various American and British military units.

About an hour outside of Ashford, we hit a series of checkpoints that funneled us toward a makeshift fort, which seemed to have been thrown together haphazardly from railroad trestles and barbed wire. Once inside, the truck pulled into an area set off by what appeared to be sandbags.

By that point we had jettisoned our driver, and it was just Babe and I in the cab of the truck. Babe looked at me with a smile as I looked at him baffled about what came next. *Wish I had some champagne for your maiden voyage, conscious that is, but here goes anyhoo, Bud,* he said.

Then I realized what he was talking about and before I could react, something that appeared to be a spotlight hit the wall of mist in front of us. There was one part of the mist dead ahead, perhaps the size of the truck, which looked darker than its surroundings. From it a small, pulsing beam shone as if someone was standing on the other side of the screen directing us with a flashlight.

Then several men moved up on either side of the truck from behind us with tanks on their back and something that looked like a flamethrower in their hands. They were aiming at the flashlight and hit it with cylindrical, laser-like beams making the darker area in the mist look like a membrane of some sort.

At that point, someone near the truck shouted, *vector primed!* With a thumbs-up to his compatriots outside, Babe gave a war cry and gunned the truck into the membrane. Everything went dark, and I had the physical sensation of squeezing through something soft but solid at the same time.

We emerged in what seemed to be the exact same place if not the same time. Had it been a minute or an hour that we had been in the limbo of space-time? Who knew?

Babe was looking at me smiling, and I responded by saying, *that was it*? My hair had been singed and my eyes and mouth were parched as if I had been walking in a desert for days but other than that, I was none the worse for wear.  The fort was gone, but a group of Army Rangers guarded the perimeter around us. About an hour after my initiation in time dilations, we arrived at a place called USAAF Station AAF-417, a major base for the U.S. 9th Air Force, which was heavily engaged in the battle to move beyond the Normandy beachhead.

We pulled up to a C-47, an olive drab hulk named, "Liberty Belle," and unloaded our gear. As I was fussing with a broken shoulder strap on my rucksack, a kid tapped me on the shoulder and said with the hint of a chuckle, *good evening, Sir, I am Ed Tierney, your chauffeur this evening on your excursion to ALG-21.*

Ed as it turned out was 21 and didn't look like he'd had a shave -- not that day, I mean – ever – but he was going to be our pilot for a flight into the battle zone. As I would learn 70 years later in life, which in the totally whacked-out time inversion thing in which I found myself, had somehow already happened, ALG-21 was a very, let me say again, very short airfield on a bluff overlooking Omaha Beach at the St. Laurent sur Mer draw where some of the most brutal fighting took place on D-Day.

The workhorse C-47, which became known as the "Gooney Bird," was perfect for something like this because it had a reputation for flying low and slow, adeptly maneuvering in tight conditions. Apart from cargo, it would ferry 50,000 paratroopers and glider-based troops into Normandy during the first week of the invasion.

The "Kid" picked up my rucksack and carried it to the *Belle* before I could protest. Hell, it was I who should be helping him – maybe a good sports massage to get the blood flowing to his brain before he took us up in a tin can that would be exposed to the hell of the Normandy battlefield, a fight that I would learn on the way to the field was then barely a week old.

*So, what do you usually carry,* I asked Ed, as I caught up to him? *We are strictly logistics now, sir, ammo, medical supplies and the like. Whatever they tell me to lug, Sir.*

*We are going to give her a workout tonight, Sir. We have nearly 6,000 pounds of 50-millimeter*

*machine gun ammo -- just got done loading it.*
*Can't wait to take her up, Sir, it's her first trip over*
*and mine too.*

At that revelation, the remnants of the very good steak and kidney pie that *Sir* had downed at Lansdowne House began to do an Irish jig in *Sir's* stomach. Telling the story of heroic 21-year-old flyers in the world war over a harmless glass of St. Emilion and a good meal in the 21$^{st}$ century was a fuck of a lot different than flying with one of them seated on a throne of live ammo.

And since I had lived most of my life 70 years later, I supposed that it was preordained that I should survive this flight to a 5,000-foot dirt track on a bluff overlooking the slaughterhouse down on Omaha Beach. Although, after London and Lansdowne, who knew anymore.

We naively think of time as a separate and discrete phenomenon with a certain purity that we can observe apart from ourselves as it would naturally unfold in our absence. However, just as our perception of ourselves is often corrupted because we are the observed and observer, can we really know whether the natural flow of time, which we mark by observing a string of events, is as simple as today building on yesterday and yesterday building on the day before?  Or is yesterday in fact a misaligned event distorted by some action in the future?

In other words, was my being here in 1944 an example of the future corrupting the past which in turn might corrupt the future, erasing me altogether?  Who the hell knew?  In the overall scheme of things, I suppose history might never miss me.

For a brief moment, I had this terrible sense of foreboding. While I was learning that it was dangerous to be me, it could be lethal for the people around me, like the 21-year-old who was going to fly us that night. Absent the Chunnel, which would not arrive for another half-century, Ed was our only ticket from Britain to France.

Despite the intense vibration and noise from the C-47's engines once we were airborne, Ed and Babe along with the co-pilot, seemed to talk non-stop through most of the flight, telling dirty jokes and stories about their adventures on leave in London, even as I encouraged Babe to let Ed concentrate on his driving.

Less than an hour into our journey, Ed pointed out the invasion armada below and it was a magnificent sight to behold. It struck me as something akin to landing at night in Los Angeles over that endless grid of lights on the approach to LAX except that in between pockets of cloud you could see ships racing from left to right and back again, parallel to the approaching coastline. The frequent flashes from those ships must have been their big guns.

Then the rain showers hit, and Ed told us to strap in. The heavy squalls slammed into our port side just as Ed was making a sharp starboard turn, and the *Belle* was thrown violently to starboard. Had I not been harnessed-in, I would have been pulverized against the other side of the cabin. Ed fought to correct, but we were buffeted again and again, and the whining of the struggling engines made it sound like the *Belle* was in her death throes.

We straightened out as the front of the Belle was thrown straight up and then we veered sharply right again drifting so that what had been vessels running perpendicular to our landward course were for the moment on the same heading. The fuselage rolled one way and then the other as Ed attempted to correct our course and bring the *Belle* into trim lest this be her first and last trip to Normandy.

A couple of times, we rolled so violently that I could look straight down through the windows on the opposite side of that cabin at the fleet below. The cabin crewman near me threw up, and I wondered if he knew something that I didn't. I hung in though, surprising myself because I had every right in the world to start crying like a baby.

And then we dropped abruptly, and I heard the flaps and slats grind into place. I prayed that we were landing, and things suddenly began to smooth out enough for Babe and me to scramble forward to watch the final approach over the shoulders of Ed and his co-pilot. I spotted the runway just as another C-47 was taking off from its far end.

We were about the length of a football field away from the edge of the strip by that point. We began to drift right toward the beachhead below the bluff ahead of us, which was pockmarked with campfires and kluge lights that provided just enough light to hint at the carnage that surrounded them. The horizon on the inland side of the strip was lit by huge flashes playing out in a staccato pattern.

There were no Automated Flight Control systems in that day and age. That responsibility boiled down to the 21-year-old who was sitting in front of me coolly fighting the yoke for (my) dear life.

We were now 50 yards from the near end of the runway at the end of the bluff and were still drifting away from the bluff and out to sea, but Ed made one last sharp adjustment on the yoke and stuck the landing. Babe and I cheered although our cheers sounded more like two people attempting a primal scream while someone else was squeezing their gonads.

It was a breezy, misty night in Normandy when we arrived, and they got the ammo off the airplane quickly while Babe and I waited for our jeep. Babe started making time with a 22-year-old nurse from Pennsylvania, who was standing next to two Red Cross trucks nearby. That nurse whose name was Jean had herself been in the war zone for just a few days.

I saw Babe elbow Ed and heard him whisper to him that she was a pretty young thing, which belied a certain air of command that Jean brought to the task that lay ahead. *All right you men,* she shouted like a drill sergeant, *it's one of me and 24 of my kiddos on this flight. Time to load our precious cargo, and I mean carefully,* as she pointed toward the Red Cross trucks. Babe and Ed were all over it, and I joined in to be part of the gang.

God those young guys were a mess. It is hard to describe because the memory of it makes me sick. I wondered how many of them would end up at Lansdowne House or make it after all.

When all was said and done and the loading complete, we all got a big hug from Jean for our good efforts, which Babe milked for as long as he could. Jean ran to the C-47 and was quickly hauled into the cargo bay by Ed's crew as the airplane began to move.

Ed wished us God Speed with a smile and a thumbs up from the open cockpit window of the C-47, whose #2 engine kept flaming out. He did a figure eight on the small taxiway in an attempt to kickstart the engine, which cut out twice more.

But damned if they weren't going to send him anyway. He finally got both engines revving as he rolled to the near end of the runway for the take-off. He gunned the C-47, which began to move down the runway leaning ever so slightly now to port or his inland side. Suddenly, the tip of the wing on that side dipped sharply kicking up dirt.

In a matter of seconds, the C-47 with those wounded men and our new friends reached the end of the runway and hung there in the void for what seemed like an eternity. God if Ed didn't straighten the damned thing out as the C-47 lumbered on, ascending slowly out over Omaha Beach and the massive armada that clung to the horizon like a jeweled necklace. We heard one of Ed's engines backfire again as his taillights disappeared into the mist.

******

Later that morning, we arrived at our destination after several hours on the road working our way through the ever-present heavy mist, which swirled in white paisley patterns around us and the great war convoy that surrounded us. Babe was like a rodeo barrel rider masterfully weaving our jeep in and out of the heavy traffic that clogged the relatively small roads of Normandy.

When circumstances allowed, the cowboy from South Philly would veer off the road and floor the gas pedal, taking his bucking bronco through the fields that flanked us, which had been chewed up by countless machines of war.

By the time we got to our destination the jeep was covered with a layer of corn stalks, wheat, dirt and manure.

He nearly ejected me in one of those fields and I ended up losing my brand-new helmet. It hadn't fit very well anyway.

My thoughts returned to Ed and Jean. I was way too flummoxed by the action that night to realize that I knew them. That is in the future, before and after my adventure 70 years earlier in Normandy on the C-47. Follow me?

Today, the strip at St. Laurent sur Mer just east of the Normandy American Cemetery at Omaha Beach is a wheat field marked by a small memorial to ALG-21 and the brave men and women who took off and landed on this postage stamp of an air strip. That stretch of beach, once the scene of unspeakable carnage, is now home to tony beach houses that line the breakwater that American troops once used for cover under relentless German fire.

Jean accompanied 20,000 wounded from the Omaha Beach area on those flights, and Ed flew many of them. Ed eventually proposed to Jean in Paris after the liberation of France, and they were married in 1946.

Jane and I met this unassuming couple just down the hill from ALG-21 at a celebration of the 69ᵗʰ anniversary of D-Day years later. It was on that day that both pilot and nurse, the kid I had flown with and the beautiful nurse who took so many of her "kiddo's" out of harm's way, received the French Legion of Honor.

Back to that night. We were surrounded by an immense number of men and machines moving in unison down the road that we were on and in the fields that flanked it. It was a mostly British formation, although one could see Canadian markings on the vehicles off to the East.

We finally emerged from behind a scrum of British Cromwell tanks. Ahead of us was a line of rooftops that looked like a cardboard cutout backlit by the arriving dawn.

*We're here, Bud,* Babe shouted above the rattle of tank treads. A road sign soon came into focus that read *Villers Bocage*.

You know, I am not the first person to say that war is an extended cluster fuck of careful planning and totally random results. I shouted to Babe, *what is today's date?*

He shouted back, but I could not hear him in the cacophony of mechanical sounds that swirled around us. I got up on the manure covered pile of gear between me and the driver's seat and shouted the same question into his ear at point blank range. This time I heard Babe say, *13 June.*

It did not take more than an amateur historian of the Normandy invasion to know that we were in deep shit and not the good kind.

# MONTGOMERY INTERVIEW XII

We seemed to skirt the west side of the band of lights that was the small town of Villers Bocage and soon found ourselves in farmland where we were enveloped by the dark silhouettes of rolling hills. All would have been idyllic had I not known that men would die in those hills before the day was over.

We came upon a stone farmhouse behind a ramshackle stone wall that in some places was barely knee-high. The house was sheltered by trees and a malignant hedgerow that combined with the trees to form a continuous canopy over the house.

It reminded me of Rastafarian dreadlocks like those of our neighbor's dog in Normandy, who used to chase me when I jogged. It had been a white dog as a puppy but today its hair had grown long, tangled and brown.

We were welcomed warmly by the farmer's wife and not so warmly by the farmer himself as he pushed past us to attend to his second set of chores that morning, this time in the fields after what looked to have been a massive breakfast of ham, potatoes and eggs flanked by a large boule of rustic, grainy bread and the remnants of homemade butter and preserves. I heard Babe's stomach growl.

We learned later from the proverbial farmer's daughter that each day when *Monsieur le Fermier* rose, he would consume two, whole roasted chickens before milking his large herd of cows after which he returned for the second round, which his kindly wife and daughter now swept off the table to start anew for us.

Marguerite, Bobby and their ever-present entourage arrived just a few minutes later ready to chow down with us. Marguerite greeted the farmer's wife warmly with a triple kiss to the cheeks, so I assumed that she was one of Marguerite's many cousins in the area.

Babe smiled and gave her a cheeky salute, which Marguerite parried with the barest of a wry smile. The two of them would make a great couple when peace came, I thought to myself. They were different, but Babe would be the ideal Yin to her Yang.

And God almighty if Marguerite, whom I had not seen since Cubitts in London, didn't walk over to me and give me a double *bis* too! I was paralyzed like my dog used to be every time he encountered the neighbor's cat, which he adored, although I hope that I wasn't quivering like my dog. Marguerite whispered in my ear, *I hope this proves to be your day, Charley.*

Yet Charley – I – knew that for every good thing that happened in this time-dilated cluster fuck of a world, fate would unleash the hounds of hell to claw it back. Perhaps it was the influence of my friends and the selfless heroes that I had encountered of late that I worried more about them at that moment than about myself.

We ate like kings or at least as well as farmers, which is pretty well. The shortages of everything 30 kilometers away on the Normandy coast were nowhere in evidence here. We ploughed through the breakfast with the same last-meal-on-earth intensity that the Jed's had shown at Rotisserie du Beaujolais, and I was one of them this time.

As I began to mellow with some ersatz coffee and the mountain of food in front of us at that old oaken table, I was blindsided by a sudden sense of dread that sent shivers down my spine in spite of the conviviality of the moment. The dim light made our rustic setting, and my companions look like an old photo that had yellowed with age.

And it made me claustrophobic, like I was being pulled down in a cramped diving bell against my will fathom upon fathom, decade upon decade to a place where I did not belong. Bloody hell, I was in 1944 and very easily could die there – then -- here. And at this point there was no clear path back to the life that I had once known or to the woman that I will never stop loving.

I managed to snap out of my momentary malaise and helped pull back the benches after breakfast so that we all could stand over a map that had been drawn carefully on a piece of silk from a parachute. The hair stood up on the back of my neck when I heard that the day's mission was to find Jane before the Nazis did and that they were fast in pursuit of her. A rendezvous with Delain and Jane was planned at a 14th century chapel later that morning at a place called the Tilly sur Seulles junction to the East of Villers Bocage.

Delain would first come alone to negotiate her return and if all went well to place her in our custody. Bobby was doing all the talking at this point, and we all the listening, but when people sensed that Marguerite was ready to speak, everyone fell silent.

*Charley, you must be aware that Delain calls Jane, Odette. This was her name before you met her, long before. I warn you that Jane may have changed since you last saw her. It is for your own good that you understand her story.*

*She did grow up in Philadelphia with foster parents, distant relatives of mine and Delain, who welcomed her when Delain and his wife put their beloved Odette through a time dilation when she was a very young girl to spare her the danger and suffering that he knew would befall France and, I might add, to conceal her from Fulcanelli. In other words, she is of this time not yours.*

I was beginning to get irritated because what I thought was going to be a homecoming celebration was turning decidedly funky. *So, I get the danger part,* I said, *but what else is going on here,* I asked in a voice approaching a growl.

Marguerite continued non-plussed by my rudeness. *Do you remember Doctor Soddy's mention of the Great Work? He was talking not just about the transmutation of metals but the experimenter as in the case of your Jane.*

*Jane has access to certain powers that are beyond our comprehension. That is also why Delain hid her in forward time.*

*We must assume that Fulcanelli has given the Bosch what he knows about the nucleic weapon and that Delain was to some degree complicit. This is why Fulcanelli entrusted Jane to Delain while unbeknownst to Delain, Fulcanelli was trying to auction her to the Germans.*

*However, Delain loves his daughter and, apparently, Jane is the only living person who knows how to use the remaining two factors that will make that awful weapon we seek to find operational. And they, father and daughter, are now on the run.*

*The transformed Jane – Odette – may not recognize you at all at this point, Charley. She may not have a side in this fight now and may use her new powers to defend herself from the Bosch and from us.*

And if this story line weren't bad enough, I finally threw them my own curveball.

I described the infamous Battle of Villers Bocage to an audience that stood around the table stone-faced and at first skeptical. But as I described the terrain, Hill 231 where the blood-letting would begin, troop movements and the orientation of Villers Bocage to the surrounding terrain, their skepticism evaporated like dry ice.

Bobby had a difficult time concealing his resentment when I described the battle as one of the most devastating ambushes in British military history, perpetrated by a single Panzer Ace, albeit one who had been credited with 137 kills on the Eastern front. His name was Michael Whitmann.

I told them that the crushing ambush, due almost entirely to the lack of forward reconnaissance by the British commanders in the area, was itself bad enough. Worse still this battle would doubly underline the fact that the British Cromwell tank was totally incapable of taking out a Tiger tank even at point blank range.

They all had to know what we were walking into. *We have a mission to complete today*, Bobby said dismissively. He reiterated the Jed policy against reengineering the present with advance knowledge of events and admonished us not to stray from the mission.

I could tell though that what I had just told all of them had hit home. So, Bobby was not leading from a position of strength.

*The Tilly junction, where we will meet Delain*, I said, *will be directly in that path of a 70-ton Tiger II tank with an 88-mm cannon and a dude who knows how to use it. Whitmann is going to turn everything in that area into cinders.*

*So, what do you suggest that we do, Bobby* asked?  Marguerite chimed in before I could respond, *if what Charley has told us about the allied bombing tonight after the Bosch retake the village is also true, we must think about the townspeople.*

I offered that Chateau Rugy should be the option for sheltering the townspeople, cheating a little on the Jed rules because that is what actually happened. Marguerite nodded to her companion, a very pregnant young woman in beret with a submachine gun strapped over her shoulder, who left immediately with two companions to get the ball rolling.

Babe challenged me halfheartedly, I think more than anything else, to help me drive home my point. *Bud, what can we really do? What will be will be, right?*

I replied, *Babe, my time spent with you guys makes me think that between each note of the dissonant musical score that we call history there is a split second that contains an infinite number of ways to influence the next beat. Dammit, just look at us – at our mission. If it's 'a what will be will be' moment, then what the hell are we doing here?*

I heard the farmer's daughter, who spoke a little English, say in all sincerity *C'est très poétique*. Babe grinned while the Bobby faction scowled.

But I was on a roll.

*Maybe we are one of those factors in the Confounding Principle that your Princeton guys talked about that may not be all that random after all, I said. We save someone today and that someone sets a random event in motion that leads to another and eventually to a short, slow dude playing for the Washington Redskins 50 years later whose house in France is burgled by two thugs kitted in World War II costumes on a mission to prevent destruction of mankind with a nucleic weapon.*

*Why the hell did you seek me out if you are so fussy about changing the course of events. I stand here as a bruised and bloodied witness to just the opposite!* My ally, the farmer's daughter with a penchant for poetry, smiled sweetly at me, so at least I was getting through to somebody.

*Those who made the reengineering policy are comfy cozy in the U.K. and U.S. and see the loss of lives as little more than a variable in a scientific calculation, I added. Blood will flow indeed, and just a minor adjustment to the trajectory of events on Hill 231 might save plenty of lives worth saving.*

Marguerite jumped in to say, *even if the die is cast, you, Charley, must let the British know if only to minimize casualties as you say. Charley, I will take you myself to see the British general staff in Villers Bocage and then join our fighters who will organize an evacuation to the Rugy cavern.*

Marguerite had won the moral high ground.

Bobby said half-heartedly, *take Babe with you. I will as planned take our team to do reconnaissance on the chapel at the Tilly junction.* No one said anything. No one moved. No one spoke up. Bobby finally did – *let's get cracking!*

# MONTGOMERY INTERVIEW XIII

And get cracking we did. Bobby left first with the partisans. Babe and I hopped back into the jeep accompanied by Marguerite for the trip to Villers Bocage.

It was barely dawn and one of those mornings in Normandy beloved by impressionist painters when the sunlight fought its way through billowing clouds to reflect off alternating fields of green and brown, creating a mélange of colors suspended between heaven and earth.

We made it to Villers Bocage as the triumphal parade of Allied infantry and their assorted war machines trundled into town. The crowds were over the moon with happiness showering the Cromwell tanks with flowers. A champagne mist seemed to envelope everything.

Young women dressed in their Sunday finest presented cider and butter to soldiers in jeeps and personnel carriers while a brass band, whose instruments seem to have been polished just for the occasion, played a peppy but somewhat dissonant march.

Yet, I knew that the exhilaration of the moment would soon be ripped apart with savage irony by both sides – a German panzer ace and our own fighter bombers. Unless we acted quickly, many of these young girls would be buried in their Sunday finest.

We had no time to spare and found the temporary British HQ in the town's Mairie, or city hall. It was amazing to watch Marguerite work to get us through to the top man. She cut through security and the formalities of a command HQ like a hot knife through good French butter. Babe and I simply rode her coattails through the roiling mass of humanity wearing brown, green and gray.

We finally barged into the inner sanctum and stood before a startled Looney Hinde, Brigadier General of the 22nd Armored Brigade and the author of this mess. There was a glimmer of something, I thought, when she introduced us -- recognition of Marguerite, resentment, perhaps?

As I followed with my elevator pitch, Marguerite faded into the group of senior officers who formed a ring around Looney. We had refined the evacuation plan on the way over, and she left to join the mayor, another cousin, in getting as many townspeople as possible to the safety of the caverns under the Chateau de Rugy before nightfall.

*So, you are a fortune teller then, Sir,* Hinde finally said with a sneer, as I wrapped up. He was a mustachioed prig that I would have loved to have body slammed. Hinde was playing to the crowd and evoked a few chuckles from the hangers on. I had no choice but to keep my cool. Babe said, *Sir, you are aware that we deal with things in our unit that are to say the least unconventional.* Babe was struggling for words because he did not want to s ay too much about the mission in front of the growing number of spectators.

I said, *Sir, we need to go now. No hesitation, now, men will die unnecessarily if we don't.* Babe interjected that we needed a jeep and an officer to get us through the roadblocks to Viscount Cranley, who was leading the ill-fated expedition to Hill 231 into Whitmann's trap.

Hinde asked us to step into the next room while he made the necessary arrangements. So, Babe and I obligingly filed into a side office and, as we did, I was sure that I caught a glimpse of Bobby in the ebb and flow of the crowd.

We were escorted by his military police who stayed just outside the door. *Bud, I am not sure about this*, Babe said, when we were alone. I told him that I had seen Bobby, and it was then that we knew we had been had. We were prisoners.

We also noticed in synchrony like the married couple that we were fast becoming that there was a WC and just past that a door to some sort of terrace at the rear of the building. We moved fast.

Babe jimmied the flimsy lock on the door, and we found ourselves on a terrace, looking down on an alley and an avocado green Citroen below us, which looked tiny from this height. My fear of heights accentuated the distance, which was barely a full story.

Babe, the ever-empathetic warrior, sized me up with a worried expression and said, *well Bud?* My friend the Army Ranger threw himself over the railing with gusto and was halfway down the wrought iron grill to the alley below before I could hitch up my drawers and make a go of it.

It took me a split second to get over the railing myself but because my sense of geometry had never been good except on a football field, I clumsily groped for support with my right hand and wrong footed the counterpart so that I had barely traversed a body length before ending up parallel to the railing and the ground -- nearly helpless.

Embarrassing. You think? I was trying to work out my next move when Babe climbed back up to yank me by the belt, and we both fell 10-15 feet. The hard contact with the ground actually felt good.  The problem had been entirely in my head.

This is not a fairytale but damn if the keys to the Citroen weren't on the driver's seat.  As if summoned from Aladdin's lamp, the driver himself showed up at that moment pulling us both up short.

I am not making this stuff up but am simply telling you what happened as you guys require but damned if the driver wasn't another one of Marguerite's many cousins. You've got to admire the fertility of her family tree.  He nodded toward the car, and we all piled in.

He was a young, enthusiastic guy, hell a boy, who was high as a kite. We had to open the windows to let the 150-proof vapor that was oozing from his pores escape the cramped confines of the tiny Citroen. But hell, he could drive.

We raced ahead up a hill paved with cobblestones behind the Mairie and through an old tunnel that was barely large enough for the car, under what looked to be a small aqueduct, crashing through shrubbery at the other end. The plan was to cut the British column off before it hit the final curve on Hill 231 that would put it barrel to turret against Whitmann's squad of massive Tiger tanks. The young guy told us that we could do it by taking a dirt tract through a dry riverbed that intersected their path at a point just below the curve.

In the meantime, the only sign of the approaching enemy was a single German eight-wheeled armored car that appeared and disappeared on the horizon to our left as we descended into the dry gulch. I knew that elements of the Panzer Lehr division, seasoned Nazi fighters, would be moving into the area to parry Hinde's surprise advance into Villers Bocage.

In a couple of kilometers, we shot out of the other end of the gulch and went airborne coming down with a jaw rattling crash in a small pasture by the side of a road that was tightly lined with trees and ascended around a curve up the hill. The high-banked road was flanked by a small wood that stood back about 25 yards.

I don't know who was more startled as we quite literally crashed Cranley's party – Cranley or us. Damned if he wasn't standing a stone's throw away in his scout car. We were lucky that his men did not open fire on us.

Most of his force was behind his car, a good thing. Unfortunately, several Cromwell and Stuart tanks and a few large personnel carriers resembling a stretched jeep had already begun to round the bend ahead.

After we gave our young driver a slap on the back, Babe started shouting and waving his arms in the air, *Sir, stop your column, turn around,* as we both rushed toward his scout car. *There is an ambush, Sir, on the high ground ahead – Panzers.* A few of his men ran forward to grab us and threw both of us up against Cranley's scout car, while our chauffeur stayed put next to the Citroen.

Babe said something that I did not quite get at that moment. It was apparently some code that only general staff seemed to know, and Cranley took charge of the situation.

Then came a sound like an airplane prop and a metallic clang followed by a roaring whoosh.  And then another and a third – damned if these weren't the first rounds from the Tigers. We could feel the explosions from around the bend before we heard them and the pressure from the blasts even at this distance felt strong enough to blow out an eardrum.

Cranley and his adjutant ran with us to the brim of the earth berm that defined the curve in the road, and we saw them. Five massive Tigers about 100 yards directly ahead on the high ground. Two had left the relative safety of the woods to move down the hill toward the now battered and burning lead elements of Cranley's force. One of those tanks would be Whitmann's.

Cranley saw that his Cromwells were no match for the Tigers and ordered his aide to get the rest of the column turned around. At that moment, a shell hit a stand of trees 50 yards to our right. We all hit the deck. *Sir, one is sighting us, we need to move,* Babe said peering uphill around the edge of the berm.

As if by telepathy, our forgotten driver revved the Citroen and drove away from us in the direction of the stand of trees, leaning on his horn. Before hitting the tree line, he did one large loopty-loop in the clearing.  I'll be damned, but Marguerite's cousin wasn't running scared. He was trying to draw the fire of the Tiger that had spotted us.

A split second before he could hit the tree line and safety, there was the snap, crackle and pop or in this case the propeller, clang and whoosh of the Tiger. The Citroen with our driver still in it evaporated in a burst of green-gray smoke, flame and burning flesh.

Cranley quickly forgot about us and rushed to retrieve as many men as he could from the carnage uphill. And unless he got the remainder of his column moving downhill, post haste, eliminating it would be like shooting fish in a barrel for Whitmann and his tanks once they rounded the bend in the hill.

As for two of those fish, Babe and I needed to get our asses down to the Tilly junction, and we soon found two bicycles on the ground that must have belonged to dispatch riders, but which now belonged to us. We jumped on

them with a whoop and peddled for our lives
away from the approaching Tiger tanks.

# MONTGOMERY INTERVIEW XIV

We were hauling ass down a very long hill. I was in the lead with Babe tight on my rear bumper. The hill curved to the right in the direction of a small ring road that we both agreed with a nod was the best route to take to the Tilly junction.

I felt like a kid, and it felt good going at top speed along the bumpy dirt tract – a balmy day, the wind in my hair and a reunion with Jane barely a kilometer or two away.

After a few minutes on the ring road, we veered off onto a much smaller unpaved country lane dominated by hedgerows on either side using the momentum of our bikes to surf the sloping road up, down, up and down again.  Not far ahead lay the intersection with the N175, the main highway that would take us straight to the Tilly junction.

I was pumping for all I was worth competing with Babe to hit the N175 first when machine gun fire hit the trees above me spraying me with debris. I had taken a slight bend in the lane and looked back to see the front of Babe's bike on the ground, but I did not have line of sight to him.

I spun out and tripped over my bike as I lunged in his direction to go look for him when I saw them, two Germans, fully kitted with ammo and those funny looking grenades tucked in their belts standing on the top of the berm directly above me. *Halt, Hände hoch,* they yelled, which I took to mean hands-up because one of the two was mimicking that move.

The other had his submachine gun trained on me. My first reaction was to get to Babe. My second was that I was bleeding profusely from a deep scrape on my left elbow and my third was that this was not part of the plan. But I did as I was told as I bled all over myself. What a fucking coward I was for not finding a way to get to Babe.

They directed me with the point of their guns to a ladder of roots in a gap in the berm right below them and hauled me up by my arms. They pushed me along the perimeter of a field bordered by the berm in a direction away from where I had seen Babe's bike. Every time I forgot to keep my hands held high, one or both growled *Hände.*

They were nervous. We were moving deliberately, ducking into the brush from time to time and waiting, presumably to ensure that we had not been detected by the wrong side.

We took a right turn at the corner of the field again holding to the perimeter staying as close to the camouflage of the trees and scrub brush as we could. I felt guilty about leaving Babe and awful about the blown opportunity to rendezvous with Jane. I got the heaves and nearly vomited. Try that trick with your hands in the air.

Had Babe given his life for nothing? Was he now just a random statistic in the "Acceptable Loss" calculations done by the generals? I couldn't help thinking about him rotting in the road – just another grotesque war photo of someone's son looking at the sky with glazed, empty eyes.

I looked for a way to break free. I could run across the field, but they would cut me down in a Texas minute. I thought of jumping off the berm, which would effectively put me on the N175, but I would probably impale myself on the shoulder-high barbed wire in the brush that was meant for cows.

No clever sleight of hand was possible here it seemed. No storybook ending. Fortunately, I was in uniform, so they couldn't shoot me for being a spy, I thought. But then again, these guys shot anyone they felt like shooting.

One of the Germans gave a warble like the large doves that lived on our land in Normandy. They thrived in the countryside and some of them grew to the size of a small dog. Jane hated them because they shit on everything.

We were answered by a warble from a stand of large cherry trees that formed the near corner of the field dead ahead. We ducked under the canopy of trees and, as my eyes adjusted to the dim light, I saw a German armored car, the kind with no roof over the driver's seat, parked there. There were two Germans in the open cockpit staring at us.

The group had been cooking because there was a flaming biscuit tin on top of a small mound of earth soaked with petrol. Ration tins were warming on top.

Then I heard a thud and the German to my right went down gurgling, a bayonet deep in his chest. My remaining captor recognized that something was up as we both came to the realization at the same instant that the two soldiers staring at us like mannequins from the driver's seat of the squad car weren't going anywhere soon or for that matter ever.

My guy, who was clearly not a true believer, dropped his submachine gun and threw his hands in the air in a gesture of capitulation when Babe emerged from the trees near the car wearing a smile and a German officer's crush cap. He was pointing that monstrous handgun of his at my captor, who we learned later was a Polish conscript as were so many in the German army on the Western Front.

I was in such a state of exultation, I had forgotten about the German until Babe pointed to the submachine gun on the ground and said, *Bud, you might want to pick that thing up before our friend changes his mind.*

*Son of a bitch* was all I could say. I wish that it had been something more profound. *Where'd you get the nice hat*, I said.

Babe smiled and said, *got it from this poor guy in the latrine gesturing to a clump of trees behind him. He was having a difficult bowel movement – a lot of blood in his stool. Poor guy.*

Babe told me later that he had gone down the second he heard the machine gun and had not been seen by the Germans. He had quickly back tracked along the other side of the field tracking our progress. He soon discovered the small reconnaissance squad hidden in the trees and systemically took out each one of them creating the tableau in the squad car to buy the split second of confusion that he needed when we arrived.

We hog-tied the hapless Pole and literally stuffed a sock in his mouth. Babe looked at the paybooks of the dead Germans and told me that it was not good news. This was an advance detachment of the 304th Panzer Grenadier regiment that was supported by 45 Tiger tanks. *Whitmann's gonna be the least of our worries soon, Bud,* he said.

******

We made our way along the N175 toward the chapel at the Tilly junction double time and could hear as we did loud reports from behind us in the direction of Hill 231 as the lopsided battle between Whitmann and an assortment of small tanks, armored cars and halftracks raged on. We could hear Whitmann's Panzer grinding its way towards us heading for Villers Bocage long before we saw the enormous hulk of the Tiger tank itself. It would be his first of several deadly forays into the village that day.

The Tiger's MG34 machine gun was blazing. About 50 yards up the road from us, it shredded an ambulance which had clearly displayed a red cross. So much for the Geneva Convention.

We high-tailed it across the road toward the chapel at the Tilly junction and hopped over the low stone wall that surrounded the cemetery to find in the tree-covered lane midway between the N175 and the chapel an M3 Stuart light tank, which the Brits nicknamed "the Honey," and the Americans called, "the Useless." There was a more imposing Cromwell tank behind it closer to the chapel.

The Stuart and Cromwell could see the hulking mass of Whitmann's Tiger across the graveyard and just up the road and bravely or ill-advisedly, you be the judge, let off two rounds from their concealed, stationary positions that did little more than bounce off the Tiger's massive frame.

Without hesitation, the Stuart moved forward down the tree-covered lane toward the intersection with the N175 while the Cromwell backpedaled to the front of the chapel. Holy shit if the Cromwell wasn't going to try to draw the Tiger's fire to give the Stuart a fighting chance.

Babe and I had the same thought at the same time and got the hell out of the blast radius of the Cromwell and hit the ground. The Cromwell took a shot and missed the Tiger altogether and, sure enough, Whitmann returned the favor slamming the front of the chapel with his own round.

A group led by Bobby had been watching the whole spectacle from the bell tower and got the hell out of the chapel a split second before a second round from the Tiger glanced off the Cromwell and hit the front of the chapel bringing down the steeple and burying the Cromwell in rubble.

This nightmare in slow motion continued as the pokey M3 Stuart finally made it the 50-70 yards to the N175 and turned toward Whitmann. The lightly-armed, 15-ton M3 Stuart was no match for the 70-ton Tiger, but the driver must have been hoping that if he steered his vehicle, the "Queen of Sheba II," as I recall, into the road, he could at least stem the monster's advance by blocking its path.

His bravery was futile though and the last thing he and his crew would hear was the resounding crack of the Tiger's 88mm cannon. Whitmann moved forward to force the disabled Queen of Sheba, now a burning coffin, off the road and turned its gun down the lane at us and the Cromwell.

The Cromwell had managed to free itself from the rubble of the chapel and, like most experienced tank commanders, the guy in charge was standing in the open turret as the Cromwell set out straight for the Tiger getting off two 75 mm shots on the run from around seventy yards away against its much larger adversary. We cheered and then groaned as we saw both shells glance harmlessly off the Tiger's thick armor.

The Cromwell would not get another opportunity. With Whitmann now fully aware of the danger ahead of him, the Tiger's massive gun trained itself ever so slowly on the hopelessly exposed Cromwell.

The German Panzer nailed the Cromwell with one shot and succeeded in blowing the tank commander clear out of his cupola, leaving him dazed on the side of the lane within a few yards of Babe and me. His driver and gunner were not so fortunate and were trapped in the burning hulk of the Cromwell.

The tank commander who was dazed and shouting incoherently was trying to get up as Whitmann sprayed the lane with his MG34 at 600 rounds per minute, which would have torn the tank commander to shreds like a branch fed into a woodchipper.  Babe and I frog-crawled over to the delirious idiot, who was trying to get up so that he could engage the Tiger with his side arm, all the while heaping profanity on him and his mother.  We managed to force him back to the ground before the worst could happen to him and to us.

Fortunately, the Tiger backed off and continued its destructive excursion into Villers Bocage.  Bobby and two partisans moved up to give us a hand.  I thought to  ask about the rendezvous but before I could, one of the partisans shook his head and said *rien, rien de tout,* meaning they had found nothing and there had been no one at the chapel.

We managed to get the tank commander to Chateau Rugy where a British medical officer treating other wounded was able to address the shrapnel wounds to his face by removing the tiny shards of metal with a small magnet.

The tank commander was damn lucky on two counts really. Had his injuries not been treated with dispatch, he would have lost sight in both eyes. And had he decided on closing the hatch, which I sure as hell would have done, he would have almost certainly been carbonized along with his crew.

******

Well, I guess that you are asking now what I was asking then and that is would I ever see Jane again. I will get to that in due course.

I didn't grow up privileged and I got my nose broken and my teeth kicked in more than a few times on the gridiron, but I had become accustomed to seeing the world from the position of privilege and opportunity. Money and influence could smooth almost any path.

But my improbable journey into the past as a servant of the future, as surreal as it seemed, was closer now to real life than the life that I had once known. Real people live in a world of random cruelty. The Gods of War amplify that cruelty a thousand-fold, and I was now subject to their whims.

In my old life, Jane and I always had a plan and faith in our ability to overcome any obstacle that stood in our way. In war time, a plan hardly mattered because you could be here one moment and gone the next obliterated without logic, without sentiment. In truth, we are all refugees in an anchorless world, where Time was a solid with a funky tubular shape that behaved erratically. Who knew? I had reluctantly come to accept that Time does not cure all ills – quite the opposite.

******

The ground shook beneath us and grit fell on us from the arched ceiling of the large cave below Chateau Rugy. Bobby and Babe were gone with a team looking for the German snipers who had taken out a few of the townspeople on their way to the cave. I helped Marguerite get the refugees from Villers Bocage sorted and settled.

The massive bombing by our guys had begun the instant the clouds had cleared that evening. The British Command had ordered Looney Hinde to retreat north by a dozen or so kilometers, effectively giving up all the territory they had gained in the approach to Villers Bocage earlier that day.

German units were advancing in their wake. The 304th Panzer Grenadiers and the dangerous Panzer Lehr were swarming around us and complicating our job of retrieving the remaining townspeople.

Wave upon wave of heavy bombers and Typhoons, our light fighter bombers, were systematically pulverizing Villers Bocage and strafing anything that moved creating a horrible muck on the ground of unlucky fighters and townspeople who had been torn to shreds.

The poetically-inclined farmer's daughter, who had fed us that morning, whose name by the way was Juline, showed up with two young studs. All were sporting hunting rifles. It was just turning dark, and they told us that a dozen school children had been rounded up by the mayor's daughter and were pinned down in an underground garage behind the Mairie.

Marguerite and I huddled at the mouth of the Rugy cavern with the three of them to map out a plan, although we all paused for a minute in awe of the massive sound and light show that unfolded before us, like the worst thunderstorm you had ever seen in your life multiplied a thousand-fold. The earth shook, and a dense fog drifted toward us carrying debris and the caustic smell of bombs and God knows what else.

Marguerite broke our reverie and flatly told us that we were about to head into town. Her radio guy showed up to tell us that the air force would give us 20 minutes at which point the squadron of typhoons that were already poised to take off from the bluff overlooking Omaha Beach would lead the next wave that was already in route over the channel.

We got our gear and Marguerite unceremoniously slammed a submachine gun in my chest and told me that I would need it. Babe had shown me the basics, although I was still convinced that given my relative inexperience, it was only a matter of time before I blew off part of my foot with one of those things – the money shot or "Blighty Wound" that the frontline British Tommy longed for – a wound that did not kill but was bad enough to get you sent home.

We left the cave while the Allies were still raining down hell on Villers Bocage and got halfway to town before the pause. The farmer's daughter and her crew were good at this and deftly steered a path that kept us under cover and away from the Germans much of the way.

We could hear their vehicles and once someone barking an order in German. Just upon entering Villers Bocage, which looked like a parking lot of burned out British and German tanks, we huddled behind one of them to avoid a patrol of Panzergrenadiers passing within a few feet of us. Much of Villers Bocage was in flames, and the roar of the fire was occasionally punctuated by the burst of a machine gun directed at someone or something nearby.

The streets of Villers Bocage were choked with rubble. We maneuvered around bomb craters at the edge of town that were so big you could drop two or three Tiger tanks into them and still have room to spare.

A sight like this gives you a sinking feeling knowing what a single bomb can do to you personally. It was hard not to be distracted from the mission for that reason even though every step we took was itself a life and death matter.

The scene in Villers Bocage reminded me of the devastation wrought on Verdun in World War I and something that Babe liked to say, *our war is a lot like the last one, Bud, 'cept the holes are bigger.*

We finally managed to pick our way to the
rear of the Mairie, which was itself engulfed in
flames. It seemed to be raining gently when we
got around to the back side where Babe and I
had escaped earlier. It became apparent,
however, that the rain was in fact molten lead
dripping from the roof.

We found the mayor's daughter and the
school children huddled in the small tunnel
under the aqueduct that had been our escape
route that morning. There were indeed 12 of
them and what looked like a very large dog in
the gloom of the cramped space. We took the
children out through the shrubbery at the far
end of the tunnel.

And then I felt them before I heard them.
My teeth started vibrating as we began to hear
the droning grow louder to the north. We had
run out of time.

The farmer's daughter and her companions
had gone ahead to scout, and we hightailed it
behind them. I carried a little six-year-old girl
who demurely gave me a kiss on both cheeks
in the French way as we introduced ourselves
when I picked her up. We caught a break that

night as I suspect the Germans nearby had already gone to ground to wait out our bombers.

We made it back to the cave in one piece – 12 children and our small band of fighters but no sign of the dog.  I deposited the little girl with her brother, who was not much older than she.

He started walking away with his young sister in tow when he shook his head as if he had forgotten something and turned heel to come back to me as his sister stood waiting, smiling sweetly at both of us. He held out a piece of canvas tied with what looked like the shoelace of a running shoe and said, *pour vous, Monsieur, du chien* or in other words -- *for you, Monsieur, from the dog.*

******

Don't ask. I know what you are thinking, but I'm just telling you like it is or like it was. Whole truth nothing but the truth, so help me God. I'll come back to the mutt in due course.

The canvas simply read "Prime -- S. Samson." Marguerite got the meaning instantly and identified S. Samson as the church in Aunay sur Odon, roughly three kilometers to the southeast. Prime is typically the first mass of the day, usually at 6:00 a.m.

Three kilometers doesn't sound like a lot, and I could have run it easily if I had to but getting there from Chateau Rugy meant navigating a jigsaw puzzle of German units that were primed to throw us back on our heels. As I recalled then, we had a limited window of opportunity because Aunay was going to get whacked almost as badly as Villers Bocage just a few hours hence.

They were dead set on going. I for one argued that this is way too dangerous and did not want to jeopardize the crew. Maybe a reunion with Jane wasn't in the cards today.

Marguerite promptly disabused me of the notion that this was my choice. Jane was the mission because as long as she was out there, she was more than likely to fall into the wrong hands.

Bobby and Babe had returned, and I moved toward Bobby because his double cross earlier that day was still stuck in my craw. I wanted answers. Babe deftly inserted himself between the two of us pounding me on the chest with his fist, *Bud, there will be time to settle scores later, but we have work to do now*, he said.

It was Midnight, and we planned to set out within the hour.

# MONTGOMERY INTERVIEW XV

So, you have already checked me out on this part of the story and, as crazy as it sounds, it is the way that it went down.

Let's back up. As you know, the Allied meteorologists working as part of a secret unit at Southwick House had been plotting the weather charts for months with an eye toward a D-Day invasion window in June, from the 4th to the 6th. The Allies needed a low tide on the landing beaches at H-hour and a full moon so that the airborne would have the proper drop conditions.

The Brits had a robust network of weather stations in Canada, Greenland and Iceland. They also had weather ships, weather flights over the North Atlantic and by secret agreement updates from weather stations in the Republic of Ireland, which was officially neutral at the time.

As rain and high winds relentlessly battered Portsmouth on the night of June 4, Group Capt. James Martin Stagg, the chief meteorologist for the Allied Command, informed Eisenhower of the deteriorating forecast and urged him to postpone the invasion of Normandy by one day from June 5 to June 6, 1944, because of uncertain weather conditions.

This was a ballsy move because it flew in the face of the American forecast which predicted just the opposite for the 5th of June -- good conditions for the invasion. In the end, Eisenhower sided with Stagg, who got it right, which was all the more remarkable because he did not have any of the technology that today's weather forecasters take for granted like satellites, weather radar, computer modeling and instant communications.

The 5th of June saw one of the worst storms to hit the coast of Normandy in a decade. If Ike had given the word to "go" on the 5th, the lives of thousands of men and massive amounts of equipment would have been lost. Victory in Europe would have been delayed for at least a year or more and the Soviet Union might have taken control of the European continent.

But that's not the entire story, is it? One of those weather stations, an old post office at Blacksod Point in the far west of Ireland, also painted a gloomy picture of conditions at its location a couple of weeks later -- rough seas, low cloud cover, driving rain and winds up to force six -- in its report on 14 June at 3:00 a.m. GMT. It  was going to be an ugly few hours, but what else was new?

At 3:05 a.m. GMT, the befuddled observers at Blacksod Point made another entry into the log reporting a picture-perfect night with a full moon or just about, big twinkling stars, calm seas and a balmy southerly breeze. In this one isolated sector of the North Atlantic, it was as if a thief had come in the night to steal a storm.

******

The trip to Aunay-sur-Odon was slow going to say the least. It was like trying to safely find your way through a lion's den blindfolded. Clouds had chased away the light of the waning moon, and we navigated by chance, encountering one formation of Germans, changing direction, encountering another formation of Germans and switching back to avoid it. We zigged and we zagged, and it was slow, gut-wrenching work to traverse barely three kilometers.

I was impressed by the Place de l'Eglise or town square in Aunay-sur-Odon where we found the imposing Church of St. Samson rising out of the gloom. It was much larger than the typical Norman church and could pass for a small cathedral. It made me think about how Jane used to describe me in relation to the hulking footballers that I competed against. She had nicknamed me "trial size."

It was a struggle not to obsess about seeing Jane and not to lose sight of the immediate business of staying alive. We learned as we entered the village that the Germans had not arrived, but it was only a matter of time before they did, as we would learn the hard way.

Babe, Marguerite and I entered the trial size cathedral, and her team posted themselves at each point of the compass on the outside of the church. I was amazed that given the bloody fighting in the area, the church was packed to the gills. Perhaps it was because of that fact not despite it.

We moved down the length of the nave toward the large altar at the point where the transept bisected the church. Juline, the farmer's daughter, emerged from the shadows of the South transept and whispered in Marguerite's ear.

Marguerite turned to me, she *can be found in the Lady's Chapel, Charley*, which was just yards from where we stood. I stared at Marguerite and Babe who stared back not making a move.

Babe looked at his feet like a shy schoolboy. I was to be on my own. Marguerite added, *five minutes and then we must be on the move…with her.*

I have had butterflies in my stomach before, but this was like having a stampeding herd of them. It was all I could do not to run as I circled the altar to the Lady's Chapel. A Lady's Chapel is typically a small chapel dedicated to the Virgin Mary that is tucked in behind the high altar bordering the Apse, at the east end of a church such as this.

I found in the gloom of the chapel a figure kneeling in front of a small ornate altar.  Her long blonde hair was covered by a head scarf, and I knew instantly from the dancer's bearing that it was Jane. I moved forward, and she turned to look at me.

Her face said everything and nothing. It was a blur and is still. She made the sign of the cross looking back at the altar and rose to meet me.

She came to me without a word wrapping her arms around my shoulders and putting her head on my chest. My emotions were so jumbled that had I tried to speak it would have come out as squeaking gibberish. In retrospect it reminds me of the country song that goes something like, "Please don't look so pretty, the next time that we meet… please don't look so pretty, and I'll try not to be a fool."

We held each other.  Torn apart for months, we just held each other and could not speak, like the two kids in my bad dreams.  There was too much to say.

She looked up at me and said so faintly that I barely heard it, *and you, you are…I wish I could…*And then we both looked up as the rumbling of airplane engines overhead was followed by ear-splitting explosions, which made the church shake to its foundations.

Our fly-boys had arrived. The stain glass in the Lady's Chapel cracked but did not shatter. It sounded like fabric being ripped.

*We have got to get out of here*, I said, and we moved quickly back to the nave  where the congregation was in a panic. Some tried to crawl under a long pew for protection. Marguerite and her brave troop tried to get others under some form of cover. In truth, had we taken a direct hit, none of it would have mattered.

I could not find Babe in the crowd but did see Bobby's sidekicks, the two dudes with the matching five o'clock shadows moving deliberately toward Jane and me. They approached from the left and the right as if to corner us. The hair stood up on the back of my neck. This did not feel right.

Jane still gripped my hand firmly as the storm of bombs raged around us. I had to get her out of here, I thought. *The crypt,* Jane said reading my mind, *the crypt,* and we ran to a winding staircase between the altar and the Lady's Chapel.

She led me to a door that was half ajar at the rear of the cramped and moldy crypt. We could hear Bobby's guys clattering down the winding metal stairs. *Will you be OK to go, I* asked? Jane nodded a yes. *Go then,* I said, *go, something is not right here,* and it was like cutting out my heart to say those words. *I will keep those two busy. Just go. I love…*

Jane put her fingers on my lips and said, *Mon amour, pardonne-moi pour ce-que je suis devenu, forgive me for what I have become, my love,* and she disappeared through the small door and, as I turned, I got the first guy with the butt of my submachine gun on the side of his jaw.

What side Bobby's henchmen were on at that moment was unclear to me and incidental. I saw red, and all I wanted to do was kill someone. I would learn later that the second guy was so badly hurt that they barely got him to a medic in time.

I returned to the nave of the church. The usually stoic Marguerite looked with shock at the blood on my hands and down the front of my shirt. Like a spring shower, the bombing stopped as rapidly as it had begun, and Marguerite's team began to take the townspeople out in small groups.

As we emerged from the church, we were greeted by a vision of the Last Judgment. The bombs had disinterred many of the skeletons in the churchyard, which in whole or in part were now scattered across the Place de l'Eglise.

This apocalyptic tableau was backlit by the red glow of the rising sun which began to illuminate the devastation around us. What had once been a square bordered by quaint homes and shops was rubble. The church's tower had been sheared off and most of its stained-glass windows were demolished but, miraculously, the nave of St. Samson stood intact, for now.

We were leading the last group of townspeople out, mostly school children and their choirmaster, when we heard them rumbling up the main drag, laboriously working their way through the rubble. It was a German column.

It was an SS Battalion flying a black banner that announced them as *Der Henker Battalion* – the Hangmen. We were compromised and could not open fire because we had so many kids in tow. The Nazis started to fan out in front of us in what was left of the square.

A command car arrived with the advance group and from it came a tall, German officer with an aristocratic bearing and a clawed left hand. He barked orders to a group of aides who looked like the same Aryan Chippendale pin-ups that I had seen in London, and I recognized him immediately from the attack at Cubitts. Also standing next to him was the scumbag who put a bullet in the head of one of our fighters when she was lying helpless in the middle of Elizabeth Street.

The pastor of the church collected as many of the children as he could and shepherded them back into the church and out of the line of fire as our hopelessly outnumbered group found cover in front of the church. I moved toward the tall German, who had seen, to get a shot off and then all hell broke loose. But it was our side that started the fight.

It was Babe and Juline, the farmer's daughter, each with a squad firing on the German flanks from both sides of the square. This was our cue to open fire from the front of the church. The rubble in the street approaching the square was fortunately too dense for the Germans to get a tank through, but two halftracks with vicious M34 machine guns and antitank weapons made it through and started to pound us.

I was still in a rage from my earlier encounter in the crypt and moved toward the tall German, again. He seemed to watch me with amusement like an animal toying with its prey.

And then it came.

First, a momentary squall hit us hard as if someone on high had thrown a large bucket of water on us. Then, we were hit with a strong gust of wind that smelled of the sea and sent an assortment of disinterred skulls and bones rattling across the square.

The clouds moved in rapidly and were thick and low leaving little purchase between earth and sky. At that point, the torrential downpour hit so hard, and the rain was so dense, one could barely see a hand in front of one's face let alone your deadly adversary just yards away. The choking winds also picked up rapidly driving the blinding rain into our faces so hard it felt like shrapnel.

To the extent that we could see or hear them, the Nazis seemed as befuddled by the tempest as were we. Gray forms regrouped around their leader's squad car. I could just make out the silhouette of Marguerite a few feet from me,  who waved me over. *We are moving while we have a chance. Get the children out through the transept and across the square in Juline's direction. We will regroup near the edge of town. There is a cider mill.*

But I hesitated because I wanted another crack at the asshole in the command car. Marguerite read my mind and said, *take them now! We need to collect our wounded while we can.* I did what Marguerite ordered while she and one or two others put down covering fire as the rest of us struggled to cross the square in the blinding storm with children and the wounded.

At a mound of rubble, we found our compatriots, and I nearly tripped over Juline. She was bloodied and incoherent and what is worse had lost an arm, which had been amputated at the elbow and cauterized by searing shrapnel from an anti-tank shell.

*Laisse-moi, Laisse-moi,* she said, but I was not going to leave her. She reached with her good arm for her weapon, which lay alongside her severed arm. She wanted to die fighting but not that night as far as I was concerned. I picked her up as gently as I could and moved as best I could through the driving rain and force six winds that had appeared from nowhere that morning and still bore down on us.

******

Aunay-sur-Odon like its larger neighbor Villers Bocage was now a pile of smoldering debris under a shroud of heavy black smoke, putrid incense to the vile God that sanctioned that day.

On each of the two opposing ridges that framed the shallow valley in which Aunay lay, stood two observers.

On one side, shielded from view by a curtain of smoke that had overcome the few remaining clouds from the storm that she had commandeered from the North Atlantic, stood a girl with a ballerina's bearing and an enormous German Shepherd on guard at her hip. She watched as more German units moved into the area. She had seen the choirmaster and his children melt into the countryside as the bruised and battered Jeds limped home tenuously making their way North through the undulating front line.

On the opposing ridge, a barely a kilometer away, stood a squat man wearing a pea coat that seemed one size too small for him and a brimmed sailor's cap. He was chewing a cigar and looked like a British bulldog and, in point of fact, he was the topmost among them. His nervous security detail stood at a respectful distance never  losing eye contact with their charge.

The man did not see the girl but felt her presence. The whole enterprise was at sixes and sevens because of the ineptitude of his general staff, he fumed, and the episode in Villers Bocage and Aunay with the American was no different. It roiled him to his core.

He pulled the cigar from his mouth and threw it to the ground, stomping on it, instantly thinking the better of it as it was the last in his  possession. If the threat of  this super bomb could not be eliminated itself,  the man on the ridge thought to himself as  he ground down the cast-off cigar with his toe, the instrument of its detonation must be addressed. In short, young Captain Percival must hew more closely to his orders upon the next opportunity and eliminate the girl.

# VI. TOMBÉ

# MONTGOMERY INTERVIEW XVI

I was in the doghouse. To be precise, I was in my house in lower Normandy during that short stretch having been sent packing to my end of the time dilation as soon as we made it back from Aunay-sur-Odon. I had pissed off a lot of people and so my removal from the front was, I suppose, the Jed version of being made to stand in the corner until I realized the error of my ways.

At the very least, they had to keep me and Bobby apart because we each wanted to kill the other. Bobby was the trained killer and I the mere amateur, so I suspect he might have gotten the better of it.

I wanted to confront his duplicitous behavior. Why did he turn us over to Looney Hinde who promptly imprisoned us before the battle of Villers Bocage? What were his guys going to do with Jane had they captured her at Aunay-sur-Odon? What was the double game being played here?

When I was a pro football player it was not uncommon to come home from the gridiron on Sunday wounded on the field of battle. Some Sundays were worse than others, but the same process always unfolded starting with Monday when you weren't quite sure whether all or any of your body parts were in their assigned places and still connected to the right things.  It was a rough day.

On Tuesday, things started out slowly but, as the day progressed, you began to feel less like a carcass hanging on a meat hook that had been used as a punching bag and decidedly more human. On Wednesday, if you were worth your salt as a pro, your outlook then swung wildly in a positive direction and your body fell into line because you were readying yourself then to kill or to be killed on the gridiron the following Sunday.

At this stage in the aftermath of the Aunay-sur-Odon fracas, I was mentally somewhere around Tuesday just before lunch.

No one was happy with my letting Jane escape, least of all me. Even the ever-sympathetic Babe was hard pressed to support me on this one. The bottom line for me was that something had not been right that night. Allegiances had shifted in Villers Bocage not just the front line.  I  felt  a perverse sense of satisfaction that I had prevented Ja. s capture.

They stationed Babe *chez nous* under strict orders not to fraternize with me. Yet Babe would fraternize with the window molding given half a chance, so his resistance crumbled in about a day, and I took advantage of it by showing him a little of 21st Century Normandy.

He was not a novice in all things 21st Century and had a special affinity toward my small Samsung smart TV and an engineer's intuition about how things like the Internet made it possible for the TV to unlock a satellite feed. I still harbored the idea of making him a permanent convert to the good life at my end of the time dilation. He would be a good friend, I thought, once we came through all of this.

Babe was also damn handy around the house. So, I would wake in the morning to find him tinkering with a leaking water heater or repairing the velux on the other side of the house, you know the type of inlaid window that you see on many French rooftops. It had been frozen shut.

He even dealt with the French cops, who continued to hound me, by booby trapping their hideout at the end of Chemin du Village. Babe accomplished this by trapping a rather large, unfriendly and, hopefully, rabid fox that roamed my property and put it in an improvised mesh cage that could be opened with a trip wire.

We made it a point to go for our evening constitutional the next time that we saw them show up and strolled by their customary hiding place just as they came tumbling out of the shrubbery screaming *Merde* at the top of their lungs!  If the locals do indeed end up hanging me one day for Jane's disappearance, I will succumb gagging and giggling at the memory of that moment.

It seemed that I was at war with everyone including myself at that time. I could not help feeling some resentment toward Jane, whom I will never stop loving, but whose higher calling placed a barrier between us that we might never be able to overcome. And that resentment made me feel like a dick.

It was all of them too. Human beings who ate, drank, slept, shit, like I did and whose commitment to a higher purpose gave them a God-like air.  And I resented it because I wanted to be selfish and reclaim the good life that was due to me and to be angry about having it snatched away from me if I damn well pleased.

I wanted to sit with Jane on the patio, get blasted over a bottle of Côtes du Rhône, and take her to bed afterwards, but these basic human desires were rendered base and even laughable by people who were quite literally sacrificing everything to make my life as a rich, spoiled ex-footballer possible.

I was stranded on one island as everyone around me seemed heroically engaged on another.

******

Soon after our return to Manvieux, Babe commandeered a forklift from the BricoPro, our local hardware store, and began to unload the five-ton army truck in which we had traveled back to my end of the time spectrum. It was not unusual to see vehicles like this in Normandy because the week-long D-Day commemoration brought out all manner of vintage vehicles along with locals kitted out in period costumes as American paratroopers, nurses, buck privates and generals.

We did the unloading carefully and quietly over the period of four nights under a waxing moon. They were large crates roughly five feet in length, three in width and about three feet high. I thought it was strange that they had

German markings including the stenciled iron cross of the Wehrmacht and a serial number SdKfz303.

I asked Babe what they were and where this all came from, and he answered with a maniacal grin that they were merchandise from a German toy store.

We laid out 10 crates each separated by several yards running in a long line down the low native hedge that ran the full length of my garden in the shadow of the tall fuck-off hedge which ran parallel to it and bordered the far side of my property. The smaller hedge is about 30 yards from my gravel driveway and the front gate that lay just a few yards beyond.

After positioning the crates the first night, my job was to break them down on the second, which exposed something the size of a go-cart that was shaped like a parallelogram. In fact, it looked like a baby tank complete with tank tracks but no turret or cannon.

All were pointed at my driveway and had a small gas motor and a storage compartment in the front. When you revved the motor, it sounded like a large lawn mower. They came wrapped in an oiled tarp, and we kept them well camouflaged under the tarp in a niche that we burrowed for each of them into the thick native hedge.

During the day, Babe would fiddle with a small electric motor attached to a battery pack in each of them that had essentially three functions: start, stop and thrust. What I mean by the latter is that there was a large, electrified pin that shot forward when the corresponding solenoid on the motor got a jolt of electricity from a remote operator.

Babe had been fascinated with a system I had at the house that enabled me to turn the lights on and off on the far side of the house and lock the doors with my iPad, which employed the same principle of delivering a small charge to activate an electric motor using a Bluetooth signal.

It took him a couple of days, and a visit to an electronics store, but he finally figured out how to use the same system to engage the pin in the electric motor, which shot forward each time that Babe clicked the icon on the iPad for my lighting system. As the pin shot forward, the lights would also flash on and off on the far side of the house.

Babe spent the next two nights tinkering with our big toys and on the last of them, we carefully unloaded another large crate full of something shaped like the gold bricks from Fort Knox. We put several into the large front compartments of each tracked vehicle as gently as one would place an infant in a bassinet.  He had me gas-up the bunch of them.

At the same time, he forced me to cut down a few of my prized *rosiers* -- wild rose bushes that lined the middle of my sprawling yard because they blocked the way between one of our toys and the driveway. He told me that we needed a clear path. I reluctantly complied.

Along the way, we also turned my dining room into an armory replete with hand grenades, submachine guns, a bazooka and even several long and skinny Bangalore mines, which eventually disappeared.  What the hell was Babe going to do with the Bangalores, I thought. We also cleared a path through  an ancient cistern that was now dry and formed a cramped tunnel from a small panel behind the water heater in my kitchen to a tight gap in the wall on Madame Jardin's property at a level several feet below my kitchen and the end of the fuck-off hedge closest to the house.

To celebrate the completion of Babe's mysterious project, we took a bottle of Calvados out to Cap Manvieux one evening. The Cap is the 60-meter-high cliff overlooking the English Channel from which Jane had allegedly jumped or been thrown.

So much for that theory.  Although, I wasn't crazy enough to attempt setting the record straight with the local magistrate, Madame Leroyer, with my tall tale of  time dilations and dust-ups with Nazis.

*So, I take it if visitors arrive, we are ready for them?* I asked after my first swig. Babe took the bottle, looked at me and said, *Bud, it is not a question of if, it is simply a matter of when.*

*They won't come through the fuck-off hedge because of the homes on Breholliere,* he said, *so our left flank is probably secure. I suspect that their first move will be a draw play right up the middle from the empty, overgrown field at the far end of your front lawn.*

*Why don't we just, 'Get the Hell out of Dodge,'* I asked.

*We have reason to believe they want to try to get to Jane through you, and it may prove to be an opportunity to flush out the double-agent in our midst,* Babe  replied.

As a dense fog crept in from the English Channel and enveloped us in the tall grass at cliff's edge, I finally got around to a subject that we had avoided on our trip back to 21st Century Normandy from Normandy 1944. We had largely avoided a real conversation because nerves were just too raw after what I had done at Aunay.

*Can I assume that 'they' means the tall man with the claw? Who the hell is he, Babe?*

*Well Bud, he is a man risen from the dead and among the worst of the worst.* I looked at him and said, *And…?*

*Does the Blonde Beast mean anything to you,* he said? *How about the Hangman?* Something struck me as vaguely familiar. *How about the Butcher of Prague, Bud?* That was the clue that nailed it.

I sat there stunned. *But he died from sepsis a week or so after the assassination attempt against him in Prague,* I said. *That is what the Nazis are happy to have everyone believe,* Babe responded.

*Himmler got a doctor over from Berlin double-time to look at his protégé. The doc used this new type of drug, something called sulfonamide, and in spite of being at death's door, the bastard pulled through.* Babe was talking about Sulfa, which at that time was the new anti-bacterial miracle drug that both sides were beginning to use on the battlefield.

*He is in one piece except for a mangled left hand that was shredded by the grenade that one of our guys threw at him when his submachine gun jammed. Tough luck for our guy.*

*Hitler and Himmler were happy to have everyone believe he was dead because they wanted to refocus their most ruthless asset on stealing the war by exploiting time.* Fuck, I thought, as I took an extra heavy shot of Calva.

I knew well that he is not only the baddest of the bad but one of the most notorious Nazis ever to have lived – Reinhard Heydrich. And now he had us dead in his sights – poor choice of words, I know.

Heydrich was the founding head of the *Sicherheitsdienst* (SD), an intelligence organization charged with seeking out and neutralizing resistance to the Nazi Party through arrests, deportations, and murders. The SD was the precursor of an even more notorious organization, the Gestapo.

He was also behind *Kristallnacht*, organized it in fact. *Kristallnacht* was a collection of coordinated attacks against Jews throughout

Nazi Germany and parts of Austria on the 9th and 10th of November 1938. These attacks, carried out by SA Stormtroopers and civilians, presaged the Holocaust.

When he was assigned to Prague by Adolf himself, he brought his special brand of cunning to the task of eliminating the opposition by suppressing Czech culture and deporting and executing members of the Czech resistance. He was directly responsible for launching the *Einsatzgruppen*, the special task forces, which traveled in the wake of the German armies and murdered over two million people, including 1.3 million Jews, by mass shootings and gassing.

He was also Hitler's right-hand man for the Night of the Long Knives. In the Spring of 1934, it was at Hitler's request that Heydrich and Himmler began building a dossier on Sturmabteilung (SA) leader Ernst Röhm in an effort to remove him as a rival to Hitler for party leadership. At this point, the SS was still part of the SA, the early Nazi paramilitary organization which then numbered over three million men.

Hitler, Heydrich, Himmler, and Göring drew up lists of those who should be liquidated, starting with seven top SA officials but including many more. In June of 1934, the SS and Gestapo coordinated mass arrests that continued for two days. Röhm was shot without trial along with the rest of the SA's leadership.

About 200 people were slaughtered during the Night of the Long Knives, which propelled Hitler into a position of absolute power to set the course of German affairs. With the SA out of the way, Heydrich began building the Gestapo into an instrument of terror.

The history books, which Babe would not have had a chance to read, say that Heydrich was critically wounded in an ambush in Prague on 27 May 1942 by a British Special Operations Executive team of Czech and Slovak fighters in Operation Anthropoid. The commonly accepted story was that he died from sepsis a week later.

Nazi intelligence falsely linked the assassins to the villages of Lidice and Ležáky. Both villages were infamously razed to the ground. All men and boys over the age of 16 were shot, and all but a handful of its women and children were deported and killed in Nazi concentration camps.

So, our adversary was an instinctive killer, some would say a monster, and he proved it before my own eyes in London and would do so again with tragic consequences for our team. It made my skin crawl to know that he had been just a few feet away.

Heydrich had been…was…such a bad dude that even a psychopath like Hitler held him in awe calling him, 'the man with the iron heart.'

Babe seemed like a distant vision now in the dense fog even though he was sitting inches away. He had pulled his exceptionally lethal trench knife out of its sheath and was running his thumb along its razor-sharp seven-inch blade as I finished the story.

He looked at me, his smile gone, as he drove his knife into the ground. *Bud, you don't want him to find Jane before we do, believe me.*

# MONTGOMERY INTERVIEW XVII

We spent the morning of what would turn out to be our last day in Bayeux running errands along the main thoroughfare. Bayeux has grown into a rather prosperous regional city, and Babe studied the sheer opulence of the 21st Century lifestyle with a certain bemused detachment. He watched the tourists with their iPhones on selfie sticks like someone watching a new exhibit of pink, three eyed sharks at the aquarium.

We got back to the car and Babe said, *Keys,* with an air of command so I turned them over to him and let him take the wheel.

*We are heading where,* I asked? *To see friends, a visit that is long overdue,* came the sharp reply.

Thirty minutes later we pulled into the parking lot at the Normandy American Cemetery at Omaha Beach. It is located on a bluff overlooking Omaha Beach and the English Channel beyond. It covers roughly 170 acres and is the final resting place of 9,388 American military dead, most of whom were killed during the invasion of Normandy, many of them on the now tranquil beach below.

Today's cemetery is on the site of the temporary American St. Laurent Cemetery, set up by the U.S. First Army two days after D-Day, the first American cemetery on European soil in World War II. About 14,000 American soldiers, who were originally buried here in temporary graves, were eventually brought home at the request of their families.

Among those who remain today are Theodore Roosevelt, Jr., the son of the President by the same name, and the former president's brother Quentin, who died in WWI but was brought here to rest beside Teddy, the younger. Another son rests beside his father, just as 33 pairs of brothers are also buried together here. Among them are Preston and Robert Niland, two of the brothers whose story inspired the film *Saving Private Ryan*.

There are also graves of Army Air Corps crews shot down over France as early as 1942 and four American women. All grave markers face West toward home – to the point closest to the cemetery in the United States, a spot somewhere between Eastport and Lubec, Maine. I had wanted to introduce Babe to all of this slowly because I was apprehensive about how he would react to his first visit to this place, at least in this century. In fact, we were barely a half-mile away from the landing strip where Babe and I helped Ed and Jean load wounded Americans onto a C-47.

So, we took the long way around past the visitor's center and its infinity pool and then along the overlook above Omaha Beach. While his origins probably made him the strangest tourist ever to have visited the cemetery, Babe managed to fit right in with the rest of the tourists and was fascinated with the interpretive maps of major landmarks on this and the other side of the Channel.

We finally emerged from the beautifully planed trees lining the overlook to immerse ourselves in a sea of white grave markers. Babe veered off without a word down one line of markers and a strange cadence ensued in which he would walk some, stop, come to attention and salute and then walk a few more paces to repeat the tribute. On and on he went.

Eventually, we both seemed to converge on the east end of the cemetery's beautiful reflecting pool and gravitate toward the Memorial Garden and Wall of the Missing with the names of 1,557 Americans who lost their lives in the Normandy campaign but could not be located. At the center of the semicircular colonnade is a statue called "The Spirit of American Youth Rising from the Waves" facing back toward the reflecting pool and a circular chapel beyond awash in a sea of grave markers.

Babe lingered at the wall as if he were putting each name to memory, so I gave him some space and took a stroll down to the chapel. I just happened to run into the superintendent of the cemetery, whom Jane and I knew from having volunteered there on occasion, and we kibitzed for a bit. I told him that I had a friend in tow, who was somewhere nearby and visiting for the first time.

When I finally checked my watch, it had been over an hour since I had last seen Babe, and I noticed some commotion at the overlook where security guards were gathering and talking on walkie talkie's. I had a bad feeling about this one and made a beeline toward them. Sure enough, if there wasn't a lone figure making his way down the steep, rough path toward the beach.

Beach access had been closed off within the last few years because of security concerns. It didn't help that Omaha Beach has turned into a major picnic destination on D-Day. Campers come from every nation in Europe, and the beach turns into one sprawling party. More than a few drunks -- French, British, Dutch and German tourists have crawled up the slope after dark to continue the party on cemetery grounds. I told the gendarmes that the man below was my friend who was perhaps distraught and managed to convince them to let me follow him. Babe, head down and hands in pockets, had made it to the beach and was heading east on its broad horseshoe like expanse.

I nearly broke my neck getting down there after him and when I hit the beach, he had a good half-mile on me. Running on sand isn't my thing, so it took me a while to catch up to him.

*Babe*, I shouted apprehensively as I closed in. He turned and smiled and kept going. I caught up with him and our conversation went something like this.

*Bud, I am a bastard from South Philly,* **Babe** said. *I was smart enough to realize it at the age of four or five because I was the only kid in the family who didn't have dark hair and a beard. Even my sisters had them.*

That elicited a double take on my part, and the Babe I knew smiled. He kept right on going.

*My dad, Mario Caffo, who adopted me, owns a laundry at 18th and Snyder and my mom, I mean the woman who gave birth to me, was a washerwoman for him. She was 17 at the time, an Irish girl who they sent away to have her baby – me – at a convent near Gettysburg.*

*I didn't meet her until I was five or six and then only once. She was with a nice-looking fellow who was dressed to the nines. He could have been my real Dad but who knows. I enjoyed the attention when they came to visit but who she was and why it mattered never really sunk in.*

*Yep, I never saw her again, but I can't say that I am the worse for it. I had a big family and a real mom and dad, and it didn't bother me that I stuck out from the bunch like the lone white bulb in a string of red and green Christmas lights.*

*My family is as traditional as Italian families come. My dad goes to mass every morning, and I went with him most of the time not because I was particularly religious. It was just something to do with Mario.*

*I eventually became an altar boy and made nothing on doing a mass but would get 25 cents for a funeral and 50 cents for a wedding. That was good money, and I socked away some real dough on weddings and funerals because there were a lot of both in South Philly in that day.*

*I was good in school and someone on some branch of my family tree must have had a good head for figures, so I went on to graduate from LaSalle with a math degree. This was smack dab in the middle of the great depression, and I was damn lucky because I had an ROTC scholarship. The Army had big plans for me.*

*LaSalle is up at 20$^{th}$ and Olney in Germantown, a working-class neighborhood like my own. I would stay with my dad's brother, who was a cop up there, during the week and come home to Snyder Avenue on Fridays because that's when the hospitals would send their huge loads of laundry into the store. Dad needed all hands on deck.*

*Mario had cornered the market on the hospital laundry trade and thanks to that we always had food on the table but not a whole lot more because most of his income went right back out the door to our neighbors who weren't doing near as well. Our dumbass Mayor, his name was Moore, used to drive around South Philly waving at us and then tell the newspapers that no one is starving in Philadelphia.*

*Yeah, wrong. If my dad found them, they had half a chance, but people were starving to death in my neighborhood, on my street. There were also these homeless camps all over the city at that time; we called them 'Hooverville's'. My sisters used to cook meals at the big one out on the Schuylkill near the art museum and, because I was a big beefy kid, they would drag me along as their slave.*

*Two of my older brothers, Dad used to call them the Bolsheviks, got involved in union organizing and general rabble rousing that struck the fear of God into the crusty Philadelphia elite, and I would often tag along with them. It was entertainment for me and cheaper than buying a ticket to the movies.*

*Dad would listen when they talked about their exploits over dinner, and he would snort, mumble a few Italian curse words under his breath but would never approve or disapprove. I knew my father well enough to know that he was a Bolshie at heart and was proud of his boys.*

*One of them was with the Budd Company and made railway cars. The other still works across the river at RCA Victor, and I marched with them more than once. I remember the food march to Reyburn Plaza where I got my first taste of a good fight.*

*We got into it with the special group of cops that the mayor had organized, mostly thugs, that they called the Red Squad. They shot a man dead that day right in front of his wife for doing nothing more than being there.*

*One of my brothers got sucked into a rumble with a group of them. I waded in behind him. It was a bad day for the Red Squad, but an Army Ranger was born.*

Babe finally took a breath.

*I know that I am just rambling on, Bud, but as bright and shiny as everything is in your day and age, I am a product of mine. If I make it back, and I am not counting on it, I still have work to do there.*

*Mario is not getting any younger and Lord knows what kind of trouble my brothers are going to be getting themselves into.*

By this point, we had made it the long way around up the Colleville gap back to the American Cemetery's parking lot near the visitor's center. Someone in uniform who clearly worked at the visitor's center was standing at the entrance near the infinity pool and reacted when he saw Babe. He made a beeline over to us waving a sheath of papers in his hands that looked like a computer printout.

*Monsieur, Monsieur, I have the additional information that you requested,* he said looking at Babe. I still think about the expression on Babe's face to this day, the profound sadness set like a jewel in his broad smile.

*Thanks anyway, Pal.* And Babe walked away without taking the information as I followed him to the car.

# MONTGOMERY INTERVIEW XVIII

We took the long way home that evening and made a stop for a few drinks in Port en Bessin. Babe had snapped back to his old self and was giving the women who ran the tabac near the mouth of the fishing harbor holy hell while we knocked back one grog after another. *Les Mesdames* were befuddled, flustered and charmed by the irreverent young American, who spoke worse French than I did.

We then swung by the battery at Longues sur Mer, which was just a few kilometers from the house, for no other reason than that we were so buzzed that Babe took a wrong turn. The battery was part of the infamous Atlantic Wall of Hitler and Rommel in 1944 and consisted of four 152-mm navy guns, each protected by a large concrete casemate.

There had been a command post, shelters for personnel and ammunition, and several defensive machine-gun emplacements. The four bunkers are intact today, and two of the guns are still in place.

It was situated strategically between the Omaha and Gold landing beaches and for that reason on the night before the D-Day landings, the battery was subjected to a barrage of 1,500 tons of bombs, although most of them landed on the nearby village.

Early on the morning of the D-Day landings it was hit again by a sustained barrage from the French cruiser *Georges Leygues* as well as the U.S. battleship *Arkansas*.

The Germans returned the favor and fired a total of 170 shells throughout the day, forcing the Allied headquarters ship *HMS Bulolo* to retreat to safer water.

Three of the four guns were eventually disabled by the British cruisers *Ajax* and *Argonaut*, although the single remaining gun continued to operate intermittently late into the evening. The crew of the battery surrendered to the Brits the following day.

Dusk had overtaken us, and the full moon arrived early to hang like a large wafer in the southern sky. We could see the twinkling lights of Bayeux and the handsome spires of its cathedral in the distance. The illuminated church steeple a few paces from my house could also be seen off to our left. Babe clamored up on one of the gun casements for a better looked and said, *Bud, get me the field glasses from the car, would you?*

I got them and tossed them up to Babe, who surveyed the horizon and lingered on the church in Manvieux. He could not see much of our house but had a good perspective on the terrain around it.

After several minutes in which Babe said not a word, he tossed the field glasses back to me and said, *catch…time to go to work.*

We took a back route to the house and parked the car at the far end of a horse pasture across the D514 from the church and the mouth of Chemin du Village which led to the front gate of my house. Instead of heading directly to the house, we veered off to the left and made a beeline to Madame Jardin's estate, jumping the fence into her yard.

We nearly collided with two huge, well-fed sheep. We grabbed two of their rather unfriendly herd-mates and used them as camouflage to make it the 25-30 yards to the other side of the field and the mouth of the small tunnel that would lead us up through the old cistern into the kitchen of my house.

As I told you, the field was about ten feet below the level of my house and garden, and we could hear the commotion above us. There were vehicles and people and seemingly a lot of both.

The moon shone now like a kluge light, and we were lucky to make it to the entrance of the cave undetected. It was clear once we made it through the tunnel and into my kitchen that there were fighters swarming everywhere in my yard, and they were not ours.

We got a better look from the window of the wood-beamed dining room where Babe, Bobby and I had shared Calvados and Coke Classic.  Two German *Kübelwagens* hit the front of the house with their head lights carving out a grimy yellow-orange tunnel through the silver glow of the full moon.

A voice on a bull horn commanded in heavily accented English, *Herr Montgomery, we only wish to talk. Join us and your friend here will not be hurt.*

My friend?  What friend, I wondered? Dead ahead at the top of the driveway was indeed a man holding a gun to someone's head. I could not make out specifics because both were backlit by the damn headlights.

Babe then said, *buy me some time, Bud, and try not to get yourself killed. And stay the Hell away from the garden when the fun begins.  The* good news is that you might be of more value to them alive than dead at this point. I was tempted to ask whether that was "more" by a lot or a little, but Babe was in a hurry.

Babe turned as he was crawling to the kitchen and said, By the way, I put the Bangalores along the sides of the driveway. They aren't armed, but the Krauts don't know that. With those final words, Babe took my iPad and hightailed back to the tunnel.

After a few more minutes working out the ground rules with the man on the bullhorn, I emerged and cautiously made my way up the driveway. He appeared to be in charge and was a young guy who was the spitting image of the stud that we had dispatched at Gare St Lazare.

In contrast to the drab green-grey camouflage capes and black razor helmets of his men who filled the yard to the edge of my property, this guy looked like he had just come from the Nazi department of central casting. He wore an officer's crush cap with a polished black leather brim and band adorned by the Totenkopf, the skull and crossbones of the SS.

He also wore a black wool field jacket with a red arm band on which the SS runes, double lightning bolts, were emblazoned. He rounded out the ensemble with knee high jack boots, which made his pants puff out. It was as if he were planning to attend a cocktail party at the Reichstag right after he took care of me.

I know that this is a lot of useless detail but if you ever find yourself in situation like this, it is as if you are in a slow-motion car wreck. Every detail is vivid as you count down to the moment of your last breath.

Damn if his hostage wasn't Madame Leroyer, the local magistrate, who was convinced of my guilt in Jane's disappearance. What the hell had she been up to hanging around my place, I thought.

Madame Leroyer was whimpering and moaning and, as I approached, I seemed to bring little comfort to the terrified woman. When she caught sight of me, she just whimpered and moaned even louder.

I walked up the driveway into the glare of headlights from the Nazi Kübelwagens hands held high in a sort of half-hearted way that would not have pleased my German captors at Tilly sur Seulles. There were enough guys in full battle gear within view to round out a college football team.

I heard a familiar motor sputter and die coming from the direction of the *fuck-off* hedge amid the cacophony of military sounds created by the group that had invaded my yard. Fortunately, no one else seemed to notice.

I was especially pissed off that they had brought their vehicles through the cider circle at the other end of my garden and that my prized collection of a dozen cider apple trees was now good for nothing more than kindling. Regardless of what happened in the next few minutes, I was going to kill someone for that reason alone.

*I bring greetings from the Reichsführer,* their leader said jauntily while keeping his gun pointed at Madame Leroyer's head. *My name is Sturmhauptführer Kurt Meyer.*

I had managed to get to within 10 feet of the guy and double-damn if it wasn't the dude who put the bullet in the head of our fighter at Cubitts and who apparently was Heydrich's right-hand man at Aunay-sur-Odon. This upped the ante for me still further if that were humanly possible given the situation I was in.

I did not react as hospitably; in fact, I didn't say anything at first. As I approached him, I studied him and the men who had swarmed around the driveway. They looked like they wanted to skin me alive. The kid who held Madame Leroyer's other arm wore a helmet that was too big for his head. He could not have been more than 16.

This must be the Hitler Jugend Division, I thought, because they were all young and bore the SS runes on their black helmets. Their fanatical defense of the airport near Caen would become legend as would their indiscriminate slaughter of men, women, children and prisoners of war during the fight in Normandy.

This included the massacre of Canadian prisoners of war, soldiers from the North Nova Scotia Highlanders and the Sherbrooke Fusiliers, on the 7th of June, 1944. Each man was shot in the back of the head in a bloody ritual near the Abbey at Ardenne.

I heard the same motor sputter again and begin humming and a second quickly follow suit. The Nazis seemed oblivious or simply assumed that it was one of their own vehicles.

*Isn't this dirty pool*, I said, as I nodded toward the Madame. *She has no part in this fight.* The young stud smiled appreciatively as if he were filing away the new American slang that I had just taught him.

*My patron simply wants to parley with you but not here and not now. Come with us, and she will not be harmed.* Madame Leroyer was beyond consoling. Her knees buckled and the young German next to her struggled to keep her upright.

A third and fourth engine began to purr or was it just wishful thinking on my part. The stud cocked the pistol pointed at Madame Leroyer's head and raised his eyebrows as if to say, *your move.*

In response, I said, *I don't care who dies including me. A lot of good people have died so far in this fucking war so a few more on a brilliant night like this under a magnificent full moon is hardly going to matter.*

*By the way, your name is what? Kurt,* he replied, obligingly. *Well, Kurt, my driveway is lined with a dozen Bangalore mines, and my comrade in the house will ignite the fuse if anything happens to me or the woman.*

*A few seconds after that, Kurt, your tiny Aryan schwanz will end up in the English Channel. In fact, we both will. I don't much care anymore. How about you?*

That got Kurt thinking. *What an ignominious way to die for the Führer, especially when you are dressed so nicely*, I said. This seemed to annoy my new buddy, Kurt, who began to fidget.

The small squad of men closest to the driveway in which we stood moved forward in response to Kurt's apparent discomfort as he surveyed the driveway for the Bangalores. To break the ice, I said, *give me the woman, and my comrade and I will consider your offer. If what you propose would help my wife, I will consider it.*

I vaguely heard two more motors kick into gear above the sound of my knees knocking. Come on, Babe. I'm running out of small talk here, I thought.

Then there was the sound of a revving lawn mower, in fact, two moving across the far end of my long front yard. Germans started shouting and their officers started barking orders and suddenly the garden was rocked by the blast from two massive fireballs.

At the same instant, my ears popped and the lights on the barn side of my house flashed on and off helping to illuminate the fragments of men and equipment that filled the moonlit sky. Meyer's men seemed to move instinctively into some sort of battle formation in the middle of my yard believing that they were being attacked from the rear, that is to say the far end of my yard.

Then the rest came as if in a dream. It was the March of the Deadly Toy Soldiers in the brilliant moonlight to the pulsing rhythm of lawn mower engines. Through the screen of moving men, I could make out four more of our toy soldiers in the eerie glow of the full moon moving steadily forward like zombies.

They came from what was now the German left flank. The first four were followed seconds later by a rear guard of the four remaining toys moving steadily toward the Germans, my driveway and me.

I did not know then what I know now but I was watching arguably the first coordinated, large-scale attack of one of Germany's most feared but little-known weapons on the battlefield – the Goliath tracked mine or what the Allies called the beetle tank.

The Goliath indeed looked like a miniature tank without a turret or a cannon. It carried a 165-pound explosive payload at about six miles per hour and had a range of seven miles. The payload of a single Goliath was powerful enough to take out a Sherman tank.

Typically, operators used a joystick control box connected to the vehicle by a 2,145-foot triple-strand control cable -- two strands for steering, one for detonation. Babe had rigged them to run in a straight line and was using my iPad to activate the bolt, which detonated each one with the collateral effect of turning the lights on and off on the barn side of my house with each detonation. Babe had never bothered to work out that bug.

The third of our first four toys hit a squad of men formed around a field car vaporizing them in a blast that reverberated with the sounds of metal being ripped apart and men in pain. As much fun as this was to watch, I had to move fast. Meyer's man had thrown Madame Leroyer to the ground as their attention turned to the carnage in my yard, which was my cue to get her to her feet and back to the house.

Then Goliath four and five went off. These explosions were closer, and the shock wave nearly knocked me off my feet. I could barely breathe from the heat and caustic fumes issuing from the blasts. German officers were barking orders to keep their men in line, but all was chaos.

There was yet another fire ball. Then two more. One of the last German vehicles to remain intact, a half track with a mounted 88 MM anti-tank gun, would take out number nine while number ten jauntily crossed my driveway unimpeded and took out my front gate and about 20 feet of my stone wall.

I managed to get back to the front door on the cottage side of the house leading to my wood beamed dining room with Madame Leroyer ready to hunker down. At that moment, the same halftrack, apparently deciding that turnabout was fair play, trained its cannon on us. Fortunately, it directed its aim first to the barn side of the house attracted by the wildly flashing lights that corresponded to each explosion.

Two rounds set our second floor ablaze. The next blew out the French doors on the ground floor of the barn side of the house shredding everything in our newly remodeled office and creating a gaping hole in the wall on the far side of the room through which one could now see Chemin du Village.

I managed to drag the very heavy and virtually inert Madame Leroyer into the kitchen as I heard more shouting from outside.

I was sure that the Nazis were regrouping and coming for us. There was no sign of Babe.

Another shell hit closer to home and took out our wood beamed dining room. The only thing that spared Madame Leroyer and me was the thick stone wall between us and the dining room.

I had lost track of my gun while I was trying to stuff Madame Leroyer through the escape hatch into the tunnel that would lead us to safety.  Getting her through was hopeless, and I reached for the nearest weapon that I could lay my hands on, which was Jane's prized copper saucepan from Mauviel. What the fuck, it was the only thing handy.

I looked through what had been the kitchen window with its panoramic view of the garden and saw a line of white flashes before I heard the syncopated firing of the machine guns that accompanied those flashes. That line moved steadily across my yard following roughly the same path as our toys and then veering toward the house. Hot lead and the debris it created were flying everywhere.

And then, a very large dog leapt through the gap that had once been my kitchen window followed by a tall figure dressed in black with a mop of hair like the Beatles, who was wearing an eye patch and toting a very large machine gun. Then I heard the figure call out in a born to the manor English accent, *Charley Dear, we must go.*

Backlit by a garden and house that were now an inferno, Rory, risen from the dead, stepped across the baseboard of my shattered kitchen window and gave me an arm up. Her companion, whom I recognized as the young black dude with the Bar Pintxo ball cap at Notre Dame, followed her and slung Madame Leroyer over his shoulder like a sack of potatoes.

After a moment's hesitation, Rory added, *Charley Dear, you can put the pan down now.*

We rendezvoused with Rory's team of fighters in a yard strewn with the bodies of Hitler Jugend who like the Lost Boys would never grow old. Babe, the triumphant toy master, joined us finally. We carried Madame Leroyer, who was out cold, to Madame Jardin's front gate where she would be found the next morning.

As we made our escape that night, I looked back at the house one last time, Jane's and mine, our cherished sanctuary, to see a plume

of fire rise with a bang from what little
remained of the second floor on the barn side.
I knew then that more than a house and garden
had gone up in smoke that night.

# MONTGOMERY INTERVIEW XIX

Note to the Reader:

This manuscript, which is here attached to the series of interviews with Charley Montgomery, originated as a letter discovered in 1974 in a lockbox at La Poste in central Bayeux, France, partially opened and addressed to him. Its authenticity in the matter of Jedburgh Team Hugo cannot be verified with total confidence, nor is it likely that it ever reached its intended recipient. Nevertheless, it remains classified material and sheds some light on two of the main protagonists in the story of Jedburgh Team Hugo's final mission.

*Hail to My Redskin,*

*Mon Cher, my cousins have me safely tucked away after our brief encounter, a memory that is with me every waking moment. Can anyone be trusted after Aunay?*

*We were betrayed. I fear that someone in the Resistance has turned on us or, perhaps, it was one of my many cousins who have helped keep me one step ahead of the Devil, at least to this point.*

*I am not much of a letter writer, as you know, so this may not turn out to be much of a letter. Nevertheless, I must put my thoughts to paper while I can as we are all here on borrowed time in the service of a higher plan.*

*I pray that you will weather the storm that I have brought down upon your strong shoulders and that my writing to you now will help you fully understand our struggle and know most of all -- I will never stop loving you.*

*I am sought after by both sides because I have a secret that could be used for good or evil. Laughably, those in my own orbit have all but deified me.*

*Yet my powers are no laughing matter, and I would give anything to return to our simple, self-indulgent and happy life together. But I suppose that we have crossed the Rubicon, you and I, and I pray that fate will one day put us back on the same path.*

*This incredible secret and I are as one and, even though I wish I had never known it existed, this is no longer possible. My body is bound to a material existence, but my soul has awakened to an ability to avoid the obstacles that the soul finds in reaching its potential to be God-like.*

*I have just laughed out loud – a real laugh, Mon Cher, my first in a long time because I had this fleeting image of how you would react to what I just wrote and how you would entertain me as you typically do with the profane sarcasm that you wield so deftly.*

*That day on my run, I encountered that strange man at Cap Manvieux and his large dog, Maia. Maia, whom you met at Villers Bocage with the children, has changed allegiances and watches over me even at this moment. That man, his name is Fulcanelli, had been stalking me for weeks.*

*His small white trailer with the Dutch license plates sat at the end of that long dirt trail leading from the D514 to the cliff and because it was barely daybreak, I missed it all together. I was running by the tall stalks of corn in the field that tapers off there toward the cliff and he sprung from hiding, tackling me as I ran by.*

*I managed to kick him and get free for a moment but instead of running toward the houses at our end of the field, like a fool, I ran toward the cliff.*

*He caught me again there. He seemed to move with a speed and agility that were superhuman. My shins were bleeding, and he knocked one of my running shoes off and over the cliff.*

*The last thing that I remember of this struggle was his looking me in the eye, his hand gripping my chin, and his telling me that he would not hurt me. I was not unconscious but from that point on found myself in something like a trance. I could observe everything that went on around me but do little about it. My fear left me completely.*

*I know what you are thinking, and Fulcanelli was in that sense a perfect gentleman if one can be thought of as a perfect gentleman after tearing someone away from the life that she cherished.*

*Eventually, he brought me to his student and protégé, Philippe Delain, in Falaise. Remember, we had lunch in Falaise when we toured William the Conqueror's castle? Do you also remember the fussy restaurant matron with the fetish for chintz who had a hissy fit when you dared to order coffee at the same time as dessert? You heathen!*

*This journey to Falaise was also a journey back to a point in time shortly after the Allies had established a tenuous foothold in Normandy. The meeting with Delain was no coincidence, and this is where this peculiar story of ours, Mon Cher, takes yet another strange turn.*

*Delain was -- is -- my adoptive father and his wife, the woman who showed me my first pair of toe shoes, was my adoptive mother. That beautiful woman had passed away several months before my capture.*

*I fell into Delain's arms the moment I saw him and into a life that I had never fully known but one that was in an instant intimately familiar, a ballet that I had danced a hundred times before and had committed to muscle memory. Returning to it was as easy as performing a gentle Tombé into the arms of a ballet partner.*

*What a strange twist of fate in this strange and twisted universe in which time plays such a perverse role that I returned as a grown woman to parents who out of love for me made the excruciating decision to send me forward in time to friends who had already made that passage to spare me from the darkness that was then enveloping France in 1940. Delain told me that he had also sent me forward to hide me from Fulcanelli, who had shown an unseemly interest in me.*

*Fulcanelli and Delain saw to my education during this period of captivity and through a series of encounters, I perceived the truth seemingly without effort and unlocked the power that I had unknowingly held inside me for so long. I was under Fulcanelli's spell and could do little else.*

*If Hermes was the mythical father of Alchemy, my provenance lies in that root stock just as humans in a faraway time were once thought to be the temporal cousins of the immortal Gods. I <u>am</u> the Jane that you know down to each corpuscle of my physical being, but I am also equal parts French country girl with roots in the Limousin and a* *descendant in the line of Hermes in this duality of time and reality, which is the crux of our story. Although, I will never know my true parents because, I am told, I was left in the sanctuary of a church near Falaise.*

*I suspect that your brave compatriots have told you something about Alchemy, and I hope that your recent trials and tribulations will give you some perspective on this peculiar story so that I do not sound like a raving lunatic. Ugh, why me? Why us?*

*We were also there, in forward time, Delain, dare I say my dear father, and I, at St. Lazare with Fulcanelli, who by that point had decided to betray us and turn us over to the Germans. My father, the compliant protégé up to that point, had finally come to his senses and would have no part of a rapprochement with the Bosch.*

*Two of my cousins who are not unfamiliar with travel between the Paris of then and now were able to manhandle Fulcanelli on the voie at St. Lazare to avoid the rendezvous with the Germans and in the confusion that ensued rushed me out through a tunnel to the Metro and then into hiding in the Marais.*

*So, how do I not sound like your high school chemistry teacher here? Forgive me, Charley, I will try not to. You must know why you are fighting and what we are up against.*

*Alchemy is real science. For example, an alchemist discovered the base element called phosphorous in his urine in the 17th century. My father and Fulcanelli demonstrated how urine could be transmuted into this element, and I now know more about urine than would be necessary in 100 lifetimes.*

*Yet in the eyes of alchemists through the ages, Alchemy is also fundamentally a spiritual discipline. Transmutation of lead into gold represents a personal transmutation, a purification that is a path to perfection.*

*Sit tight, patience, Mon Cher.*

*My education was less about a party trick like making urine glow (cow urine is the best for this because of their diet) than the evolution of the spirit. In literature, the key to this evolution is called the Philosopher's Stone.*

*Its goal is not the transmutation of common metals into gold but the evolution of the spirit from an imperfect, corruptible and ephemeral state toward a perfect, healthy and everlasting state. My kidnapping, indeed, everything that has happened to you and me since, was the price of my enlightenment in this hidden spiritual truth and my unity with the Philosopher's Stone.*

*Still with me?*

*I first understood just how frightening this unity -- power -- could be, the duality with time that is my essence, the day of our escape in Aunay. A storm answered my summons and was our ally that day in the service of Good and made plain why the Germans so urgently want me and why I will never let them take me alive.*

*It is at its root, Mon Cher, the power to bend time and matter to one's will, which we have both experienced, and it makes one question what is real and what is not. Is our reality something that has unfolded naturally despite an occasional disruption from God's sloppy design of Time or is history nothing other than the bitter fruit of his sloppy workmanship?*

*To know the secrets of the Philosopher's Stone is to know that time is in fact a two-headed arrow. There are those of my line dating back to Hermes, who was no myth, who can move back and forth freely, to and fro, in a mirror universe where time also moves in the opposite direction.*

*I know that you must think I am crazy but think about what you have experienced recently. Those who master this duality and thus the battle between* good and evil, win more than a war. They will control all that we know as real.

Mon Cher, I must wrap this up as painful as the thought of it is to me. The time draws near when we must move again to a new hideaway, and Maia, whose instincts are impeccable, is growing more restless by the hour.

Do you remember the video I showed you about my first role as principal dancer at PBC while I was finishing my senior year at Penn? It was during the time that I lived over Jim's Steaks in West Philadelphia and went to ballet class every day smelling of Philly cheese steaks. It wreaked havoc among my bulimic ballet classmates who couldn't figure out why they felt so hungry the moment that I walked into the room.

Well, anyway, the ballet was Orpheus and Eurydice. I don't think that you liked it very much because you didn't like my ballet partner, remember, the one with the blonde dreads? I thought you were simply jealous, which I found very flattering. He was only a passable partner but, at that stage in my career, I was not yet in a position to dictate the choice of my partners.

Do you remember the legend of Orpheus and Eurydice?

*Eurydice was the love of Orpheus' life, who died on the day of their wedding, bitten by a poisonous snake. Orpheus was shattered but resolved to do the impossible and to journey to the Underworld to confront Hades and bring his bride back to the World of the Living.*

*In myth, Orpheus is the Father of Music, and his singing before the gods of the Underworld let his immense pain shine through. The gods were so moved that Hades allowed Orpheus to bring Eurydice back to the World of the Living on one condition. Orpheus was not to turn back to look at Eurydice's face until they had reached the light of the sun.*

*Orpheus took his love by her hand and started to go upward to the light. But, on his way, he was overcome with doubt and worried that he had been deceived, that the hand he was holding was not Eurydice's but rather the hand of a creature belonging to the Underworld.*

*He forgot his promise and so looked back at her and in the instant when their eyes met, Eurydice disappeared, and Orpheus was powerless to prevent his bride from dying a second time. He understood that this time, death would be eternal, and nothing could be done to save her.*

*My love, we find ourselves bound to this legend, believe it or not, forced to confront the darkness and to retrieve each other from the confines of Hell. You would be hard pressed to tell me that our current situation isn't Hell, and it is no myth.*

*Orpheus had no confidence in his deepest intuitions and motivations and did not trust in a higher plan. Mon Cher, you must.*

*So, in the humble saga of Charley and Jane, we must look only toward what is ahead, for to look back will cause us to lose that which we cherish the most, a future filled with light that knows loss and so cherishes what has been saved.*

*Je t'aime.*

*Your Jane*

# VII. ACHILLES GRIEVED

# MONTGOMERY INTERVIEW XX

One side took to the offensive attacking in force up the enemy's center. The opposing line collapsed, and the protagonists seized the opportunity to encircle its Enemy's right flank within striking distance of the goal. In classic flanking moves like this, it is not uncommon to gain the advantage on one side while leaving one's other flank fatally exposed.

And then came the inevitable counterattack from the left, which split the protagonist's attacking force in two. Precious momentum was lost, causing confusion in the forward ranks.

*Florian, le ballon, le ballon,* I heard as I followed the perimeter of the pitch on which the two opposing sides, all six to nine-year-olds, coaxed a soccer ball to and fro maintaining control for a few feet only to wrong-foot the ball to an opponent who repeated the same awkward sequence in the opposite direction.

Poor Florian, perhaps the youngest of this young band, sat in the middle of the pitch as the action swirled around him admiring the blades of grass that he was plucking from one of the few remaining tufts of grass in the largely barren field trampled by these combatants and earlier in the day by the Queen's Horse Guards who used the same pitch in Hyde Park to drill.

Florian, who was clearly not destined for glory in the world of sport, was oblivious to the ebb and flow of the battle being waged around him. I spotted a seemingly relaxed and smiling Bobby on the other side of the pitch, and as I moved toward him, I heard once more the exasperated coaching of someone who must have been Florian's mother, *le ballon, Florian, le ballon!*

It was the first time that I had seen Hyde Park since arriving in London, the Hyde Park of the London Blitz, because as you can see from the other interviews that you have done concerning this deadly Jed mission, it was February 1941 at the height of the German bombing raids on London.

The Blitz was the most intense bombing campaign Britain had ever seen. Between September 7, 1940, and May 21, 1941, there were major raids with more than 18,000 tons of high explosives dropped on 16 British cities.

London was attacked 71 times and bombed by the Luftwaffe for 57 consecutive nights.

More than one million London houses were destroyed or damaged and more than 40,000 civilians were killed, almost half of them in London.

Major cities like Birmingham, Liverpool, Plymouth, Bristol, Glasgow, Southampton and Portsmouth were each hit several times. There was also at least one large raid on eight other cities.

Apart from the generalized gloom of everyday life in London under these circumstances, the heavy mist on a day like this draped you like a wet blanket carrying the aromas of cordite from munitions, theirs and ours, wood from fireplaces and cooking stoves, dirt from the debris that seemed to be everywhere and the body odor of people standing next to you who through no fault of their own probably had not had the means to bathe in a fortnight.

My heritage is mostly British with a dash of Welsh scoundrel and this short stay in a good place at a really bad time left me with new respect for the average Brit. I know it seems like a cliché to say but if you live through even one bombing, as I did, when you become convinced that the next bomb must surely have your name on it, you know that everything that has been written about the bravery of the British in the face of the German onslaught is a vast understatement. Yet if you put this proposition to one of them, he or she would demur with the proverbial stiff upper lip.

The football match was a regular weekly event for the ex-pat community in London. The small crowd sounded like cast-offs from the Tower of Babel. There was a Polish military officer, a group speaking French, a subdued Scandinavian family with two large twin boys in the match, and somewhere within earshot there was the thick sibilance of someone speaking Castilian Spanish.

Bobby was chatting up a strikingly handsome woman wearing a bright blue beret that struggled to contain a riot of glowing blonde curls that brightened the gloom of that late February morning. She briefly wrapped her arm in his, and I assumed from their rapport it was Bobby's wife because his seven-year-old boy was among the combatants on the pitch.

I turned the corner of the pitch on the final approach to Bobby's corner just as the blonde hurried past me in the direction of the Serpentine with her head down leaving the scent of daffodils in her wake.  It struck me that this was not my first encounter with her, but I could not put my finger on why.

I caught up with Bobby just as another attractive young woman arrived. She was demurely British in a tweed suit and introduced herself as Gwendolyn, Bobby's wife.

Bobby and I had patched things up after they deposited us at a small camp near Southampton where Jed Team Hugo was reunited after the conflagration in Manvieux. Rory disappeared as quickly as she had appeared that awful night but not without telling me that her father and my old friend, Roddy, would be proud of what a badass I had become.

I needed a compliment like that spoken in the born to the manor patois of a striking warrior princess to take the edge off the memory of my home in Normandy going up in flames. It had been yet another futile milestone in my quest to reunite with Jane.

They had kept word of Rory a closely guarded secret after the fiasco at Cubitt's. Once they had patched her up, she and her team had started operating in a clandestine fashion, putting out fires in current and forward time of which there were many. As she bid me farewell, Rory forewarned that our paths would cross again soon because, she said, once you start playing this dangerous game, it never loses its grip on you.

Bobby and I had planned to rendezvous that morning in London to head over to the Dorchester for our first briefing. When the match reached its conclusion, Gwendolyn and the boy set out in the direction of the Albert Memorial while Bobby and I took the opposite direction toward Park Lane weaving our way through a Hyde Park that bore a scant resemblance to the one we know today.

If Bobby had seen me approach when he was arm in arm with the mystery blonde, it did not seem to bother him. I did not broach the subject to keep the peace.

Apart from the all too numerous bomb craters, which in many cases were being filled in with the debris created by the Blitz in West London, Hyde Park was a military installation.

There were bivouacked troops, tanks and artillery pieces everywhere.

Just before we arrived at the massive Achilles statue on Park Lane, we had to maneuver around a checkpoint that restricted access to FSB-Archangel or in other words a fire support base with an impressive battery of 20 3.7-inch anti-aircraft guns that could propel a shell upwards as much as four miles. They were arranged facing the tony hotels on the other side of Park Lane and pointed skyward, fortified within a series of reinforced concrete berms draped in barb wire that followed the convex contour of Park Lane.

This did not discourage Londoners, however, from using Hyde Park as they had always done. Daylight raids by the Germans were largely a thing of the past now and had been rare since the Germans failed to establish air superiority in the Fall of 1940. If the Germans were coming now, the first wave would take off from their bases across the Channel a few minutes before dark and arrive over London a few minutes after dark.

So, Londoners were in the habit these days of enjoying those activities in the daylight that they might have done in the evening hours. At the edge of the Serpentine closest to Park Lane, there was a small bandshell, where a fittingly small orchestra from the Royal Opera was playing something that sounded like Bellini's *La Sonnambula*. I wondered if that was a sly joke because during nighttime raids, one got very little sleep indeed.

As we arrived at the statue of Achilles, there was also a theater company at its foot reading what else but Homer's *Iliad*.  We stopped for a few minutes -- remember I was with a classic's professor in civilian life -- to hear the actor  bellow:

*As Homer said of Achilles, the great hero of the Trojan War,*

*'He was a man already dead,*

*a victim of the part that loved, the part that was mortal.'*

Yes, we were indeed headquartered at the Dorchester just across Park Lane from Achilles. What great digs, huh? The Dorchester would earn the reputation of being one of London's safest buildings, a reputation that would be put to the test soon.

At its opening, the builder declared it to be 'bomb-proof, earthquake-proof and fireproof.'

Even though the Dorchester was often clobbered by bombs during the Blitz, its belly of steel and reinforced concrete helped to ensure that the only damage inflicted on the building by the Luftwaffe was chipped concrete and broken windows.

The Jeds assembled for our meeting in what had essentially been a storage room near the underground gymnasium and Turkish baths, which themselves had been converted into a bomb shelter. We bunked in rooms on the topmost floors of the Dorchester, which would have been prime real estate at any other time than the height of the London Blitz, but which now tested the luck and life expectancies of their occupants.

The hotel at one time or another during this period housed or entertained everyone from the Royal Family and General Eisenhower to Chaim Weizmann, a leader of the Zionist movement, and, ironically, a group of upper-class British anti-Semites.

The Jeds were 'assigned' to this time and place because this is where it was believed that Jed leadership had been first compromised by the double agent who had thwarted our efforts at St. Lazare and who exposed our meeting at

Cubitts to an ambush by the Nazis. Heydrich had someone, perhaps more than one person, in his hip pocket and, what is worse, in ours.

Jed Team Hugo had been reassembled to find the spy – Bobby, Marguerite, Babe and Professor Soddy. Marguerite was squarely in charge of this mission, and that reassured me. It was about time in my book.

Once we had been briefed in the dank confines of the storage room, I asked the obvious question or at least it was obvious to me. The future events that we were trying to prevent by finding the traitor in our midst had already taken place.  Follow?

If we caught this person or persons, would the setbacks we endured in the future simply be erased along with our experience of them? I was thinking about the movie *Groundhog Day*, which my Jed teammates would never have seen, so I didn't mention it.

Soddy, never one to pass up his moment at the lectern, rephrased my question, *could history be manipulated or even reversed by eliminating one or more contributing factors, in this case, our informant? Yup, I believed that is what I asked*, I replied.

Soddy then began to patiently knit together a theory that began to make some sense to us but only because we had been living it. It would, however, make no sense to the average Joe, who was lucky enough never to have encountered more than one-time continuum in his life.

*Charley,* Soddy said in his best professorial baritone, *an event leaves its imprint and cannot be erased but can be prevented. Moreover, as we know full well, an untoward event in the past can change the future. It is a paradox, yes, but we have measured its validity in small ways. We cannot reclaim the lives lost at Cubitts nor redo the moments leading up to when we lost track of Jane at St. Lazare, whose provenance was the treachery of the traitor among us. However, with proper foresight, we could have prevented them.*

*We know,* and Soddy paused for emphasis, *we know that Heydrich and his merry men have acquired the penultimate element to make the nucleic weapon operational and require one thing and one thing only – the elusive Jane and whatever she brings to the equation. We do not, I say, do not want to tempt fate by allowing the Germans to complete their nucleic weapon in the here and now with the untold consequences that would follow.*

*We are in London during this unhappy époque for that reason and that reason alone. We cannot erase the harm that les Mouches, as our French brethren like to call informants, have wrought. We can prevent new harm being done, however, by working backwards to the point in time when we hypothesize that the trouble began.*

*We also hypothesize that there is a relationship between our mishaps and the systemic elimination of some of our better resistance teams among the Macquis. If we find the German operatives who have infiltrated the leadership structure of the Macquis at its base here in London, we may well find our very own Mouches.*

*I thought that it was virtually impossible to infiltrate the Macquis because of its command structure,* I said. Soddy beamed and responded by saying, *Jolly Good, Charley, my boy, you have done your homework, Bravo! Yes, it has been for much of its existence.*

*As you know then, my boy, the most famous, and perhaps ingenious security device of Resistance groups is the use of a pyramid command structure. The pyramid structure ensures that no member of a partisan group ever interacts or conducts operations with more than two other members of the organization.*

*No records of membership are kept, and messages are sent only by word of mouth. Each resistance member knows one commanding member and one other partner member. Members keep strict confidentiality and rarely meet in groups larger than their operational units. This structure ensures that enemy infiltrators and captured partisans can positively identify no more than two resistance operatives, leaving the rest of the organization unscathed.*

*As our team can appreciate better than most* (Soddy looked at the three Jeds sitting across from me) *this same structure affords other operational advantages. Ambushes and assassinations of German officers have been, will be,* oh bugger that, *carried out by a group of three men.* I was glad to see that tenses for those of us adrift in time confused someone other than myself.

*I beg your pardon, Marguerite, fighters, male and female, I should emphasize,* Soddy continued nervously under the stern gaze of the French leftenant who had barely scratched the surface of her 20's. *One serves as a decoy, the other carries the weapon to shoot the victim at close range, while the third member of the team takes the weapon after the shooting and walks away from the scene.*

*Often the actual assailants will remain at or near the scene until authorities arrived. As they possess no weapons, they are typically cleared of suspicion. Because resistance fighters in most urban areas do not keep their own weapons as a security measure, weapons used in attacks were returned to their stockpile via courier, often a child who seldom arouses the suspicion of Gestapo agents.*

*These same cells also support our underground railroad system to smuggle downed Allied airmen from the front lines back to Britain, an effort in which Team Hugo has and will continue to excel and which brought our compatriots Bobby and Marguerite together in the first place. The traffic of Allied servicemen between one safe house and cell and the next also facilitates communication not only between diverse Resistance groups but between the fighting front and elements of our military command.*

*If we fail to find this Mouche or nest of Mouches, there will be dire consequences, I fear,* Soddy declaimed. *The Macquis are one thing, but Heydrich has Jane in the crosshairs. When and if he can get to her, he will have the means to unleash a bomb that will make the Blitz in its entirety look like a Punch and Judy show.*

Marguerite used the moment that Soddy finally took a breath to retake the reins of the meeting and to make assignments. Bobby was to take the communist branch of the Macquis, which he knew well from his days getting downed flyers over the Pyrenees and out of France as a member of the Special Operations Executive.

The Resistance as it came to be known comprised small groups of armed men and women who were generally called the Macquis in rural areas. In addition to their guerrilla warfare activities, they were also publishers of underground newspapers, providers of first-hand intelligence and, as Soddy had pointed out, guardians of escape networks that facilitated safe passage for Allied soldiers and airmen trapped behind enemy lines.

The men and women of the Resistance came from all economic levels and political leanings of French society, including émigrés, academics, students, aristocrats, conservative Roman Catholics (including priests) and also citizens from the ranks of liberals, anarchists and communists. One of the most important elements of the Macquis were Spaniards.

After their defeat in the Spanish Civil War in early 1939, about half a million Spanish Republicans fled to France to escape imprisonment or execution. Thousands of these Spanish escapees joined French Resistance groups and formed their own autonomous groups which came to be known as the Spanish Macquis who, like Raoul and his team in the Limousin, were among the most effective fighters in the Resistance and had apparently borne the brunt of the recent betrayals by the spy in our midst.

In the early days of the war, there was enormous in-fighting among the elements of the Resistance including Communists, Socialists, Gaullists, Armenians, Zionists and Anarchists, you name it. Depending on your allegiance, you were just as likely to be killed by someone from a rival Resistance faction than by the Nazis.

Eventually, most factions would coalesce into a coordinating body called the *Francs-Tireurs et Partisans (FTP)*, which would bring some order and operational coordination to the Resistance. But for now, and especially in London where most of these groups were headquartered, it was the Wild West.

Marguerite and Babe, for their part, were going to attack the problem from another angle and pursue leads in the Gaullist Resistance, which reflected the prickly and overbearing personality of its namesake and had cultivated a talent for inflaming an already volatile situation. There were fears that the Gaullists had been infiltrated by elements of the Vichy government, the Nazi puppet regime, while they were preoccupied with fighting their own compatriots in other Resistance groups.

Soddy and I were to join forces. *We want you to insinuate yourselves into a small clique of aristocrats which happens to have established itself here in this hotel,* Marguerite said. *They are the upper crust of British society, and we believe they are linked to Monsieur Fitzmaurice.*

You may recall that Monsieur Fitzmaurice was in fact Bertie, the now deceased 5th Marquis of Lansdowne, who had come very close to dispatching Babe and me to our eternal rest at Lansdowne House during my convalescence there.

Marguerite continued, *we are almost certain that there is a direct link between this group of confirmed anti-Semites, Fitzmaurice and the attempt on your life at Lansdowne. We just do not know what that link is or, better said, who it is. If we find that link, we may be able to eradicate the traitor who threatens us.*

I could not argue with that but what was unclear was how we were going to rise through the ranks of British society lickety-split. Soddy chimed in that he knew Cookie (here we go again with nicknames) Hinshaw, Baroness of Rothmere, whom he had bumped into in the lobby of the Dorchester just that day.

Soddy added, *her husband and his brother had been super luminaries in the British Union of Fascists, or BUF, which had been a fascist political party in the United Kingdom formed in 1932 by Oswald Mosley. I rowed against her brother in the CRA Bumps; he was St. Ives Rowing Club and I the blue on blue of St. Neots.*

To blank stares all around, Soddy soldiered on, *BUF changed its name to the 'British Union of Fascists and National Socialists' in 1936 and, in 1937, to 'British Union.' It was finally disbanded and banned last year amidst suspicion that its remaining supporters might form a pro-Nazi 'fifth column.' But let me tell you this, they are still pursuing at this very moment albeit in a Sub Rosa fashion their misguided agenda and quite energetically so.*

*Alors,* an impatient Marguerite challenged Soddy, *is Cookie, our way in?* Marguerite's Gaelic pronunciation of Cookie gave us all pause, and Soddy reacted with a vacant expression that left no doubt he did not have a clue about how to answer this question.

*I might have the answer,* I chimed in, as everyone turned to me with anticipation. *What if we presented ourselves as press people with an interest in how the British elites are supporting the war effort?*

*And before you ask the obvious question, I have a new-found friend who may be able to give us a hand here. He is a fellow by the name of Ernie Pyle, and I met him on the train ride up from Southampton the other day. He writes for Scripps Howard and maybe just maybe, he would be interested in helping us and could finagle a set of press credentials for me.*

My compatriots did not know Ernie Pyle, as it would be a year or two before he would earn wide acclaim and a Pulitzer Prize for his spare, poignant accounts of "dogface" infantry soldiers from a first-person perspective as he followed them through North Africa, the Italian Peninsula and the breakout in Normandy.

I knew the name because he had been a childhood hero of mine. His reports from the front had inspired my love of history and all things World War II, which in large part is why Jane and I had put down roots in Normandy in the first place.

During the war, he would be welcomed into some 14 million homes stateside with his personal letters from the front. Families would pray for Ernie just as they prayed for their own kin in harm's way.

He never made war look glamorous.  He hated it and feared it. He simply wrote about his own emotions as he watched many men get wounded and some of them die. He got people at home to understand life at the front like no one else.

And like a boyhood dream come true, he was  now my friend. They had split up the Jeds for the trip to London, and I was assigned to a train up from Southampton that had been packed with soldiers in full kit with their rifles. Each of them had so much gear that they took up the room of two or three normal people.

I was about to squeeze into a compartment with a bunch of them when a porter looked at my papers and steered me toward a first-class compartment where I found a slight, wiry guy whose face seemed permanently imprinted with an expression that hovered between worry and curiosity. Damn if it wasn't Ernie.

After some preliminaries, we were summoned to a first seating in the restaurant car. My dad had always been fascinated with trains, and I know that he would have loved this one.

The restaurant car was paneled in dark wood of some kind and the floor was covered with well-worn oriental rugs. We were directed to deep easy chairs at a table where they brought us soup, lamb, boiled potatoes, canned fruit and coffee for eighty-five cents.

We both shared the dregs of a bottle of Calvados that we had seen on the bar counter. As Ernie put it, *I can't taste the apples, but this stuff sure hits the spot!*

I got a very good sense of Ernie as an interviewer that night because he peppered me with one question after another over the course of a conversation that covered just about every topic imaginable because Ernie seemed to be interested in just about everything. There were obviously places that I couldn't go with my background, so I patched together what I thought was a plausible cover story.

I must have given Ernie the impression though that I was a covert operator of some kind because he began to treat the boundaries of my story with some respect and my silence on some things as speaking volumes.

We finally made it to London in the wee hours of the morning although it was hard to tell where we were most of the trip because the windows of the restaurant car and our compartment were blacked out. So, we really couldn't see stations coming or going.

When we got to London, we both had escorts who met us at the train station. Mine looked like a goon, which only reinforced Ernie's conclusions about what I did. Ernie invited me to come to dinner at the Savoy, where he was planning to stay, and I said I would gladly take him up on the offer once I knew what was in store for me.

*C'est bon ça…Allez*, Marguerite said matter of factly with a nod of her head, which I took as a green light to involve Ernie. After a call to the Savoy, a conversation with my bemused,

new friend and Soddy's overture to Cookie in
the Dorchester bar, dinner for two reporters
and a gaggle of British anti-Semites was set for
that evening – first seating at 7:00 p.m. sharp at
the Dorchester.

# MONTGOMERY INTERVIEW XXI

Soddy, Ernie and I arrived at the appointed hour. The Jeds had to do some quick thinking because I did not have any formal clothing, so they found a butler working at the Dorchester who was about my size and borrowed one of his black suits. It wasn't a perfect fit but worked well enough.

Soddy was every bit the image of the suave London socialite of the day and Ernie the appropriately rumpled newshound in a brown suit and red tie emblazoned with the logo of his alma mater, Indiana University.

We were greeted in small anteroom by a glass of Dom Perignon and Cookie, the Baroness of Rothmere, along with three other dinner companions. We were first introduced to a distinguished looking fellow by the name of Henrik Laborde de Montlezat, who apparently had some ties to both the Danish and now-defunct French royal families. He was tall and imperious with a permanently cocked right eyebrow that, as an Ernie said later, made you feel like he was constantly looking down on you, which we agreed he probably was.

Laborde de Montlezat had gained some notoriety as G.K. Chesterton's publisher and occasional anti-Semitic muse. Chesterton who had died several years before had done it all. He was a writer, poet, philosopher, dramatist, journalist, orator, lay theologian, biographer, literary and art critic, and one of the most influential British literary figures of his time.

Standing next to Laborde de Montlezat was a smartly groomed British military officer in a khaki wool uniform replete with a leather Sam Browne belt. He was Cookie's nephew, and his name was Basil Templeton Graham-Colleville, the 5th Baronet of Stanhope. He was a young and handsome guy of about 25.

Basil was as friendly and informal as Laborde de Montlezat was not. He was keeping a watchful eye on our final dinner companion, his grandmother, the Baroness Stanhope-Colleville. The Baroness was, as Soddy had forewarned, delightfully daft but, in her day, her salons both in London and East Anglia had been to upper crust British fascists what Gertrude Stein's Saturday evening salons at 27 rue de Fleurus had been to the world of art and literature in Paris.

The Baroness was a close friend of Queen Mary. She was still regal if not all together operating in the here and now and on that evening wore a breathtaking diamond necklace for the occasion that had reputedly belonged to Marie Antoinette, along with a pair of diamond chandelier earrings.

There were hundreds of us packed into the sprawling basement of the Dorchester made over to look like the grand ballroom of Buckingham Palace. I did not see them, but Ernie told me later that Eisenhower and Churchill were a hop, skip and jump away.

Our dinner conversation started well enough, and we indulged in small talk while orders were taken and Henrik chose the wine for the evening. The Baroness sat fixated on her gin and Dubonnet, which the attentive wait staff seemed to replenish every few minutes.

Both Ernie and I noticed that a stocky attendant, who seemed to station himself just behind us, would swoop in early with refills before the Baroness had finished the drink in front of her. Once he made it back to the cover of the palm trees near the kitchen, he would down the remainder.

I had passed myself off as a reporter for the San Francisco Chronicle and Henrik himself a publisher, knew the Chronicle's publisher well. He peppered me with some questions that I should have been better prepared to answer, but Ernie came to the rescue and redirected us to a discussion of the war effort as waged on the home front by the leaders of British society.

Cookie got us going by talking about her work and that of the "responsible nobility" in the St. John Ambulance Brigade, which worked side by side with the British Red Cross delivering emergency aid during the Blitz including running first aid posts in London's tube stations. *We also provide much needed anti-gas and first aid training to civilians*, she said proudly.

The doddering Baroness seemed to reconnect with the conversation at that point and blurted out, *oh dear Cookie, you are too modest. Tell these lovely gentlemen about that horrible incident in the Underground in the East End. All of those people crushed to death by the Chosen Race. Whitechapel…So deficient…so, so cowardly.*

Cookie, Basil and Henrik stared at the Baroness speechless. They reminded me sitting there on the other side of the table, three in a row, of cringing notes climbing a musical scale, each successive note more horrified than the one before. At this point, the Baroness, who sat directly to my right, gave us a crisp hiccup and drifted back to the world from whence she had taken a brief detour.

Soddy jumped in providing a safety valve to the pressure that had just jumped off the charts and explained to Ernie and me that the Jewish quarter of Whitechapel was one of the first areas to be heavily blitzed with the natural result that swarms of Jewish refugees redistributed themselves throughout London. He said that it was at about this time that a strange accident occurred when a crowd, frightened by a bomb-burst nearby, fled into the mouth of an Underground station with the result that over a hundred people were crushed to death.

*The very same day, all of London whispered that the Jews were responsible, compounding the indefensible outlook that already held some in its sway that Jews behaved in an exceptionally cowardly way in the air raids in Whitechapel. It was horrible business and a decidedly shameful reaction to place blame where in truth none was due,* Soddy said.

*Cookie, you are wholeheartedly to be commended for the brave and caring attention that you gave the victims of all backgrounds. It must have been hell, in extremis,* Soddy added.

Henrik jumped in suavely to say, *Naturally, no thinking person would do anything but protest the wholesale condemnation of a people regardless of their origins. Yet a notable minority of refugees have behaved in an exceedingly tactless way, and the feeling against them necessarily has an anti-Semitic undercurrent, since they are largely Jews.*

Well, what had started out as a promising plea for tolerance seemed to end in a roadside ditch. At that moment, the Baroness turned and winked at our stocky attendant, who was back with another gin and Dubonnet, and he lowered his head. As Ernie and I tuned in, she said, *Malcolm, you are a Scot, am I not correct?* He nodded assent. *Have you heard the story of the Jew and the Scotsman?*

The gist of her joke was that there was a Jew and Scotsman who went together to a meeting which has been advertised as free. Unexpectedly, there was a collection, and to avoid it, the Jew faints, and the Scotsman rushes to carry him out. Soddy told me later this was of a common genre of humor called the "Jew Joke" that poked fun at the stinginess of both races but seemed always to credit the Jew merely with cunning and avarice while the Scotsman is also credited with goodwill and physical hardiness.

Basil, who had been quiet much of dinner, had also overheard the joke and said, *oh, Grand Mama, please.* He then turned to me and Ernie and said, *please do not misunderstand. Antisemitism as a fully thought-out racial or religious doctrine has never flourished in England. There has never been much feeling against intermarriage or against Jews taking a prominent part in public life. We are, are we not, fighting their war, one that they are exceptionally clever at dodging?*

*Basil, dear, perhaps you could introduce them to the smart crowd that you have attracted to the January Club and to your charitable endeavors in the Aldgate Underground,* Grand Mama suggested. Aldgate station, as it would turn out, was to become one of the largest bomb shelters in London, sleeping 10,000 people a night, one that Ernie would write about and call Double-X. It was in East London, more specifically Whitechapel.

*Grand Mama, these people, I should think, have much better things to write about than our distributing bedding and a little bit of good cheer,* at which Henrik deftly jumped in to take our orders for an after-dinner drink.

This bit of verbal gymnastics and nimble change of direction did not escape us.  Soddy told us later on the way out that the January Club was a discussion group founded in 1934 by Oswald Mosley, the aforementioned father of the BU and British Brown Shirts and chum to the departed Bertie of Lansdowne, for  the purpose of attracting Establishment support for the fascist BU.

Soddy went on to say that he thought the January Club had disbanded. Its members, who  had reveled in Mosley's mercurial ascent in British politics, had fled like the fallen angels to the four corners of the earth to distance themselves from the BU in the wake of Mosley's equally precipitous downfall.

*What about Basil,* I asked later. *He doesn't strike me as the goose-stepping, Mosley Brown Shirt type. Quite right, Charley,* Soddy responded. *I think that a fine brandy and an evening of small talk with his fascist friends in a fashionable salon is more his style.*

Soddy added, *however, Charley, my boy, the January Club…active…congregating in a bomb shelter in the East End. Dodgy…quite!?*

******

Dinner ended as it had begun with polite small talk. After saying goodbye to Soddy, Ernie and I decided to clear our heads and take a stroll through the West End.

We set off in the direction of Shepherds Market, and he said, *thanks, Charley, for getting me involved in this tonight. I am always after a good story, although I am a live and let live kind of guy, and the folks back home have enough to think about than how one person or one bunch of people looks down on another.*

*These people live in a paradox of their own making,* I replied. *Jews are accused of offenses like bad behavior in food queues to merely rationalize one's anti-Semitism, while the accusers remain fully aware that their outlook is indefensible.*

*You can't help but wonder,* Ernie said, *if some mysterious lubricant in the machinery of modern thought isn't missing and, as a result, we are all subject to this lunacy of believing that whole races or nations are uniformly good or uniformly evil.*

*Ernie, I appreciate the sentiment. Thank you as well for providing the cover and thus my entrée to the evening's festivities,* I replied. *From the serious look on your face, Pal, I won't push you for the who, what, when, where and how about your motives for this evening,* Ernie replied. *Thanks, Ernie,* I said.

Shepherd's Market had taken a couple of direct hits and was a mess but since the bad weather had kept the Germans at bay that night, I decided to get some exercise and help Ernie negotiate the debris at least as far as Piccadilly Circus.

If darkness could be thought of as a solid, we navigated the solid murk of Half Moon Street in the direction of Green Park by instinct. The city was a dense field of black – black ruins, blacked out windows, blacked out head lights, and scarcely the hint of dark forms moving in all directions. Your eyes eventually adjusted to the profound darkness but barely.

Halfway up the block, someone to our right lit a cigarette lighter, which stopped us dead in our tracks because he was barely a foot away standing in the shadows. His right arm was raised with what looked like a set of brass knuckles as if he were about to bring it down hard on our heads. Shit, we were about to get shaken down, I thought.

There standing next to him in the glow of the lighter was a young girl who was half his size and ours for that matter with an imposing head of hair, which she wore like a helmet.

She said, *good evening, Gentlemen, I am Melody Schwartz, may I have a word?*  She was pointing a large handgun at us, so Ernie broke the ice by saying, *well, darlin, we are all ears.*

# MONTGOMERY INTERVIEW XXII

To say that what happened next was a rollicking good time would be a vast *under* and *over* statement. Our captors threw us into a panel van that stunk of gasoline and rotten eggs and forced Ernie and me to sit together on something that felt like an old army blanket in the small lorry's cargo hold.

The girl, Melody Schwartz, who pronounced her last name as if it was several syllables long, sat in the shadows facing us from the jump seat behind her burly companion in the in the driver's seat of the van. This interlude had put me in a foul mood, so I taunted the oaf behind the wheel by saying, *they didn't give you a gun, big boy?*

Melody came to his aid in a flash and said, *no we don't and lucky for you. Gun in hand, he is more likely to use it than not.*

Melody wasn't a Brit. Was she American, I wondered? She had a distinct accent that was vaguely familiar but hard to place.

Ernie said, *I know you, big boy. You are the Scot who served us, and it was you to whom the Baroness told her little joke. Malcom, correct?* The oaf nodded, eyes fixed on the road.

Melody again protectively jumped in, *if you want to pick on Malki, perhaps I should give him the gun. My colleague's name is Malki, not Malcolm, short for Melchior – that is 'My King' in Hebrew for your information.*

Ernie shot back, *our apologies, your highness,* and then buttoned his lip.

Our deranged chauffeur was taking a course that continuously threw us from one side of the truck bed to the other. I knew London pretty well and could roughly track our progress toward East London in my mind's eye.

From Half Moon Street, we took a sharp left on to Piccadilly for a long stretch past Green Park and the Ritz, swerved around Piccadilly Circus hitting another straight shot, much longer this time. Then came a bruising series of left and right turns.

All of this was in virtually total darkness because of the blackout, like the ride at Space Mountain. All streetlights were turned off. Even the red glow from a cigarette was banned, and a man was once fined for striking a match to look for his false teeth.

The truck's headlights had been angled downward and were covered by three horizontal slits of dark cloth. White lines were painted along the middle of the road to help drivers as were curb edges and car bumpers. The speed limit for night driving was officially 20 mph, but the lunatic with a death wish driving the lorry was going at a speed that would have been dangerous even in daylight.

Melody and Malki had apparently done this kind of thing before because they were the epitome of calm. *Where are you taking us, I asked?*

*To someone that you need to meet and before it is too late,* she said.

*Too late for what,* I asked.

*Remains to be seen,* Melody replied. The accent, Philadelphia Mainline, I thought?

After another 10-15 minutes of rocking and rolling, Malki grunted, *where,* and Melody replied, *the bottom of the Saint Botolph tunnel, near the tracks.*

And lickety-split we came to an abrupt halt as the rear of the truck fishtailed throwing us against the side of the lorry one last time for good measure. Malki opened the door and yanked us out and led us to two large steel doors that were slightly ajar and then into a tunnel large enough at that point for a couple of double-decker buses running two abreast.

The tunnel led us up and down and up again narrowing all the while. The last stretch toward the bright lights ahead reminded me of jogging down a stadium runway to the field with the Skins on a Sunday afternoon just before kickoff.

And then we were there. It took our eyes a minute or two to adjust, but we found ourselves in a bright, cavernous hall with vaulted ceilings soaring high overhead. Damned if it wasn't Double X, the massive bomb shelter in London's East End some six hundred feet below street level that Ernie would eventually write about in his dispatches to the home front.

Double X was the nexus of several tube lines and stations in the vicinity of Aldgate making it one of the largest in London. We had come in on a mezzanine of sorts. Below us, there was the hustle and bustle of hundreds if not thousands of people milling about. It was loud but not as bad as it could have been. The sound at our level seemed to dissipate into the endless firmament of ornate ceiling medallions above us.

I heard, Ernie mumble, *Gosh almighty! It's bigger than the Indiana State Fair.*

For me it was like Dorothy's first glimpse inside the City of Oz. There was a central promenade where people went about their business or simply strolled back and forth to see and be seen. It was all very orderly.  The central promenade seemed to go on forever, and we could not see the far end from where we stood.

As Ernie would later write, 'Double-X is a big, jolly city, all under one roof. Its inconveniences are overshadowed by its personality. It is a gigantic human omelet, fried in war.' And that personality struck me at that moment as oddly cosmopolitan and convivial.

On either side of the central promenade were activity stations that served a variety of purposes. We could see and hear a jazz band entertaining a swarm of people. There was also a stand with a beer keg where they were grilling something that smelled like sausage and a first aid station with nurses screening patients and leading some to small spaces behind khaki curtains.

It appeared that we were in a central hall that connected several Tube stations because there were named tunnel entrances at intervals along the mezzanine level, and I could make out corresponding entrances on the level below us.

Beyond the promenade and the stands that flanked it, the great vaulted space was divided into a series of bays each housing roughly one hundred people.  As we learned later, within each bay there was a system of self-governance in which the residents elected submarshalls.

Our "hosts" hustled us along the mezzanine on the side of the hall where we had entered and then down a series of metal stairs that took us to the lower level and along a side wall parallel to the central promenade. We passed what appeared to be a very large makeshift library and several other bays where they were installing bunk beds. The only thing missing from this tableau were industrious munchkins singing *The Wonderful Wizard of Oz* in cheery unison.

We came to another bay concealed by large gray curtains and guarded by two stout young men in yamaka's. Melody, who  handled her weapon with the panache of Jesse James, waved it in the direction of the small opening in the curtains and the guards nodded us in.

We found ourselves in a spacious bay that had been tastefully furnished like a Mayfair townhouse. There was a credenza on the far wall with, I would venture to guess, a priceless delft epergne as its centerpiece. There was also a Georgian writing table to one side and huge stuffed leather armchairs to the other.

Everything seemed afloat on a sea of oriental rugs. The Persian Isfahan that lay in the middle of the space was probably 16th century and priceless in today's market.

*Please be seated*, Melody said. *Charles will see you shortly*. Ernie looked at me and rolled his eyes.

It was barely five minutes before we were joined by a distinguished looking, professorial type in wide wale corduroy pants and a rumpled blazer accompanied by a male aide and Melody. There was no sign of our buddy Malki.

He approached us straightaway to shake our hands as we both struggled to get up from our plush armchairs and looked us squarely in the eyes. *Hello, I am Charles Weizmann. I must apologize for the circumstances under which we brought you here tonight.*

He was in his sixties with gray hair that cupped a broad, dome-shaped forehead. A short gray beard covered a strong jaw line. There was something yeoman-like and sturdy about the guy. His English was perfect with a hint of something else to suggest he was not a native Brit.

Melody stood off to the side beaming, rosy cheeks barely discernible under her helmet of hair. She had taken off her trench coat and without her gun looked far less imposing. In fact, she was tiny, and there were just enough strategically placed curves under her thick turtleneck sweater to distinguish her from a page boy.

And then it dawned on me. Soddy had pointed him out at the Dorchester. Charles Weizmann was in fact Chaim Weizmann, one of the most important Zionist leaders of his time, who served as President of the World Zionist Organization and later would become the first President of Israel. Weizmann would go on some years later to convince the United States government to recognize the newly formed state of Israel.

Weizmann was a biochemist by trade who had developed the process for making synthetic rubber through the bacterial fermentation of acetone, butanol and ethanol. Synthetic rubber was hugely important to the Allies in both World Wars. He was Russian but had spent his early career in Germany before emigrating to Britain before World War I.

Weizmann had also been instrumental in persuading British Prime Minister Arthur Balfour, when he was Foreign Secretary just before World War I, to support a Jewish homeland in Palestine, the original Zionist ideal.  Perversely, the British establishment at that time had been pushing a plan to establish a new Jewish homeland in Uganda of all places.

The story goes that Weizmann asked Balfour, *would you give up London to live in Saskatchewan?*  When Balfour replied that the British had always lived in London, Weizmann responded, *yes, and we lived in Jerusalem when London was still a marsh.*

*I know of your work Professor Weizmann, I* said. *Your colleague, Frederick Soddy, pointed you out to me the other day at the Dorchester.*

*Yes, my dear friend the ever-gregarious Freddy! The Dorchester serves as our Embassy and base of operations as it were when the Germans are not, as your Bing Crosby would croon, 'Raining Pennies from Heaven' down upon us.* Ernie chuckled.

*Here*, Weizmann was distracted for an instant as someone brought in what smelled like strong coffee and set it on the table between us. *Please*, he said, *help yourselves,* which we did.

Weizmann continued, *I have spent a good part of my adult life in Britain but still have not acquired a taste for its tea. It is not well known or appreciated that Germans are passionate not just about their beer but about their kaffee and were among the earliest Europeans to embrace it.*

Out of the blue, Ernie abruptly chimed in, *I need to have coffee, coffee; if you want to give me a treat, pour me coffee. Bravo,* replied Weizmann, *Johann Sebastian Bach, another German transplant, oh circa 1732, I would venture!*

I looked at Ernie in surprise, and he said, *what, what, do you think we Indiana University grads only study the chemical composition of cow chips? Ah, here we are...the final ingredient,* Weizmann said, as someone placed a bottle on the tray in front of us, *and of course, if you would like to fortify your drink, we have a bottle of our best schnapps from Stockvogler's of Vienna, recently smuggled in via Bremen.*

Ernie and I required no coaxing to help ourselves to a liberal dose of fortification and then looked at Weizmann expectantly. I said, *Sir, we must assume that we were brought here at gunpoint by your thugs for a reason.* I chuckled and glanced at Melody, still standing at attention, who blushed scarlet as I continued, *and that it was not simply for a friendly coffee klatch.*

*Yes, of course,* Weizmann replied, *we will come to that shortly. Freddy has informed me that you are not without resources, Charley.* Ernie turned inquisitively toward me, but I let it pass.

*As you may know then,* Weizmann got the ball rolling, *apart from the struggle that ebbs and flows as it were pertaining to Palestine, our current work is to ensure that the British government approaches the question of Jewish immigration with some elasticity of mind and policy. We are hearing reports that defy the imagination about what is happening in Germany not just to my fellow Jews but to anyone who does not conform to the Aryan ideal.*

*My young colleagues,* Weizmann emphasized the word *colleagues, some of whom you have met, are also helping me develop the Jewish Brigade to assist in the war effort.* Weizmann nodded warmly toward Melody and the aide standing at attention off to the side. Melody was now blushing with such pride that it looked like her head was about to blast off from its launching pad.

*We are aware, Professor,* I said.

*You may not be aware,* Weizmann said with a broad smile on his face, *that our efforts may well culminate tomorrow night in a meeting at the Dorchester with the British Prime Minister, along with Bernard Baruch, representing your President, and my dear friend Dolly Rothschild, and that most impressive man, Eisenhower. My dear and insightful Dolly has offered to underwrite a plan to amplify the impact of the Jewish Brigade on the war effort if the politicians are willing to make just a few simple concessions on immigration.*

*Among those immigrants, in fact we have her to thank for our schnapps, is the wife of my former colleague Ze'ev Stern. I would like you to hear Helga's story. She will join us in a minute.* And as if on cue, it was barely a minute before she did. After introductions, Weizmann said, *Helga please.*

Helga appeared at first to be a slight, shy woman, but it soon became apparent to us that her seeming frailty belied a personality of steel forged in the furnace of Nazi Germany.  *My Ze'ev was invited by a former colleague at the University of Konigsberg to join a project sponsored by the National Socialists. This was a little over three years ago,* she began.

*To say that he had any choice in the matter is laughable. It was join and work or find oneself in a KZ, that is a Konzentrationslager. You call them concentration camps.*

*It was then that we began to make plans for me to get out with our two daughters. They are now 16 and 18.  Thank God for Chaim.  We were among the last to make it out under his good offices.*

*Ze'ev's project was called Unternehmen Seelöwe. I think that you would say Sea Lion, Operation Sea Lion that is.*

*It contemplated nothing less than the invasion of the United Kingdom in concert with the bombing that we now endure. Ze'ev was forced to develop the Seilbomben, which would be dropped just prior to the Wehrmacht landings. This was a secret weapon which would have been used to blackout the electricity network in southeast England.*

*This weapon worked perfectly in tests but because it involved dropping charged wires across high voltage wires from specially modified aircraft,*

*Ze'ev would say that it was probably more dangerous to Luftwaffe crews than to the British.*

*Ze'ev heard rumors of something called the Black Book, a list of a few thousand people who were to be arrested by Einsatzgruppen, death squads, during the invasion. The Einsatzgruppen have also been tasked with liquidating Britain's Jewish population.*

*The architect of the project is an awful man. Ze'ev knew him at Konigsberg and Chaim as a student at the University of Berlin. Weizmann nodded his head encouragingly.*

*He is an acolyte of an even more horrible figure, and the last thing Ze'ev told me before he disappeared was that there was a power struggle over whether the invasion should take place at all and that its proponents were trying to move up the timetable to make it a fait accompli.*

*Who is it that we are talking about,* I finally said? Helga hesitated looked at Weizmann and replied, *his name is Franz Six and his patron is one Reinhard Heydrich.*

Weizmann studied my reaction as if he knew this bore special significance for me. It did indeed.

Ernie jumped in by asking, *and what does this have to do with us.* Weizmann kept his gaze on me.

Helga hesitated, and Weizmann answered for her, *improbably, impossibly, my friends, Six and his operatives are now here in London. Indeed, they have assumed residence here in Aldgate and appear to be the guests of your dinner companions this evening.*

# MONTGOMERY INTERVIEW XXIII

Weizmann then ushered in a strapping young guy who looked like he had been carved from a block of granite by the Fuhrer himself. His father was German and his mother, a Polish Jew, who taught at the University of Krakow. His name was Szymon, pronounced Simon, and he had apparently inherited his father's Aryan good looks.

Szymon was an undercover member of the Jewish Brigade who had been befriended by a member of the January Club. Szymon had resisted the man's overture for a tryst at a seedy West End hotel but convinced him of his past membership in the Brown Shirts and his family's origins as aggrieved German refugees from the Sudetenland.

Szymon had proven himself as a key operative of the fledgling Fifth Column that had taken root in the January Club. His current assignment was keeping watch on the needs of the Club's newly arrived guests.

*They appeared as if they had simply walked through a door that led from the Unter den Linden to East London,* he said. I didn't have the heart to tell Szymon that this might just have been the case.

*It is Franz Six and several bodyguards although we are told that there are more of this group here in London. Leftenant Graham-Colleville is their liaison here.*

*What are they up to, I asked?* I had by then perfected the art of asking the obvious question. *It is unclear and naturally very secret. Only a very few know all the details, but something is imminent because the pace of activity has accelerated in the past few days, Szymon* continued. I suspected that it would not be the invasion but still what was a contingent of dangerous Nazis doing hanging around a London bomb shelter?

I had all sorts of ideas and plans swirling around in my head. It made perfect sense to sound the alarm with the Jed's, but Szymon said, *they are gone and not expected to return for an hour, possibly two. I can get you into their bay now for a look, but we must be fast because they will almost certainly return soon.*

So much for rallying our forces. There would not be enough time. Ernie looked at me and said, *I'm game. Ernie, this is not your fight,* I replied. *Maybe not, but I smell one hell of a good story here, so you will have to clobber me to keep me from tagging along,* he replied.

*How do we do this*, I asked Szymon and then looked at Weizmann for his ideas. Szymon said, *I can pass you off as members of the January Club.* Weizmann added, *we will have Melody and her team follow at a discrete distance in the event that there is trouble.*

Szymon went on to add, *you must remember how the password goes. I am told that whatever this operation is, they call it 'Erzangel.'* Weizmann translated – *Archangel.*

*The challenge is a phrase from the "Horst Wessel,"* Szymon said. This was a song named for Horst Ludwig Wessel, a ne'er-do-well Nazi activist who was made a posthumous hero of the movement following his violent death in 1930. He wrote the lyrics to the song "Die Fahne hoch" or "Raise High the Flag," commonly known among card carrying Nazis as the "Horst-Wessel-Lied," which became the Nazi Party anthem.

*Der Tag für Freiheit und für Brot bricht an!*

*The day of freedom and of bread dawns!*

*The challenge will be either Freiheit or Brot, and the response is the other and then the word Erzangel.* We practiced the routine a couple of times.

As we were leaving, Melody handed me a gun. *Walther PPK, 9 mm,* she said matter of factly.  Who was I to argue? I gladly tucked the gun under my belt.

She, Malki and Weizmann's aide followed us at a safe distance. It wasn't a plan. It was barely the contours of a plan, maybe even no plan at all, but we needed information. Anything that would help us determine what Franz Six was doing here was critical because it was most certainly evil-personified if Heydrich was behind the whole thing.

The bay, which has been commandeered by the January Club, seemed to be at the far end of the massive bomb shelter from where we set out. Szymon took us on a winding course to our objective and twice made us take cover, apparently to avoid a couple of Six's men who casually patrolled the complex.

We arrived at the Bay to find two young Brits who, had they not been forced to wear civvies, would have been proudly sporting their snazzy brown shirts. They were guarding the entrance to the bay and as they and Szymon went through the password ritual, they came to attention and clicked their heels.

There would be no Fuhrer salute, however, not here.

We entered a large bay that was loaded with supplies ostensibly reflecting the charitable mission of the January Club. There were bunk bed frames, blankets, something that looked like K-rations and a bin of toiletries.

Strangely enough there were also deck chairs stacked off to the side with striped canvas backings like those one would find at the beach. A few were arranged in the middle of the bay as if several people had been lounging in them having a casual conversation.

Beyond the main section of the bay, there was a smaller room that we accessed with a key that Szymon carried with him. To the back of this room there was a narrow, tunnel-like hallway that led out to an exterior bay where, Szymon told us, there was a loading dock. Someone had thought of everything.

There were signs of activity. Clearly a large group of people had eaten here as remnants of a meal remained on a large trestle table near the door.

There were also two large, non-descript lockers that Szymon opened with another key loaded with firearms and ammunition including a couple of cases of hand grenades. Ernie whistled when he saw it all and said, *how thoughtful of the January Club.*

The floor in the back room was like slate, and it appeared that the occupants of the bay had drawn a large map on it with chalk. The map had been erased for the most part, but one could make out a few shapes. One area with the biggest smudge looked vaguely familiar, and I could make out two curved, parallel lines forming a quarter circle like the interval between Noon and 3:00 or 4:00 o'clock on the dial.

Off to the left of what remained of this image, there was a squiggle that looked an awful lot like the contours of the Serpentine. This was Hyde Park, I thought, but what was it that this picture was really showing me?

And then the shit hit the fan.

Voices came from the direction of the loading dock, and Syzmon immediately moved forward to greet them. There was roughly a dozen of them, and the only thing that saved us in the end is that they were crowded into the tunnel-like hallway standing two abreast.

Ernie and I stood behind Syzmon, while Melody and Malki, who had joined us in the back room, were farther back near the lockers. We heard a loud *Scheiße* from the hallway when the leader of the group angled his head around Szymon to survey the rest of us.

He was a handsome kid with two black eyes and a face that had been nicked badly in several places and, son of a bitch, if it wasn't the son of a bitch Kurt Meyer, the dapper but murderous leader of the Hitler Jugend, who had held a gun to Madame Leroyer's head in my yard in Manvieux. He did look like shit, and I vowed to finish the job that our beetle tanks had started or die trying.

When he saw me, he pulled his gun. It occurred to me that I had one of my own, so I drew too. Kurt's squad started the shooting, but it was a ragged, ineffectual effort at first because they were so crammed into the narrow hallway that they were more likely to hit one another than one of us.

I stepped in front of Ernie returning fire while I pushed him back toward the door to the main bay with my body. He tripped, and I pulled him up ripping the collar of his nice brown suit.

We both stumbled through the door into the main bay, and I caught a glimpse out of the corner of my eye of two people coming through the curtains into the bay just at that moment, who instantly turned tail when they saw me and heard the chaos in the back room.

I left Ernie in the bay and returned to the back room to see that Szymon was down, and Melody was shielding him from the Nazis while trading fire with the group huddled in the hallway. Malki and Weizmann's aide returned fire from behind the now overturned trestle table.

Melody shouted to me, *get him out,* nodding toward Syzmon, and I could see that it was possible to get him to his knees and to the door, so I got him under the shoulders and helped him bear-crawl to the door. Ernie was at the door waiting and helped pull him through.

I felt a bullet singe my ear as it ricocheted off the door frame and I turned around just in time to see Malki move himself between us and the Nazis who were now using a pile of their dead comrades as cover at the mouth of the hallway. Malki staggered two, possibly three times as he was hit by gunfire, but that bull of a man did not drop.

I wanted to go back and put a bullet in Kurt Meyer's brain, but I had two lives to save and two to hunt down. The image of the two people I had seen come into the bay returned to me in that instant as I tried to catch my breath in a cloud of gunpowder and daffodils.

******

Weizmann took charge of Szymon and the situation in the January Club's bay and quickly got Ernie and me back to our respective hotels using the same elegant means that had brought us to Aldgate, except that this time we got to ride in the jump seats. Ernie was mildly shell shocked but otherwise none the worse for wear. The last thing I heard him say as he walked into the Savoy mumbling to himself was, *I need a bourbon and a hot bath.*

Much of the day that followed is still a blur. After sounding the alarm when I made it back to the Dorchester, I took a few minutes myself to grab a shower in my room while the Jeds assembled. The Dorchester butler who loaned me his suit was really going to be pissed when he saw what shape it was in.

My room overlooked Hyde Park and the Achilles statue next to the row of antiaircraft guns that curved around the bend of Park Lane. At that moment, however, the fog gripped my window in its solid white fist so there was little to see.

The meeting of the Jeds that soon followed was to say the least grim. The three Jeds and Soddy listened, troubled faces set like an angry Mount Rushmore as I gave my account of Aldgate starting with my arrival at the soccer pitch and chance encounter with the woman with dazzling blonde curls trailing the scent of daffodils as she rushed by me.

*She was also there at the Aldgate shootout,* I said. *She and Basil Templeton Graham-Colleville turned tail as soon as they saw me, but they had walked into the January Club's headquarters like they belonged there. Who the hell is she?*

It was Bobby who spoke first, *her name is Marita Salthar. She is Norwegian and one of our operatives and quite a good one at that. Marguerite and I have known her since our escape to Spain.*

*Her husband had been a Falange fighter in Spain and a bastard. He was Franco's liaison to the Nazi Condor Legion, which was a unit of military personnel from the German air force and army that supported Franco and the Falange during the Spanish Civil War. He worked with the Condor Legion to develop methods of terror bombing which they now use so prolifically on us and that produced the atrocities at Guernica back then. He was captured by the Republicans shortly after Guernica and was never seen or heard from again.*

*Marita was a double agent at that time for 'La Pasionara,' or the Popular Front, which was a mulligan stew of factions opposed to Franco and the Nazis. When Marita's husband disappeared, she went to ground and was recruited by our agents shortly thereafter.*

No one questioned what she had been doing with Bobby in Hyde Park, so I suspected that his liaison with Marita was a secret to no one. Bobby's explanation trailed off and you could see in his eyes his mentally replaying every moment that he had spent with Marita to find a reason for her betrayal and the missed clues that could have prevented the damage that she had done to us and the Resistance.

*At the very least we need to talk to her, and she must not know that we have any suspicion of her loyalty,* Marguerite said. *She could have been undercover with Graham-Colleville for all we know, so we will not judge her quite yet.*

Babe who had been deep in thought delivered the coup de grace to Marguerite's plea for tolerance when he said looking at me, *Buddy Boy, remember the night that we ran into Bertie in Lansdowne…the heavy fog…the tall guy, Bertie's handler, whom we now believe to have been Heydrich himself? What else do you remember?*

*The blonde,* I said without hesitation. *And what we thought was Bertie's after shave. I called it Narcissus – fucking daffodils.*

Marguerite sent word to Marita through normal channels that Bobby and I were missing and that her services would be required the next evening in an effort to locate the two of us. She and Bobby would confront Marita. Their rendezvous would be at the Achilles statue in Hyde Park.

I returned to my room later because I had left my handgun there during my brief respite earlier in the day, actually both handguns – Jed standard issue and Melody's gift, the Walther PPK. It turned my stomach to think about what might have befallen her and her comrades. There had been no word.

The fog had lifted and what remained of it had become a low cloud deck that now hovered just above the hotel. Had I the inclination, I could almost have reached out to touch the bottom of the cloud from my hotel window.

I could see Hyde Park. It was sunset, and a sliver of sun glowed red on the Western horizon and reflected off the cloud deck to burnish the scene below of the home guard clearing the park for the night. It also appeared as though several large military units were vacating the park to parts unknown.

I sat down for a minute because I was dizzy from lack of sleep and the tall glass of Irish whiskey in my hand. I must have dozed off briefly because I came to as the air raid sirens came to life. Their high, undulating wail always made the hair on the back of my neck stand up and signified that German bombers had been sighted over the Channel. In the gloom, I also saw the 20 or so 3.7-inch antiaircraft guns in the battery below swivel left and then right, loosening up like athletes before a big competition.

It was then that I got a call from Ernie who was waiting in the lobby, a development that I had not expected. He told me that Weizmann had invited him to cover his meeting with Churchill and Eisenhower that would soon take place in the hotel's Plantagenet Suite. It was a massive complex of rooms several floors below me that nearly covered the entire floor. It also had a killer view of the park from its long bank of floor to ceiling windows.

Ernie invited me for a quick drink and said that he would wait for me in the lobby, adding, *the girl and Syzmon made it but the big lug, well that's another story*. I thanked him for the update and said that I would have to take a rain check. I put the antique telephone back in its antique cradle and realized I needed to draw my blackout curtains and get going.

It was then that something odd happened. In the faint amber light, I could see the long barrels of the powerful antiaircraft guns drop one by one until they were not quite parallel to the ground, and a few of them at one end of the line swiveled like a group of synchronized swimmers to point squarely at the Dorchester at an elevation several floors below mine.

And it was then that Six's plan and the depth of my own stupidity hit me like a pulling guard on an end run. What was that place called? The gun battery that Bobby and I had passed in the park. Hell, why did it take me so long!?

It was Fire Support Base Archangel or *Erzangel* to Six. And it was about to unleash its fury not on the Krauts approaching from the Channel but on the Dorchester, and I thought I knew why.

******

As implausible as my theory sounded, Marguerite did not waste a second. We had feasted on the implausible of late.

Twenty Jed fighters seemed to materialize from nowhere as Marguerite also got word to Rory to proceed posthaste with her team to Archangel.

We had minutes not hours to make something happen. Babe found Ernie and got Weizmann's party out of the Plantagenet Suite to the basement over the objections of Churchill who could be heard muttering angrily, *does this have something to do with that bloody American?*

I was sure that the target of Operation Archangel was Chaim Weizmann's meeting at the Dorchester. The elimination in one blow of the luminaries in attendance would be the master stroke that Franz Six was looking for to reignite Hitler's interest in an invasion of Britain.

His *Einzatgruppen* or death squads had been formed to eliminate anti-Nazi elements in Britain including the detention of some 2,300 individuals immediately after the conquest of Britain. This list included politicians like Churchill and financiers like Baruch, who would attend this meeting. Others on the list were members of the Cabinet, writers like Sigmund Freud, even though he had died in September 1939, the philosopher Bertrand Russell, and members of exiled governments. A separate list named organizations to be dismantled like the Jehovah's Witnesses and even the Boy Scouts.

Marguerite, Bobby and I along with our fighters sprinted across Park Lane to find Rory and about 50 members of her team engaged in a firefight with the occupants of Archangel. Rory told us that Bruno had led a small squad into Archangel to do reconnaissance, and the original British crews were gone, most of their bodies haphazardly stacked behind the command center.

*It must have been an inside job,* she said, *fast and clean to avoid raising the alarm.* It was at that point that Bobby pointed to his watch and split to go after Marita.

Bruno, as you know, was the strappingly fit black dude with the Bar Pintxo ball cap that I had encountered on the banks of the Seine near Notre Dame and who had retrieved Madame Leroyer from the wreckage of my house in Manvieux. He was also a football fan who as a kid followed my exploits with the Skins, a real part of my life that now seemed unreal to me in this unreal moment.

Bruno said, *we lucked out some. By our count we caught them only part of the way through the loading process. Most of the shells are still on the rollers leading to the gun cabs or in the cradle but not yet locked into a barrel. Though a handful of guns appear to be fully loaded.*

*No help is coming from surrounding British units. They all seemed to have pulled out earlier in the day,* he added.

Rory summarized our predicament, *we can keep them pinned down and unable to fire the antiaircraft guns for now, but this time portal that they are using is disgorging Nazi fighters by the score, and they are good ones. They could be approaching battalion strength, so it is only a matter of time before they become too strong for us to stop them from using the loaded guns.*

Marguerite replied, *Rory, you know what needs to be done…execute both prongs of the operation.  Lovely,* was all Rory said in response. She signaled Bruno to join her before they disappeared.

Marguerite turned to me and added, *Charley, Bobby may have need of your assistance but stay out of sight until he confronts Marita. I will remain here with Rory for the moment. We need to find Six in this melee.*

I sprung loose from the fight at Archangel wondering what was meant by "the operation" as Rory and Marguerite led the desperate delaying action. I ran at full tilt toward the Achilles statue in the direction that I had seen Bobby go.

Bobby had a good ten minutes on me, and I finally caught up with him in the surreal glow of hand grenade bursts to my rear at Archangel and the man-made thunder and lightning on the near horizon from marauding Luftwaffe bombers in North and East London. I found two figures standing in the gloom about 20 feet apart with handguns pointed at each other's heads.  It was Bobby and Marita.

Marita was standing on the first pedestal at the base of the Achilles statue looking down on

Bobby. Neither one even attempted to use cover. It was a lover's spat that was one itchy trigger finger away from being settled.

Bobby said, *put down the gun, Marita. We must talk. About what Bobby?* she replied. *Why is it I betrayed you? Is that what you wish to know? Why is it I found meaning in the arms of Heydrich and not a heroic Jed? Are your feelings hurt?* They were shouting at each other amidst the din of the fighting that surrounded us, but Marita's sarcasm rung as clearly as Big Ben.

*I was never yours, and it was just as well that you never left your obedient wife, Bobby. It was all part of the game…a grand distraction as I turned every piece of information that you and your comrades provided me against you…against the Communist scum you adore who tortured my husband… that American witch whom we shall soon bend to our will.*

And it was at this point that this crazy night got even crazier.

First, a figure emerged from the shadows to put his gun to Bobby's head, cocking the trigger. For some damned reason, I considered this my cue to emerge from the shrubbery and move quickly toward the figure holding the gun to Bobby's head to nudge his head with my cocked Walther PPK to find that it was the head of none other than my execrable Nazi best bud, Kurt Meyer, who now looked even worse than he had at the shootout the night before.

So, there we were, a daisy chain of loaded and cocked  pistols.  To the asshole's credit, Meyer like I, appreciated the theatrical absurdity of this tableau. He announced to the group, *what are the odds, meinen Freundin?*

Couldn't argue with that. War teaches you that fiction can never come close to the reality of war for its perverse barbarism.

Then to make our rapidly dwindling life expectancies more interesting, young Basil Graham-Colleville chose that moment to stagger out of the shadows of a disintegrating Hyde Park. The semi-delirious Basil seemed to be bleeding from just about every place imaginable, but he gamely pointed his gun at my head from about six feet away.

And then, we heard someone else say, *Buddy Boy, don't move or you will end your days feeling hot steel from the stick I have in your back.* It was Ernie with nothing more than the pipe in his trench coat pocket poking Basil's  back.

Later, Ernie told me that he had learned this move from his favorite Bogart  movie.

It was Marita who finally lost patience with the lot of us and flicked her arm left in the blink of an eye to put a bullet into the right temple of the still babbling Basil with the ease of Annie Oakley shooting whiskey bottles off fence posts.  Ernie dove into the shrubbery as Basil crumpled where he stood.

Marita then took a shot at Bobby, and he returned the favor.  The ill-fated lovers lurched backward with each shot as they absorbed the deadly insults each visited upon the other. They were warriors who could take burning steel.

At that moment, Rory and her team came flooding through the trees nearby to add to the chaos.  That was Meyer's cue to get the hell out of there but not before he slammed his revolver against the side of my face putting me on my ass.

Rory bellowed with an air of command, *we have 90 seconds*, as for a moment, we all gazed skyward, mesmerized by a massive projectile at the end of a parachute, backlit by the detonations surrounding us.  It seemed to have come from nowhere and, as if guided by an unseen hand, it glided lazily over the Dorchester toward Archangel.

*Move your arses, move,* Rory yelled again.

At that point, Marita pulled a hand grenade from her pocket and the pin from the grenade. Bobby reacted instantly and ran full bore toward Marita, smothering her in his arms and using his momentum to push her across the width of the first pedestal to the other side of the Achilles statue away from our fighters.

There was a flash and an ear popping bang at which I rolled to my feet starting toward the far side of Achilles statue, but Rory intercepted me saying, *there is nothing that we can do now. Run, now, run!* I did run but not before I remembered Ernie, who was still in the shrubbery. I pulled him to his feet using the belt on his trench coat, and we both ran like hell.

We had just made it to a stand of stately oak trees on a low berm that bordered the field where we had seen Bobby's son play soccer. I looked back to see the projectile appear to hesitate for a split second directly above Archangel on the end of a now flapping parachute and then drop toward its target as I knocked Ernie to the ground and threw myself on top of him. Faces in the cold, wet dirt, we felt the ground ripple like a massive earthquake, and then the concussion of the blast flatten us like a steamroller, squeezing the breath out of us.

It had been a parachute mine, a naval weapon packed which could be packed with as much as 1,800 kg of high explosives. It was the largest weapon at the Luftwaffe's disposal. These huge cylinders were attached to parachutes to act as blast bombs that detonated at roof level rather than on impact to maximize the aerodynamic effects of a blast. Because the shock waves from the explosion were not cushioned by surrounding buildings, they could take out an entire city block.

In this case, the reinforced concrete berm along Park Lane acted as a backstop that projected the force of the blast away from Park Lane and toward the Serpentine vaporizing every living thing in its path. It left those of us on its periphery relatively unscathed along with the other side of Park Lane and the Dorchester.

Where it had come from and how it had been so deftly targeted at Archangel was a mystery.

******

The debris cloud and the rain of choking grit that fell from it would have overcome most people, but there stood four stoic figures in the early morning hours after Archangel had been secured staring through this grim veil in silence from what remained of the bandshell that had brought *La Sonnambula* to Hyde Park. It had been ruined in the blast, and most of its faux Corinthian columns and had been reduced to rubble along with its concave roof.

The anti-aircraft station was now a veritable Hell, twisted metal lacquered by the searing heat of the blast with an indescribable organic mélange worthy of Picasso's Guernica. There was still the sound and light show of the waning German raid off in the distance, but it was less intense than before. The Nazi plan had been to keep their bombing off to the North and East of Hyde Park as a diversion.

*Dear Charley will not like having been left in the dark on our little plan*, one said in her mellifluous born to the manor British accent. Marguerite was the first to speak and with a hint of rueful sarcasm said, *Rory, your dear Charley has proven that he is much more effective when he doesn't know the plan, when there is no plan.*

*It is a rare talent that Bobby possessed,* and then Marguerite's voice clutched for the barest fraction of a second. She stopped speaking as abruptly as a soldier comes to attention on a drill ground.

After what seemed like an interminable pause, the girl with the bearing of a ballerina looked toward Marguerite hesitating at her discomfort and then turned back to look at Archangel as she scratched the head of the very large animal sitting at her hip. Jane said, *I could not allow him to see me...yet…to give him false hope….*

*We now have Six and may soon have a better idea of where Heydrich has the nucleic device if Six cooperates,* Marguerite said. *If his ravings can be believed, we have very little time to prevent its use.*

*Regardless of what he says,* Jane continued, *our Garden of Gethsemane approaches, mine and Charley's. It is not something that I would wish on someone I love, but Charley and I must become the bait that will snare this monster once and for all.*

And then a single, continuous note reverberated thróugh the night sounding the *all clear* as Achilles grieved.

348

# MONTGOMERY INTERVIEW XXIV

I met Ernie at the Anglers Arm, his favorite pub, which was a short walk from his office on the Strand. It was his favorite pub not because it was noted for its hearty food or libations but because on the night of November 1, 1940, during the height of the London Blitz, one of the hundreds of German bombs that would rain down on London that night came crashing through the roof of this pub as a crowd of men sat drinking beer.

The bomb exploded blowing the place to pieces killing some people in the house across the street but hurting not a soul in the pub. It was the kind of irony that Ernie liked to write home about and did.

There was just enough of the place left so that it could stay in business. I got there first and nursed a beer. Three-quarters of a beer later, Ernie casually sauntered in through a hole in the wall that now served as the door. The barkeep brought us a round, and we sat there in silence for a few minutes.

Ernie finally broke the ice and said, *Charley, I stayed up all last night trying to write this up for the folks back home. If there were such a thing as a scale of unbelievability, this past week has damn well busted that scale.*

*The piece, well I tore it up, as I suspect your compatriots want. I do this with some reluctance because a good newshound like yours truly could never pass up something this juicy for the folks back home who are counting on us.*

*Shucks, the other night stole a page from HG. Wells or Jules Verne and if I had a hankering to dabble in the downright weird, I would damn well send a story home. And the next thing that would happen is they would send me home too, wrapped up tightly in a little white jacket with first class accommodations in a padded cell. So, I tore the damn thing up.*

*Thank you, Ernie,* I said. I had been delegated to ask him to bury any story about the events of the last week. And in Ernie's elliptical and folksy style, he had just done me a huge favor.

We ruminated over another round of beers. He told me that he had trashed his ruined brown suit but would keep the trench coat. Too many good memories, he said.

Ernie also told me that he was going to ship out soon. He couldn't say where, but I knew because I had read his books voraciously as a kid. It would be North Africa and so it would be the last time that I would see him.

We lingered for another beer or two and finally got up and left together through the hole in the wall and shook hands. Ernie said, *Charley, you are as good a soul as they come and an odd duck. I can't quite place why, but there is something about you that makes you stand out from the people I am used to knowing. Maybe you also come from a page in that H.G. Wells or Jules Verne book that we were talking about. Wouldn't surprise me one bit.*

*I've enjoyed your company, Pal, and I hope that our paths cross again,* Ernie went on to say, *I would like to introduce you to 'That Girl' someday and exchange tall tales as we all sit on my porch at the ranch in New Mexico and admire the lonely mesa out back.*

*Ernie, I would like that very much. It has been a privilege to know you even for such a short period of time. More than you know. God speed. Take care of yourself, OK?*

We shook hands again, and I watched as he sauntered casually in the direction of Fleet Street just as the plaintive air raid sirens awoke for the night.

Ernie would make it through North Africa and up the Italian peninsula from Sicily. He would be blown out of the press headquarters during the landing at Anzio and in the breakout from the Normandy beachhead in France would nearly be killed by our own bombers near St. Lô.

One of my favorite quotes of his was about the experience of life at the front. He said, "(It) works itself into an emotional tapestry of one dull dead pattern -- yesterday is tomorrow and Troiano is Randozzo and, O God, I'm so tired."

On the 18th of April 1945 in the waning days of the Battle of the Pacific, Ernie would be cut down in a burst of enemy machine gun fire in the battle for a small island called *Ie Shima*. He died instantly among the men he admired and who revered him.

# VIII. INTO THE VALLEY OF DEATH, INTO THE MOUTH OF HELL

# MONTGOMERY JOURNAL ENTRY XXV – IN THEATRE

This will be my first entry since receiving this dictation device, a tiny 21$^{st}$ century gadget that I am forced to conceal here midway through the summer of 1944.

The ICA guys, who understand the physics of the time dilations that we now travel as if we were going back and forth through the Holland Tunnel, want me to substitute a journal for our interviews, which have become less practical as I am drawn deeper into Jed Team Hugo's pursuit of the nucleic device that could change the course of history.

The scuttlebutt is that it would have been detonated by now but for the missing ingredient, who is still missing, my wife Jane.

I often find myself in the netherworld between sleep and wakefulness in a state of depression in the early hours of the morning. I lie there processing battles won and battles lost in this crazy story in this crazier world that now holds me in its grip, where time is not simply the backdrop to life but a protagonist. Everything that may have gone wrong or could go wrong, something I had failed to do or that might threaten us still, hits me like a tidal wave. You've been there or perhaps not.

I have had these repeated bouts of nocturnal anxiety and self-doubt throughout the years, which I suspect may be a purely physical phenomenon. Perhaps, they are simply a function of cortisol surges triggered by a full moon or my blood alcohol level or the latest kick in the head by an opponent on the gridiron when I played cornerback for the Redskins?  Who knows?

It was something like that the night before the big meeting with top brass at the American forward command post.  I was sacked out with my Jed compatriots in a damp potato cellar somewhere near St. Lô and my mind would not shut down. There were a bunch of us. Rory and her team were due to arrive soon, so something big was in the offing.

Invading my sleep were roiling, repetitive images of Bobby's tragic and heroic last moments in London, the shootout at Double-X involving Ernie Pyle, Melody and her team who were pitted against the Nazis working hand in glove with British anti-Semites, the home in Normandy that Jane and I loved so much going up in flames, Rory stepping over the sill of my blown out kitchen window to find me, and the smiling face of that pretty-boy, Hitler Jugend bastard, Kurt Meyer, who seemed to be at the center of it all. He is Heydrich's henchman in the plan to grab Jane in order to set off a nucleic device with the force of a modern-day atom bomb.

At one point in this disjointed dream, I was my tackling the Teutonic stud who was going after Babe, gun drawn, at Gare St. Lazare followed by the oozing gray goop from his head after Marguerite neatly put a bullet in it, which I proceeded to serve like Calvados to Bobby and Babe by the Godin stove in my wood beamed *salle a manger*.  Yup, fucked-up.

Then I saw through Marguerite's eyes the death of her brother Freddy somewhere in the Loire, obliterated by German bombers on their retreat from Paris. I know that this memory more than any other thing gave the young leftenant in the Free French Army her backbone of steel.

And then there was the sickening blood-spattered eating room at Cubitts, our waitress spread eagle at the base of the bar, arms akimbo, vacantly staring with a fixed expression of horror at the gaping hole that had just been blown in her chest by Heydrich's men. I saw Jane watching from the street and tried to get to her through the mayhem only to find myself hovering above the church at Aunay sur Odon helpless to keep Bobby's men from coming for Jane and me when we were together in the crypt and to control the strong sense of betrayal that I felt.

To fix all of this, I would try repeatedly in my dream to find the right mixture of lead and Coke Classic to create gold in the hope that such alchemy would please Jane and appease the gods enough so that she would come back to me and never go away again, but the love of my life would always go away again.

This sequence of events would repeat itself in a continuous, looping, permutating, nauseating bad dream that I was helpless to change to the good.

******

A coded message had been intercepted by *Ultra,* the Allied intelligence source that tapped the very highest levels of encrypted communications in the German military, and this time its origin was none other than the Abwehr, Germany's military intelligence service. Damn if the message wasn't directed toward us, and its agents desired a meeting on a subject code named *Hölle*, which is the German word for Hell.

Admiral Wilhelm Canaris, the head of Abwehr, thought to be a leading member of the July 20 plot to assassinate Hitler, was a complicated figure who had maintained an open channel with British Intelligence during Operation Barbarossa, the German invasion of Russia. He had also intervened to save victims of Nazi persecution, including Jews.

For example, he was instrumental in getting five-hundred Dutch Jews to safety in May 1941. Many of them were given token training as Abwehr "agents" and then issued papers allowing them to leave Germany.

In our case, the Abwehr appeared to be tuned into to Heydrich's efforts to detonate a nucleic device. Canaris and Heydrich were bitter rivals but, more importantly, Canaris was a principled man who understood the toll that Heydrich's plan would take on both sides and the course of history itself.

Babe clued me in later that this had been a topic of back-channel conversation with the Abwehr for some time. The communications from the Abwehr typically took the form of a coded message from the German Naval Command to U-Boat 246.

This particular message prescribed that the meeting would take place 48 hours hence. The location would be a church in a small hamlet called St. Gilles, roughly 15 kilometers southeast of the St. Lô-Periers road. This road now served as the front line for American forces that were massing for the anticipated breakout from the Contentin Peninsula and soon thereafter Normandy itself.

This would be a dicey excursion because there had been so much confusion on the Cotentin Peninsula caused by the fragmented and porous front line that our units on maneuver were just as likely to be attacked by our side as by the Bosch. In the same vein, we were setting off for a church that today was 15 kilometers inside German territory, but who knew about tomorrow.

The Abwehr offered that its agents in the Wehrmacht or German army would look the other way for the 48 hours in question in a narrow geographic corridor that would essentially be our route to St. Gilles. However, they could not guarantee that we would not face the remnants of the once mighty *Panzer*

*Lehr* division which was massed in that area but had been degraded by the Allies into small units.

These *Panzer Lehr* units were still fighting fiercely to hold their positions, but they did not form a continuous line and were susceptible to being outflanked or bypassed altogether. Abwehr assurances notwithstanding, it would be our job to thread this needle if we were to make it to St. Gilles.

To make this official, we needed to meet with the American Commander in the sector, Lieutenant General Lesley McNair. It was Marguerite who entered the lion's den, in this case McNair's command tent, situated in the middle of an overgrown field of pear and quince trees.

Babe and I hung outside, not having been invited in by McNair, and we listened to McNair bellow at the top of his lungs for much of the meeting. Marguerite was apparently not returning fire in kind, and we never heard her raise her voice.

We learned later that McNair had warned Marguerite about Operation Cobra, which the Allies were about to launch to break out of Normandy from positions near St. Lô, the major communication hub in the area, whose capture the Americans had paid for dearly in a siege that took over a month. Cobra would unleash a hellish 72 hours that would overlap with our mission, McNair said, and he did not want to commit good men to chaperoning us on what he called a fool's errand.

In the end, the top brass in London gave him no choice, and he was forced to give us a full Company, nearly 250 men. Two hours after she went in, Marguerite emerged from the tent, apparently none the worse for wear.  She looked at us in her exquisitely deadpan fashion and matter of factly said, *we move at dawn.*

And move we did. It was Jed Team Hugo -- Babe, Marguerite and me, along with Jed Team Zeke and B Company of the 119th Regiment, 30th Infantry Division.  A gray mist swirled up from the marsh nearby like vapor from a newly opened bottle of champagne as we set out. A sliver of red between earth and sky on our left flank signaled the coming of dawn.

After crossing the St. Lô-Periers road, we moved cautiously down a narrow country lane that snaked this way and that to stay roughly in line with a winding river on our left flank. A reconnaissance platoon probed forward for enemy resistance.

It did not help that we were in countryside that was dominated by some exceptionally large hedgerows. They loomed over the country lane, and by and large, they had to be at least 15 feet high and as wide as six feet at their base behind which were fields, each roughly the size of an American football field.

My favorite writer on all things D-Day was Stephen Ambrose, who wrote, "No terrain in the world was better suited for defensive action in World War II than the hedgerows." He got that right. German defenders could station large cannon and field guns in the curve of a narrow, sunken farm lane like the one we were on and destroy any American tanks coming up the path.

Worse still, German infantry would dig into the sides of the hedges and use the tangle of trees, shrubs, and prickly brambles as natural camouflage to cut down attacking Allies. German soldiers were meticulous in digging into their defensive positions and turning every bucolic pasture into a well-prepared kill zone. Their snipers would also climb high in the trees to have full view of each small battlefield.

German defenders would frequently retreat in the face of an Allied onslaught, luring our guys into seeking cover in foxholes, which the Germans had created in the fields between the hedgerows, where our guys would then be pulverized by German artillery in the rear that had sighted these same foxholes. It was also not uncommon for the Germans to retreat and use cleverly positioned tunnels to return to the field and attack us from the rear, not unlike what both sides were trying to do to each other on a different battlefield – Time.

German machine gun positions in the corners of the hedgerows gave them interlocking fields of fire, meaning that each gun's range overlapped another gun's range. This intersecting fire called an *enfilade* could saw a man in two.

Mortars behind the opposing hedgerow were also targeted to locations in the middle. In short, all the Germans had to do was wait for a head-on attack.

In the early days of the Battle of Normandy, American troops obliged and would charge directly into each field, hoping their numbers and bravado would force the Germans back. Tanks attempting to go up-and-over the hedgerows would expose their lightly-armored undersides to deadly German anti-tank weapons.

Such assaults proved to be suicide missions, leading thousands of men to their deaths. One ill-fated Company in the 331st Infantry Regiment lost 90 percent of its original men just three weeks into the hedgerow combat after repeated frontal assaults into these fields.

Our small convoy of jeeps with a Sherman tank in the lead and one bringing up the rear ventured deeper and deeper into the jaws of the Minotaur waiting for us in its lush labyrinth. We would stop and duck from time to time as both sides lobbed mortars over our heads and hesitated at frequent intervals as small arms fire crackled to our left or to our right.

The driver of my jeep was a guy by the name of Manny Martins, who described himself as a Jew from Brooklyn who loved killing Germans. He was a gregarious guy who chewed compulsively on the butt of a cigar and seemed totally unfazed by gunfire or the periodic mortar round.

Babe was with Manny and me. Marguerite rode up toward the front of the convoy with the Company's captain.

It had been a couple of hours since leaving camp. The convoy's slow progress came to an abrupt halt as the country lane t-boned into a gargantuan that loomed over our column.

A runner came back from the lead tank and told us that the road we had planned to take off to the right was blockaded about several kilometers up the line by a large German formation. So, we were going to probe the hedgerow dead ahead and move across the field behind it. St. Gilles would then be several kilometers due south of the other side of the field.

Most of the Company moved forward as the rest fanned out to each side of the road to guard our rear and our flanks. On one side was a small pasture with two bloated, rotting Guernsey cows. The smell was disgusting but your senses adjusted to the rot of warfare the longer you were exposed to it.

To the other side was a wide opening in a scraggly section of a hedgerow and a pastoral scene worthy of Norman Rockwell -- a wooden barn about 50 yards away that was largely intact next to which stood a large hayrick full of hay with a conical top that looked like a Viking's helmet. We took up positions in a gully on the side of the road facing this scene along an old wooden fence laced with barb wire.

Babe had gone up front to determine whether he could bring his unique set of skills to bear on the effort to cross through the hedgerow onto the field beyond. Jed Team Zeke hovered in my area and appeared to have the assignment of keeping one eye on the bad guys and one on me. Manny sat in the jeep chewing on his cigar leaning back in the driver's seat with his helmet pulled down over his eyes catnapping.

We waited as the Sherman tanks both equipped with Rhino's worked to plough through the base of the imposing hedgerow in our path. The "Rhino" was a technological innovation cooked up by a young sergeant named Bud Culin, a New Jersey boy, who heard a young soldier joke that the Americans should put teeth on the front of tanks to saw through hedgerows. Culin took the idea and ran with it, welding sharpened metal teeth on the front of Sherman tanks.

Using steel from German beach defenses, more than 500 tanks were eventually equipped with "Culin Rhino" attachments. With these modifications, tanks were able to quickly break through individual hedgerows. The Army also got a whole lot smarter about communication between ground forces and tank commanders, which had been virtually nonexistent during the early days of hedgerow fighting.

And then the shit hit the fan.

Up ahead, we heard the high-pitched sound of "Hitler's Buzzsaw" indicating that Germans were there to welcome us with M42 machine guns whose high cyclic firing rate gave it this distinctive sound. And then the first shot from the direction of the barn came our way, and the private who had been standing shoulder to shoulder with me took a bullet between the eyes, toppling over, stiff as a two-by-four. Damned if it wasn't a sniper. Everyone hit the deck.

A second and third shot rang out, and I saw another man go down up the line. They say that if you are unlucky enough to be killed by a sniper you never hear the sound of the shot because the bullet arrives first.

We were trying to spot the guy, and the most logical place to look was the loft of the barn.  After a few minutes, a tank moved back from the hedgerow and turned its turret toward the barn and let off a few rounds, setting the rustic barn ablaze.

Our guys waited, crouching. Then there was another shot that seemed to ricochet off something just to my rear and then another, but I had seen it. *It's the hayrick,* I shouted.  *The hayrick!*  There had been a puff of smoke from the top of the hayrick near the crest of the helmet.

*We need tracers. Bring up the 50 millimeter,* the sergeant in charge of the group toward the rear yelled. That was one brave dude who drove the 50-millimeter gun mounted on a jeep up into the gap, which the sniper was exploiting.  The gunner jumped on board just as the 50mm arrived and started pumping round after round of tracer fire into the hayrick immediately setting the hay ablaze.

Tracers are bullets or artillery rounds built with a small pyrotechnic charge in their base that burns brightly. It had become standard operating procedure for addressing snipers in hayricks or haylofts. If the machine gun didn't get the sniper, the fire from the tracers would roast him alive.

As the fire-fight at the head of our column intensified, those of us toward the rear began to collect ourselves and our dead and wounded after waiting several minutes for the hayrick to broil the guy. I turned to catch a glimpse of Manny on the other side of the jeep with the 50 mm gun still napping in his jeep, although the gnawing at the cigar between his lips had ceased.

My stomach did a flip as I walked over to him. He sat where I had left him in his jeep frozen in place and time and in his hatred of Germans. The final sniper's bullet had pierced his helmet and taken him.

******

It had been a small force of Germans, who had hastily dug into the hedgerow opposite our column, but we lost valuable time trying to root them out. After a few hours of intense fighting, we eliminated all of them.

Babe and I looked the other way as the platoon that did the clean-up work dispatched a handful of German wounded, who were begging for their lives. *Fucked up, but who am I to judge,* Babe said as we walked back to our jeep. No prisoners of war would be taken that day.

We were too far into enemy territory to risk sending our wounded back to our starting point with a small detachment of men. We had two medics with us, and we did the best that we could. We left our dead – six men including Manny in shallow graves for retrieval on our return.

How cavalierly we say six men dead these days. These were human beings who were a mother's son, cherished their wife and children, were afraid on their first days of school, cheered their favorite sports teams, had a first holy communion or bar mitzvah, and whose dogs loved them and vice-versa. Perhaps, the same could be said for the Germans we neatly stacked like two by fours under a stand of apple trees.

But we had become hardened and immune to the toll this war was taking. There were the 2,500 American boys lost in one day on D-Day. On any other day in the last several weeks, it was not uncommon for hundreds of men to exchange their lives in a matter of minutes for 50 or 100 yards of a muddy wheat field far from home.

They say in Normandy that if you don't like the weather wait 15 minutes. The sunny and bloody afternoon had turned into a misty dusk which at this time of year came at about 22:00 hours, as we arrived in St. Gilles.

Babe went ahead with Jed Team Zeke to reconnoiter the area around the church and, as had been agreed, lit a small orange flare and tossed it into a clearing in what must have been a car park on the side of the church. We had seen Germans in defensive positions around the church on our approach, who at the sign of the flair seemed to melt away into the gloom.

I joined Babe, Marguerite and the other Jeds, and we approached the church cautiously. The medics with the wounded followed closely behind us while the B Company created a tight perimeter around the place.

There was movement in the church and more than one person talking, and we entered with guns at the ready to find that the church was a German field hospital. It was run by an Austrian surgeon who was not exactly welcoming but who took one look at us and matter of factly directed the medics to take our wounded to the main and side altars that had been jury rigged as operating tables.

The surgeon's name was Hans Faber, and he was assisted by a German nurse and two women from the village. German wounded were trickling in through a door in the left transept of the church and were being sorted by a couple of German orderlies who glanced nervously in our direction. Marguerite sent word to the captain of B Company not to interfere with the influx of German wounded, and our medics began to pitch in.

The church in St. Gilles was connected to a natural cavern set in the hillside by something akin to a cloistered walkway. Apparently, a group of Benedictine monks made Calvados here and used the cavern as a cellar.

We were less than 12 hours away from the launch of Operation Cobra, and anything within several miles of the St. Lô-Periers road was at risk of being annihilated. I urged Marguerite and Faber to begin moving those who could be moved to shelter in the  cavern.

Indeed, on the morning of July 25, 1944, Operation Cobra would get underway at 09:38

hours when 600 Allied fighter bombers attacked strongpoints and enemy artillery along the strip of ground bordering the St. Lô-Periers road that was about 300 yards wide.

Then, for the next hour, 1,800 heavy bombers of the U.S. Eighth Air Force would saturate a 6,000 by 2,200 yard area just to the south of the road, followed by a third and final wave of medium bombers. All told, one of the greatest assemblages of air power in modern warfare, about 3,000 U.S. aircraft in total, would carpet-bomb a narrow section of the front, with the Panzer Lehr Division taking the brunt of the onslaught.

While St. Gilles was not in the targeted rectangle, miscommunication about the path of the bombers and a strong breeze that blew smoke and dirt everywhere obscured the target zone and would kill over one hundred of our own men behind our lines, wounding several hundred more. Barely a minute or two of hesitation by crews of the B-17 Flying Fortresses and B-24 Liberators, which flew at about 300 miles per hour, could send their bombs raining down on St. Gilles instead of their planned targets.

If our fly boys didn't get us, the 170,000 artillery shells, which the artillery units of the 7th and 8th Corps had been given to put the icing on the cake, could finish the job. The Germans had known nothing about Operation Cobra when they selected St. Gilles as the site for our rendezvous. How could they have?

Speaking of the rendezvous, around midnight Babe and Jed Team Zeke faded away into the misty night as I was helping Faber hold down a delirious Hitler Jugend, who had a broken jaw and a left foot that was dangling precariously from his leg by a piece of cartilage. Faber looked at me and shook his head indicating that the young Nazi was near death, but before he fainted, he rolled his head over and murmured, *Heil Hitler*.

I had just come back from taking a wounded man to the Calvados cellar with the help of one of the nervous German orderlies when there was a commotion at the main door of the church. In walked Babe holding a Thompson submachine gun and wearing a look that told you he would use it if necessary.

Babe was followed by a tall German, a general judging from his long leather field coat and the gold insignia on his peaked cap and shoulders, who was followed closely by an aide flanked by two members of Jed Team Zeke. The rest of the general's entourage was being entertained by B Company's captain at the perimeter of our defense.

Marguerite moved toward the general and I with her, but he did not seem to recognize her as our leader. *I am Generalleutenant Hans Speidel. Whom may I address,* he said firmly, as he looked with concern at the remaining German wounded, some too weak to be carried to the cellar.

Speidel stood ramrod straight and had the face of a hawk that had just spotted its prey. I noticed that he wore a Knight's Cross of the Iron Cross that hung from his neck and rested on the front of his leather coat. This meant that he was not your average field commander.

Marguerite answered by saying, *I am Leftenant Marguerite Martragny of the Free French Army and for our purposes tonight, your counterpart, General.* There was a flicker of bemusement on Speidel's face as he sized up the young and determined woman who stood before him but just a flicker that was replaced in a heartbeat with respect as the tall German removed his cap and placed it under his arm, bowing his head and softly clicking his heels.

Not unlike Canaris, Speidel was an important figure in his own right. He had been a committed German Nationalist but detested Hitler's racial policies. He was chief of staff to the Desert Fox, Irwin Rommel, who commanded Army Group B on the Western Front. Like his boss, he saw as inevitable the collapse of the Reich once the Allies secured a foothold in France and consequently became involved in the July 20th plot to kill Hitler.

He had been delegated by anti-Hitler forces to recruit Rommel to the conspiracy, which he had cautiously begun to do prior to Rommel's injury in a Canadian strafing attack on the 17th of July 1944, just a week before our meeting at St. Gilles. He would continue as Chief of Staff for the new commander of Army Group B, the ill-fated Field Marshal Günther von Kluge.

Speidel gestured with a nod of his head toward the baptismal font located in a rear alcove of the church to his right, and our small group moved as one to gain some privacy. He asked Faber to join us for a report on causalities, which he accepted gravely.

*War is the worst possible way of breeding the best type of human being...the best blood is lost,* Speidel said as he surveyed the remaining wounded before dismissing the good doctor.

Speidel then got to the point in his thickly accented English.

*Der Teufel or if you prefer the Devil is moving at night with the device and while we have a sense of where his trajectory will take him, we are still unsure about the final location he has chosen. We believe it is high ground to the East of the town of Falaise overlooking the Orne, and we continue to monitor the situation.*

Wittingly or unwittingly, if this were true, Heydrich was angling to locate the nucleic device in the vicinity of what would become the Falaise Gap. Barely a month later, the remnants of two once-mighty German armies would occupy an area roughly twelve miles long and five miles wide as the Allied armies bore down on them from the North, West and South. A gap at the Eastern end of this pocket that ran North-South for about five miles provided the narrowest of escape routes for retreating German forces across the Orne and Dives rivers to the relative safety of the Seine River Valley.

Perhaps, Heydrich did not have the scruples of the Jeds, which prevented them from stealing intelligence from the future to change the present. Did Heydrich know about the Falaise Pocket – the *Trap with a Gap*? Was he going to spring his own trap on converging British, American and Canadian forces?

*It was our hope that you would be able to share more to justify our social call tonight, General,* Marguerite replied unobligingly.

*Then, let us get to the point, Leftenant,* he responded. *As you may know, we have had not one but two short truces during which the Allies handed over German nurses; the most recent was in the Caumont sector involving the 2nd Panzer Division. The chivalrous treatment of these nurses by your forces made at that time a deep impression on the entire division and the Field Marshall himself.*

*We propose yet another such exchange once we have determined der Teufel's fixed  location. And pinpoint it we must for we get one chance at this.*

*This time, it will be a small team of your fighters posing as German medical personnel, whom we will guide as far as Heydrich's camp. I am sure that you have the appropriate costumes at your disposal.*

*How much time can you give us,* I asked? Marguerite was doing just fine without me, but I knew how much chaos lay ahead and was skeptical about whether Speidel could pull this off. Speidel looked at me as if to size me up and after a brief pause continued.

*Your team will be escorted as far as possible by my most loyal men, and you will have as much time as we can give you to complete the destruction of Der Teufel and his toy. Whether that is four hours or 24 hours, I cannot say at this moment. As you can see,* and at this he motioned as if looking outside, *our circumstances on the Contentin seem to change by the minute,* Speidel said with irony but no humor.

*Now, I must go,* he said. *You will hear from us again, God willing, by regular channels.*

Speidel concluded our meeting by looking each one of us in the eye lingering on the self-assured young woman before him. As he turned to leave, he nodded to Marguerite respectfully and said, *bonne chance, Leftenant, ou nous reverrons bientôt en enfer.* In other words, Speidel had told Marguerite, *Good luck, Leftenant, or we will soon meet again in Hell.*

******

Shortly after Speidel's departure, Faber and I shared a hit or two of Calvados, which doubled nicely as an operating room antiseptic, as Babe and Marguerite huddled by the main door of the church. When the conversation had finished, he saluted Marguerite with what could only have been called affection. He might as well have just hugged her but for military decorum.

Babe was detached to get me back across the front line before all hell broke loose. Marguerite was going to hunker down in the Calvados cellar with a machine gun platoon from B Company, the medics and our wounded in the hope that our side found them before the other side did after Cobra had been unleashed.

We flew like bats out of hell, retracing our tracks back to base.  The calculation was that we would be much more vulnerable to destruction by our waves of bombers and the shit storm of artillery that would follow than by a random attack by the disorganized Germans in that sector. We did, however, stop briefly to retrieve Manny and his comrades.

The great bombing that would soon be unleashed by Cobra would create a landscape that looked like the moon. Scarcely a human being or animal would be alive in an area of many square miles. The bombing would leave a horrid stew of every type of truck, gun and machine reduced to tortured and twisted rubble on a deeply scarred landscape. In some cases, Panzer tanks would be flipped on their backs like turtles.

It was estimated that the Panzer Lehr division lost over 35 tanks, fifteen assault rifles and 2,000 men. When Marguerite was finally relieved by one of our units, she and Faber emerged from the cellar to find German walking wounded aimlessly wandering around among our troops babbling like punch drunk fighters after the sustained, concussive bombardment.

As we crossed back into our territory and put some distance between us and the Saint Lô-Periers road, I thought about Erne Pyle, who was somewhere nearby and would nearly be killed by errant American bombers, as well as the Americans GI's who would be buried in their foxholes, many of whom could only get an arm or a leg up through the dirt and had to be dug out.

Among the dead on the American side would be Lieutenant General McNair himself who would leave the safety of his command car shielded behind a tank to go forward on foot for a better look at the big show. His death would be kept a closely guarded secret for some time.

We got back to the potato cellar by late afternoon at which point Babe told me to clean up and get into a change of clothes. There were no showers, but there was a small stream with crisp, cold water so we both dove in to wash away the grit, sadness and tension of the last 48 hours.

After a snack of K-rations, Babe said, *Bud, time to saddle-up*. We had one more mission to complete this evening, he said, although he was not particularly forthcoming when I tried to get at what he was planning.

After about 45 minutes in the jeep, we found ourselves in front of a secluded wooden cottage attached to a small water mill that sat astride the proverbial babbling brook. Babe gave me instructions in faux military fashion and a cheeky salute before tearing back down the country road from whence we had come leaving me standing alone at the front door.

# MONTGOMERY JOURNAL ENTRY XXVI

I opened the door slowly not knowing quite what to expect and the scent of roasting chicken hit me softly like a warm wave on Waikiki. I found myself entering a rustic main room that combined the living and dining areas. It struck me that a large family lived here, or used to, because the long oak table looked like it had come from the refectory of a monastery and the room was full of the tchotchke's that families collect over time.

There was a roaring fire off to my left on the far side of the oak table, which bore a double line of flickering candles of various sizes and shapes down its center. Two places were set at the far end.

There was a flash of movement to my right and, at this point in my life and this story, I had been conditioned to assume that it would be someone trying to kill me, so I turned sharply, ready to deflect the blow and to counterpunch.

And there she was. It was Jane, and something about the way she smiled told me that it was my Jane, the real Jane, not the wan, mythical creature that I had last seen in the crypt of the church in Aunay sur Odon and whose fate had consumed me and the Jeds for so long.

Her straight blonde hair fell to her shoulders, and she wore something that looked like a simple peasant dress that could have been a costume from one of her ballets. It had a tightly drawn bodice of course brown material like suede, which gave way to a sheer, cream colored skirt that flared at the waist.

Despite the lighting or because of it, it was evident that this was where the costume ended. Her first words were, *soldier, do you want to see the Washington Monument?*

I laughed, and months of stress evaporated like dew under a warm morning sun. Jane, my Jane, the real Jane, was referring to an episode early in our courtship when I brought her to Washington, D.C. for a sightseeing trip. She had never been.

I was playing for the Skins and had a place in Old Town Alexandria at the time, while Jane had a Trinity townhouse in a small alleyway just off Rittenhouse Square in Center City Philadelphia.

I was so anxious that day to show her the sights that I ignored the fact that Jane had draped herself seductively across my bed. Sightseeing won, and I lost. Jane barely spoke to me the rest of the day.

*What do you think,* I said? *Where?*

Jane nodded toward the table. *Shall we show the monks a thing or two?*

*I suppose it won't be the first time that we have ended up with splinters or an unholy rug burn,* I responded.

And in an instant, the dress made a bed for us on the long oak table after we hastily shoved the candles to one end. The ballerina who had occupied my dreams and once occupied the dress, lay waiting for me on the tabletop.

******

Never had cold chicken tasted so good. We devoured it later, along with some now soggy roasted potatoes and a wheel of strong Livarot cheese with bread. Homemade cider and some hearty, non-descript red wine punctuated our Bacchanalian feast. And, holy moly, it was a feast in so many ways.

As we devoured the meal in the light of the roaring fire, Jane asked if I had received her letter. I told her that I had not. Obviously disappointed, she proceeded to tell me about her capture by Fulcanelli and her reunion with her adoptive father, Philippe Delain. I asked her about the bloody running shoe, and she filled me in on that too.

*Did you try to escape,* I asked? *I did but Fulcanelli had a power over me that I could not resist, at least then,* she said. *He is a man whose understanding of nature is timeless, and he hoped that he and Delain, the dear man who had adopted me, could seduce me into their scheme. The memory of my adoptive father's betrayal is bittersweet.*

*The experience at first was like being hypnotized. I could do little that Fulcanelli and Delain, his compliant protégé, did not dictate, but some of the real me, my conscience and character, remained hidden in a small corner of my psyche waiting for the opportunity to break free. It would not let the person that I really am be snuffed out completely.*

*Fulcanelli and, dare I call him my father, had been holed up in a disheveled chateau in Crepon, which is where Fulcanelli first took me after snatching me at Cap Manvieux. This was in forward time, but it was not long before they both became apprehensive that we were being watched. They were less concerned about the incompetent local Gendarmes than they were about Heydrich's fanatical pretty boys, whom they suspected to be operating in the area.*

*So, they brought me back here, that is to say, back to 1944 where they felt more in control of the environment, but not before torching the house in Crepon to leave no trace of our presence there.* Mondher had really been on to something, I thought to myself.

*Fulcanelli and Delain saw to my education during that period and unlocked the power that I had unknowingly held inside me for so long. I suspect that your Jed colleagues have by now taught you more about Hermes than you would ever want to know in this or any other lifetime, but he is the mythical father of Alchemy and in truth the patriarch of my real family tree.*

*We who are his descendants live in a duality like Christ himself, who bore the burden of being half human and half God. But for us at least, the latter has a basis in physics and, in days past, what people called Alchemy.*

*To Alchemy,* I said raising my glass as did Jane with a smirk on her beautiful face, as I indulged in some good French profanity. *Putain!*

*I am the Jane that you know down to each corpuscle of my physical being,* she continued, as she took my hands in hers. *Yet there are people like me, descendants of Hermes, who knowingly or unknowingly carry the power to manipulate the physics of the universe in a very real sense. My ancestors planted us in each of the 11 major branches of the Indo-European language family from Wales and France to Iran and India.*

*Then who is Fulcanelli,* I asked.

Jane gave me a sour smile and said, *my ancestors exist to this day though not in a physical, human form and do not seek to influence the direction of time and reality except for one. Fulcanelli is the son of Hermes, and this is real. Just as Lucifer fell from God's grace, the same is true of Fulcanelli's relationship with his own father.*

*Fuck, let me grab another bottle of wine,* I said. Jane did not let go of my hands and listed toward me to give me a tipsy kiss. She was flushed and hot to the touch. *Let's take a break,* she said, *and save the wine for when I pick up where we left off. You'll need it.*

Jane's sense of timing was perfect, and it was an hour, maybe more, before we picked up the thread of her crazy story.

*The circumstances around my primer in the mysteries of Alchemy began to unravel when Fulcanelli appeared to cast his lot with the Bosch,* Jane continued. *His plan was to turn me over to them, and the trap was set at St. Lazare. I did not see you, but my cousins told me about the stocky American who had tackled one of the Nazis in the train station and the melee that followed.*

*The Germans got only Delain, who had finally come to his senses and arranged to have his nephews in Paris squirrel me away to a hideaway in the Marais. The Germans also got the badly bruised and battered Fulcanelli in the bargain and were furious about his failure to turn me over to them.*

*That is not the end of it. Fulcanelli knew how to get word to me through Delain's nephews and proposed to return him, no strings attached. We knew it was a trap because with Fulcanelli there were always strings attached. But we had no choice but to try.*

*Fuck,* I said. *You really do need to expand your vocabulary, Mon Cher,* Jane said with a sly smile on her face.

*We met in Paris in forward time under a full moon at Place Dauphine at around 2:00 a.m. several days after the encounter at St. Lazare. Their*

men were at one end of the Place and ours at the
other.

My cousin Robert and I met Delain who looked
like he had been badly beaten and Fulcanelli, who
was accompanied by a very large dog, the one that
nipped me at Cap Manvieux. Her name is Maia.

Fulcanelli wanted me to reconsider and to hew
to my true heritage, which simply meant that I
should obey him. He talked like a maniac about
changing the course of history. There was
something in that moment, a flash of insight, which
gave me the sense that I was no longer completely
subject to his powers, and I scornfully told him to
go away and if he knew what was good for him
never to approach me again.

It was at this moment that a shot rang out and
Delain fell at my feet as a young man emerged from
the shadows pointing his gun at us. He smugly
said, 'Enfin, la belle Jane.' Fulcanelli pleaded, 'no
Kurt not now, not here.'

I know that son of a bitch, I said. Jane nodded
and continued, Fulcanelli lunged for me but at
that instant Maia attacked Fulcanelli taking his
arm in her mouth and pulling him to the ground in
one motion. Perhaps, she made the same
assessment as I had about the new balance of
power between me and Fulcanelli.

*Kurt swung the gun toward Maia but did not fire for fear of hitting Fulcanelli by accident. Maia then released her grip on Fulcanelli and bounded toward me as Kurt turned his gun on us but hesitated. He was clearly confused.  At that point, the Bosch still believed they needed me along with Fulcanelli to detonate their bomb.*

*He moved toward me, but it was then that it happened. You have seen fossils that have been trapped in amber, I am sure.  Well, it  was  as if Robert, my cousin, Maia and I were enveloped in our own field of amber, an encasement that gave us the protection that we needed to  return unscathed to our compatriots with my father's, that is Delain's body, while the young German stood helpless to penetrate the solid barrier that had grown  up around us. His smug expression turned into a combination of hatred and fear.*

*I remained in hiding after that night protected by Maia and my cousins until they managed to make contact with Marguerite several days before our brief rendezvous that awful day in Aunay. Marguerite took me under her wing but did not let Bobbie know of my whereabouts.*

*I take it that Marguerite brought you back through one of those strange time tunnels of theirs,* I asked. Jane hesitated and said, *No, I brought* us back my way. Okey dokey, no feelings of inadequacy here. What the hell could I say to that?

Jane then proceeded to talk about her powers and until then I had not realized that the storm at Aunay sur Odon had been her handiwork and the cause of her weakened state in the crypt of the church. *The power I possess is drawn from a constellation,* she said, *called Auriga, which in Greek mythology represents Myrtilus, yet  another son of Hermes, who died in a chariot battle.*

*I take it that he was real too,* I said, fighting my sarcastic streak.  *You bet,* was all Jane said in reply.

*In my other reality, this is history rather than myth.  The dominant star in the constellation is one called Capella, which is yellow like our sun and more powerful. It is one of the brightest in the sky and the direct source of this power.*

*So, Alchemy is real. It is a real science that utilizes these truths,* she said.  *At its root, is the ability to use physical energy like that from Capella to bend time to one's will, which we have both experienced. This reality views time not simply as the passive backdrop to our lives, like a proscenium stage in the theatre, but as a malleable thing like the four elements -- Earth, Air, Fire and Water. It is the fifth element, one might say.*

*Yet in the eyes of alchemists through the ages, including my ancestors, this fifth element makes Alchemy a fundamentally spiritual discipline. It is a personal transmutation, a purification that is a path to understanding the powers that I have been granted but never desired that have now turned our happy, predictable lives – yours and mine – into a living hell. By the way, I have seen our home in Manvieux, Mon Cher. Someone will pay, I assure you.*

By this point, we had consumed every form of alcohol that our bungalow had to offer. And there were just a few hours until dawn. *I know what you are thinking,* Jane said, *because I know you. Hard to swallow but thank you for putting that silly, inbred sarcasm of yours aside to take me seriously.*

A prisoner of my own tendencies, I pressed on by saying, *I had no choice, Cherie, otherwise you would have instantly propelled me to some weather island in the North Sea.*

She stuck out her tongue and then answered with her own, *fuck you.*

*So, let me guess,* I said, *you also had a hand in our tussle with Franz Six and his crowd at*

*Archangel…the little episode with the flying torpedo…its unusual pinpoint accuracy. Yes, just a tiny bit,* Jane said with a sly grin.

*I was Marguerite's insurance policy in London all those years ago just after my joining forces with her 70 years later. The paradox here again stems from something real. Time moves in two directions and 'the before' along with 'the after' can actually run in parallel or out of sequence altogether,* she said.

We laughed and then groaned at the absurdity of this statement, as well as our situation and just leaned into each other, forehead to forehead. We were both too tired and too buzzed to do much more.

At that, we called it a night and as we began to doze off on a straw mattress in what went for the master bedroom, I asked, *but what about the nucleic device?*

*It is unsophisticated by modern standards but no less lethal,* she answered. *You cannot even tell that it is a bomb. The entire thing is contained in an old urn that is about chest high and as wide as two men.*

*The Bosch may have an alternative to me, but the outcome would be unpredictable. For it to reach its full potential, they need me during the ascendancy of Capella. Think of me as a transformer in a power distribution system, an antenna that can relay and even amplify the exotic force of this faraway star.*

*Even without me, I am afraid that the device could devastate a huge area of the countryside. I also may be the only one who can destroy it or at least blunt its force.*

As we lay there in each other's arms, both sinking into a pronounced divot in the center of our straw mattress, I yawned and asked vaguely, *so what's the plan?*

Jane moved closer to my ear, her eyes barely open, and gently bit me there. She responded by saying, *phuff, unfortunately, I think that we both know the answer to that question, Mon Cher.* At that, we both dozed off but not before I saw the silhouette of a very large animal silently enter the room and lie across the doorway.

# MONTGOMERY JOURNAL ENTRY XXVII

Several days later, my Jed compatriots and I were up before dawn to apply as much spit and polish as humanly possible to our rumpled and dirty uniforms in anticipation of our meeting with the top brass and the Old Man himself. Jane had been shepherded away to another, undisclosed location to keep her one step ahead of our adversaries. That would all change soon.

We arrived at the outer edge of Patton's sprawling Third Army encampment by mid-morning and traversed successive layers of security, phalanx upon phalanx of unfriendly men and 50 caliber M2 Browning heavy machines guns. Babe drove the jeep, and it was a good thing he did, because we had to constantly dodge the comings and goings of Patton's reconnaissance units, which he used to great effect.

Patton favored speed and aggressive offensive action, and he typically deployed these highly mobile scout units by sending them forward to determine enemy strength and positions. Self-propelled artillery moved with this spearhead, ready to engage German positions.

Light aircraft such as the Piper L-4 Cub, which seemed to swarm above us that day like honeybees, provided airborne reconnaissance and served as artillery spotters. Once enemy positions were located, the armored infantry would attack them using tanks as infantry support. Other armored units would then exploit any breach in the enemy lines, keeping the pressure on withdrawing German forces to prevent them from rebuilding a cohesive defensive line.

For our part, we eventually penetrated the center of this frenzied beehive to find scores of tanks lined up in geometric formations with the lead units of the infantry division that they supported. It was the first sunny day in a week, and crews were camped out next to their tanks, some lounging shirtless, but most adding soft provisions to the larder, loading ammo, or tuning up the massive engines of their immense killing machines.

I sat next to Babe in the jeep, who reveled in every moment. If there were something akin to a martial version of Disneyland, the grin on Babe's face suggested that this was it. The ever stoic and self-possessed Marguerite rode in the back casually surveying the scene.

The lead jeep in front of us veered off at a makeshift crossroads. Straight ahead on a hill that someone had labeled "Golgotha" stood a large headquarters tent and a small complex of supporting facilities. This was where Patton lived and worked at least for the moment.

We turned south to a less impressive complex of tents on another hill that turned out to be Patton's air reconnaissance headquarters. Patton was to be an innovator in many respects in creating the American version of the Blitzkrieg, and no innovation was more important than the way he used air power. The speed of the advance that Patton sought forced his units to rely heavily on tactical air support.

The Third Army pioneered the technique of "armored column cover" in which close air support was directed by an air traffic controller in one of the attacking tanks. Each column was protected by a combat air patrol of several P-47 or P-51 fighter-bombers. Using coordinated ground and air power in this way, Patton sought to avoid casualties by using this symbiotic relationship with tactical air support to encircle static German positions while covering his flanks as his armored columns raced around these German formations.

We were eventually deposited in an auxiliary tent that smelled of mildew and that contained little more than a map table and several folding chairs. There we waited for the better part of two hours in stifling heat.

Then, in walked the man. Patton was accompanied by an aide de camp and a Colonel from G2, his intelligence unit. My heart was pounding away in my throat, Babe looked like he was having a beatific vision and Marguerite, well, Marguerite was Marguerite.

Patton was taller than I had expected him to be after watching George C. Scott play the role in the film. He also looked like he was in pretty good shape.

Historians and contemporaries described Patton as foul mouthed and uncouth with a theatrical style that included a polished helmet and ivory-handled pistols. He wore no helmet on that day but was packing an ivory-gripped and engraved, silver-plated Colt Single Action Army .45 revolver on his right hip and an ivory-gripped Smith & Wesson .357 Magnum on his left.

Patton had not forgotten to wear  his trademark riding pants and high cavalry boots. He also arrived wearing his "war face," a stern expression that he had cultivated over the years to motivate his troops.

You know, I have played in a Super Bowl, caught the game-winning interception in an NFC championship game and made all-pro more than once, but I found myself at a loss as to how I should stand, where I should put my arms, whether I should smile or try the war face thing myself. In short, Patton's take-no-prisoners persona made me feel a little wimpy by comparison.

And his attitude went unchanged over the 90 minutes that we spent with him. Marguerite laid out the case for why Patton should approve our mission while Babe and I stood "at ease" behind her. The latest *Ultra* message had raised the stakes by suggesting that Heydrich may have the means without Jane to detonate a nucleic blast.

If true, both sides would lose tens of thousands of men in an instant. The *Ultra* message, presumably from Canaris, offered a two-point plan.

First, the Third Army would agree to hold firm in its position overlooking the approaches to Argentan and would not move on Falaise to close the gap at the Eastern end of the Falaise Pocket. Indeed, a pocket had formed with the Canadian occupation of Falaise to the north and the breakout from the hedgerow country of Patton's Third Army, which was driving toward the Seine River, forming the Western and Southern borders of the pocket. The German Seventh Army and most of German Army Group B could be trapped if Patton's troops turned the corner to go north to link up with the Canadians and close the gap at a small village called Chambois.

The written history of the Allied failure to close the Falaise Gap describes this episode as a major blunder. It is written that Bradley over-ruled orders by Patton for a further push northward towards the Chambois-Trun corridor by his 5th Armored Division, an order that effectively stalled the pincer movement leaving an exit for the German forces struggling to escape the Falaise Pocket. Ostensibly, the decision was taken because Bradley and Eisenhower were reluctant to stretch Patton's already over extended resources across an additional 20-kilometer front.

Closing the German escape route in the narrow gap between Chambois and Trun would in Canaris' view amount to little more than a Pyrrhic victory for the Allies who would soon find thousands of their men incinerated by a nucleic blast. It was a bitter pill to swallow for Patton and his boss, Omar Bradley, the commander of the American armies in France, but they were not going to take the chance that Canaris was right and that the forward elements of the American, British and Canadian breakout from Normandy would be lost in one blow.

A skeptical Patton read the last line of the Ultra message, an admonition from Canaris to both sides, *those of us who have engineered this carnage should burn in hell, but our heroic men should know only honor*. This made an impression on Patton. He hated Nazis, but he respected fighting men like Canaris and Speidel. And thus, the cover story was crafted for posterity.

Patton's displeasure was writ large in the pulsing veins in his neck and one preternaturally large vein that dominated the center of his forehead. After hearing the first German proposal, Patton simply growled, *continue, please!*

Marguerite jumped to the second proposal repeating Speidel's plan, which was to contrive an exchange of nurses, theirs and ours, which was not uncommon on the Western front. Medical personnel were one of the most valuable resources on the battlefield in Normandy second only to the sheer bravery of its fighting men.

Both sides would declare a four-hour cease fire ostensibly for purposes of the exchange. Except during that four-hour period, a group of Speidel's most loyal fighters would lead a Jed team to the location of Heydrich's operation.

Patton's purported flamboyance masked a deeply learned and analytical military mind. Our mission depended on the analytical rather than the theatrical Patton showing up that day, and it appeared that this was the case. It was clear that Marguerite had him thinking.

We were fortunate about one other thing. Patton believed in reincarnation. So, when Omar Bradley's people had briefed him ahead of this meeting about time dilations and their connection with Alchemy, they found a kindred spirit.

Patton in fact had claimed he had seen combat many times before in previous lives, including as a Roman legionnaire. So, it would be hard for him to look askance at the notion of our traveling on the four-lane expressway called Time, which most reasonable people would view as sheer lunacy.

During the 1943 invasion of Sicily, British General Harold Alexander told Patton, "You know, George, you would have made a great field marshal for Napoleon if you had lived in the 19th century." Patton responded by saying, "But I did." Patton also believed that after he died, he would return once again to lead armies into battle.

*Leftenant Martragny, what do we expect to accomplish in four hours*, he asked? *Sir,* Marguerite responded in a professional, measured cadence, we *believe that we can find and neutralize Heydrich's encampment, which we understand to be reachable from where we will make the exchange of personnel.*

*You mean what, a dozen of you against a thousand of Hitler's lethal young bastards swarming around the encampment?* Got to hand it to him. I felt the same way about the *Hitler Jugend* and the odds.

*Sir, unless we are willing to carpet bomb a 100-square kilometer area, we may not be able to destroy the nucleic device. And even then, we may not be successful at that. It is a risk, bien sûr, but one that we must take. There is no other tactical option.*

Patton replied, *this isn't tight. We have not nailed down all contingencies. Can you tell me how we avoid making this a fool's errand?*

Patton's eyes drilled into Marguerite but for the first time he made real eye contact with Babe and me. The three of us had talked about this moment and had a ready answer. It was mine to give.

*General Patton*, I said, suppressing the giant frog in my throat, *we will set a trap that will lead to their destruction in the end by giving them what they want…my wife Jane. Speidel's men will let Heydrich know that they have her after our men have time to get into position. With Jane as the decoy, the Jeds will attack the camp and destroy the nucleic device.*

Patton asked a few more questions. He continued to be skeptical and concerned that Speidel's men or the *Hitler Jugend* would kill Jane on the spot. *Our theory, sir, is that they have too much of an investment in finding Jane to do something precipitous with her because they may still need her powers to achieve a full detonation of the nucleic device. And for that matter, the one person whom they have believed all along was critical to detonating the device may be the only person with the power to destroy it if Speidel's men can get us close enough,* I said.

Patton then left as abruptly as he had arrived, and we were taken to a mess tent for some grub. Marguerite is not the pat on the back type nor someone who would readily let you give her a hug, but Babe and I both congratulated her with a coffee toast for what she had accomplished with Patton.

We waited yet another two hours and then the word came in a brief visit from the G2 officer. *The general asked me to convey the wish -- Godspeed to you all --* then the G2 man hesitated, *and carpet bombing will commence the instant that the allotted four hours comes to an end.*

# MONTGOMERY JOURNAL ENTRY XXVIII

*Roddy, My Friend,*

*I am making this tape, which I will get to Rory shortly, to let you know that Jane and I have been reunited. Exactly how is a long story dating back to the day that I had you burgle the files at MI6 for information about Jed Team Hugo.*

*Your Rory, the warrior princess, who is every bit her father's daughter, can provide you with the color commentary once all is said and done, and I am confident that all will be said and done soon. If Rory demurs, I am quite sure that you are clever enough to find the reams of paper that probably memorialize my interviews with the high command stashed away deep in some vault on your side of the battle line for Time.*

*She is the real Jane, my Jane, the Jane that you know so well. There are many ways that I can tell, not the least of which is that she still to this day cannot tell the difference between a flea flicker and a draw play in American football.*

*She is every bit the Jane that knocked me head over heels in love like a 300-pound offensive lineman hitting me in full stride although she now comes in a different wrapper.*

*I don't know whether it is that of a goddess, superhero, avenging ballerina or what to call it. Her story makes me wonder if the life that I, you, all of us, have known is real or little more than a happy illusion shaped by the elemental battle between good and evil, strength and weakness, which provides the real energy in the universe.*

*I remember how Ophelia used to tell her ballet students that in art there are no upward limits. This whole episode has forced Jane and me to confront this idea in the context of a fight that we did not pick in our callow and comfortable lives. Yet now we must find the strength to surpass our own boundaries and to overcome our deepest despair.*

*We used to watch you and Ophelia, in fact study you both together, because you made being in love look so effortless. I can say honestly that it was not so at first for Jane and me – a rough and tumble footballer and an introspective ballerina.*

*We do not plan to lose each other again nor what we have gained. The next chapter in our lives and the storied history of Jed Team Hugo are now inextricably linked as will be made clear in due course.*

*Perhaps I have had one too many crazy rides in a time dilation or taken one too many shots to the head over the past weeks and months, but I am happy, and we are happy because we have discovered the secret, the point of this crazy story. It is that to feel love, to be loved, one must become a person worthy of it. Absent that, the trappings of being in love are as substantial as thin air.*

*And this love will soon enough bring us to another boundary, one that we will happily cross together to join those before us who confronted their mortality to achieve the eternal.*

*As you used to say, especially when the two of us were drinking too much, Fortune favors the bold. That is a good synopsis of our life plan today and, back at you, my friend.*

*Jane sends her love. Bonne Chance, Roddy and, as always, God Save the Queen and Hail to the Redskins.*

*Charley and Jane*

414

# HUNTER INTERVIEW XXIX, CONTINUED

Yes, for the record, my name is Rory Odile Hunter, MI6, recently attached to Jed Team Hugo for Operation *Hölle* in the Orne River Valley, also known as the Falaise Pocket.

And yes, the operation was a bloody cock-up, plain and simple. No, I can't say that I am being hard on myself when lives were lost.

And no, to be crystal clear, this is no criticism of Leftenant Martragny. None. It was her level-headed leadership in the face of the deadly web spun for us by the three sisters of fate that in the end brought so many of our fighters home in one piece.

The *Ultra* communique set a rendezvous with Speidel's forces at dawn on 17 August at a logging camp that had been reduced to rubble near a crossroads in the shadow of Hill 262. Yes, the same Hill 262 was the storied Mont Ormel.

Charley and Jane and Jed Team Zeke were kitted out in uniforms of the German Medical Corps and were ferried to this point for the so-called prisoner exchange in a German command car and ambulance bearing red cross insignia. My team followed providing support. Babe drove the German command car with Charley and Jane whilst Jed Team Zeke occupied the German ambulance.

The German retreat in the Falaise was so chaotic at that time that Germans were abandoning their vehicles in the face of intense harassment by our air forces to attempt an escape on foot. There was such confusion amongst the retreating Germans that the movement of our teams in the area was a surprisingly simple matter barring a flyover from our own air forces.

Many Germans hid from our fighter bombers during the day if they could. At night, they attempted to make their way to the Orne River where they could cross to the relative safety of the Seine River Valley beyond. As agreed, Patton would see to it that our air forces avoided this sector from 06:00 hours to 10:00 hours on the day of the mission.

My team, comprising a dozen MI6 operatives, followed the command car and ambulance at a close distance on one flank using motorcycles commandeered from the retreating Germans. Marguerite, who was in command of the overall operation, came in on the other flank aided by a small detachment of the Free French Army from General Maczek's 10th Dragoons. As you well know, the Polish 1st Armored Division was operating most capably in the Mont Ormel sector at the time of our operation.

When Charley and Jane arrived at the appointed site, Speidel's men, identified by arm bands with the red cross, were there waiting. Humanitarians they were not. There were 25 of them, give or take, grizzled, severe looking veteran fighters. Overall visibility in the area was poor, as we arrived in a heavy, soaking mist.

Speidel's men were to accompany us to the point on the Coudehard Ridge above the rendezvous point to which Heydrich's device had been traced. It was our mission to take it from there. This long, steep ridge runs North-South roughly parallel to the Orne River and at a right angle to Mont Ormel.

The ridge looked down on the roiling chaos of the German retreat in the Orne Valley below. In a matter of minutes after our rendezvous with Speidel's men, when they were readying to set out, other fighters appeared like ghosts in the mist blanketing the thin stand of trees just ahead on the steep slope of the ridge looming over us. They were clearly German with guns at the ready and a wide phalanx of them moved steadily but cautiously down the hill toward us. The leader of Speidel's group sent a couple of his men forward to get a handle on what was happening.

These men did not get more than a few yards before they were cut down by the approaching Germans, who began to lay down fire against the rest of Speidel's men who took cover and immediately returned fire. Babe got Jane and Charley to cover behind one of the command cars and then joined the fire-fight with Jed Team Zeke and Speidel's men. My team supported them from their left flank.

The attacking Germans hooted and screamed like savages. It was as if we were American pioneers whose wagon train was being attacked by marauding Apache Indians. And then as they got closer, we saw that they wore the *Totenkopf* on their helmets, the skull and crossbones that marked these men as SS. It turned out to be a force of *Hitler Jugend*.

There were too many of them. We had one dead man on Team Zeke and two wounded. Bruno took a few men forward from my team to pull them out of the melee. Babe was nowhere to be found.

Speidel's squad to its credit fought to the last man leaving only two people in the clearing alive -- Charley and Jane, who were still crouched behind the command car. Jane was in Charley's arms, head down in his chest. My team and Marguerite's remained concealed and held fire after Speidel's squad had been eliminated to assess the situation in the hope that we could still salvage the operation.

Suddenly, another command car followed by a small, covered Kübelwagen tore down a dirt track at high speed on the hill from whence the German force had come.  It ground to a halt in the clearing opposite the car where Charley shielded Jane from harm.

An SS officer jumped from the car with such a theatrical flair that he could have been performing a grand jeté in La Bayadere. There was something familiar about him – the theatrical flair and the fact that he was wearing a uniform better suited to a reception at the Reich's Chancellery than the meat grinder of the Falaise Pocket.

Quite right, it was that shit in the bed dandy, Kurt Meyer. His men had found Charley and Jane by then, and Meyer promptly waived them off smugly saying, *nein, nein. Lasse sie sich nähern. Sie sind meine Gäste,* essentially, *they are my guests.*

Then, in the same breath, he turned to Charley and Jane to say, *are you here to help us make history on this beautiful day, Comrades? Please, this way. His Excellency, the Reichsführer has been expecting you.*

He ordered his men to separate Charley from Jane, and a couple of them threw Charley into the back of the *Kübelwagen* whilst Meyer made a show of being the perfect gentleman to Jane albeit one with a Luger pointed at her temple.  We could hear him tell Jane, *if you cooperate, and your sorcery is put to good purpose today, no harm shall come to him.*

As he got into the command car, Meyer surveyed the perimeter of the clearing nervously and ordered his men back up the hill double time.

As I said a few minutes ago, it was a cock-up indeed. We had clearly been double crossed and had lost Jane and Charley in the bargain.

But whilst we had lost control of the situation, Jane and Charley were in play as planned.

I looked across the clearing to Marguerite for instructions, who gave the signal to move forward.  Back on plan?  Not exactly but close enough to make a bloody go of it.

******

Our team beat Meyer to Heydrich's camp by following his men who took a direct route straight uphill on foot to the summit of the ridge.

Meyer's command car and the Kübelwagen got sidetracked by indiscriminate shelling from tanks in the area. In the thunderous confusion of the Falaise, it was difficult to know whether the tanks were ours or theirs.

Eventually, we made it to the top and took up positions. Marguerite and her team were concealed to the south along the summit line toward Mount Ormel to seal a dirt road through a shallow ravine used by the Hitler Jugend to resupply the base.  My position was about the same distance from Heydrich's camp to the north along the ridge line.

Our teams were barely at half-strength as some of my men and the Free French platoon had attended to our dead and wounded in the clearing below.  Nevertheless, we were effective in taking out the first line of German sentries on the approach to Heydrich's camp without raising the alarm.

Marguerite and I were able to rendezvous behind a boulder within earshot of the clearing where the camp stood. It was a foul place and had apparently been used as a latrine, but we had dealt with worse.

The camp was a beehive of activity.  It became clear to us that most of Heydrich's force had pulled out.  This was an ominous sign that we were not far away from his showstopper -- the detonation.

It was also an odd scene. The camp was set against a large stone outcropping from which several springs, starting as small fountains, turned into rivulets that would ultimately feed the Orne and Dives rivers in the valley  below.

The rock outcropping and a stand of very large, very old oak trees created a canopy over the enemy camp. The whole thing could have been a stage set in Tannhäuser or some other Wagnerian opera that evoked a certain romantic Aryan mysticism.  The only thing missing was the white knight and a band of lusty troubadours – Aryan of course.

Heydrich's second line of defense was a more complicated problem as it formed a perimeter of sandbags around the camp with machine gun emplacements every few feet. The sandbags covered three sides of the camp, which was protected to the rear by the massive, overhanging rock formation.

Behind this line of defense was a large tent with a peaked top. With all of the comings and goings, mostly the latter, blocking our sight line, it was difficult to tell what force we would go up against, but we estimated no more than a Company was left. We were still outgunned but had to make a go of it if the opportunity presented itself.

Once there, Meyer helped Jane out of the command car, Luger still held high, and ordered his adjutant to enter the camp to announce his arrival to the Reichsführer whilst for some inexplicable reason he and two of his men casually lingered outside the sandbag perimeter.

Charley emerged stumbling from the *Kübelwagen* on the opposite side of the clearing. A steel helmeted German propelled him forward, holding a gun to his back. Our impulse, mine and Marguerite's, was to cut our losses and rescue these forlorn figures, Jane and Charley, at all costs. But we knew that the consequences of an act so precipitous would be unfathomable and could lead to the annihilation of three approaching Allied armies in a single blast.

It was then that the German guarding Charley again pushed him forward roughly, actually pushed him out of the way. Bloody hell if it was not Babe doing the pushing. He took two quick shots dispatching the two sentries standing on either side of Kurt Meyer, who was slow to realize what was happening.

Babe and Charley exchanged words briefly. Before Babe retreated to the edge of the clearing, he chucked a sheath that contained his large and lethal trench knife to Charley with the words, *good hands, Bud*.

And then everything seemed to happen in a blur. Yes, this is more than a figure of speech. It started with a distortion in our visual field, and the only thing that I can compare it to is looking down on a table as someone takes a tablecloth and ripples it over the top of the table.

The scene with Charley, Jane and Meyer seemed to ripple like this creating a syncopated rhythm in their movements whilst the activities of the Germans in the camp behind them seemed to flow normally in real time. Another way to think about it was that you were watching a stage play with three characters performing a scene at one speed whilst a movie with a different cast of characters was projected on the screen behind them moving at a completely different cadence.

Meyer trained his Luger on Charley, a look of anger washing over him like a massive wave crashing against rocks. As he did, he threw Jane to the ground.

But Charley was too quick for Meyer closing the ground between himself and Meyer in the blink of an eye and slicing the Luger from the Nazi's hand along with a few of his fingers an instant before he was able to pull the trigger. Meyer screamed pitifully, but I did not pity him.

*You've caused us -- my wife, my friends and me a lot of grief, Arschloch, or for future reference even though you have no future to look forward to, Asshole, as we say in my country. See, I have been brushing up on my German dreaming that this moment would come.*

Meyer tried to turn and run toward the safety of the camp, but Charley grabbed him by the collar and spun him around so that the two antagonists stood face to face for a brief moment. Meyer screeched half in agony, half in the fanatical style of the Hitler Jugend and said, *you are too late. There is nothing you and that witch can do. We are barely minutes away from the glory we seek.*

*Let the witch and me work that one out,* Charley said and, as he uttered those words, he drove Babe's knife into Meyer's gut.  The Hitler Jugend leader gasped, tried to pull away, but could not because he was literally hoist on the proverbial petard that Charley held firmly in his gut. Charley withdrew the knife with some difficulty as Meyer screamed again in  anger and agony and drove the knife into Meyer again, this time under the chin driving the blade up through Meyer's jaw and into his brain.

Meyer then seemed to freeze in place, arms akimbo. His handsome and expressive face had turned into a rippling pond of fear and agony. Blood shot from his mouth, which moved as if to scream once more, but there was no sound. His eyes flicked left and right and then his head rolled back as Charley let him drop to the ground dead.

Charley left the knife in the blood-soaked corpse. He must have known then that from this point on there would be no need for self-defense. It was also at this point that Babe made it back to our position. *We need to get the hell out of here*, he said. *Charley and Jane have had their own plan all along. Get the teams running north and south along the upper ridge line but not, I repeat, not down the slope.*

And we did run like hell but not before we saw Charley and Jane fall into each other's arms over the inert form of the *Hitler Jugend* leader and kiss. The kiss was a short one, but they lingered in each other's arms, each looking into the other's eyes, smiling all the while.

They set off for the compound still enveloped in the warped visual field in which the drama with Meyer had unfolded. The frenetic activity of the Hitler Jugend camp sped by on a different plane as Charley and Jane casually walked into the camp seemingly unnoticed.

I was a stage rat at Covent Garden because Mother was a dancer in the Royal Ballet. I had seen it all, and in Opera the death of young lovers was considered sensuous and the suicide of one or both downright sexy. It is the way that our ancestors looked at the world and the meaning of love and death in that time.

I shall forever be angry with Charley, my father's best friend and my second father, for lying to me about their intentions for the mission. But I shall never forget the two lovers, walking together into the jaws of evil, Charley's hand on the small of Jane's back as if he were casually guiding her across Walnut Street in Philadelphia for a Spring stroll in Rittenhouse Square.

Marguerite and I got back to our teams and covered as much ground as we could in the time that we had. It was 10, possibly 15, minutes before we heard something that sounded like a low groan at first, which then grew to such an intensity that it was as though we were listening to the collective moaning of the inhabitants of Hell as the ridge seemed to buck under our feet.

My team hunkered down in a dry riverbed and, over the course of the next several minutes, lay as flat as we could because the forest and everything in it was swirling  crazily around us. One of my men was nearly decapitated by debris, which buried us in the riverbed.

And, as you know, we had chaperones overhead that day. However, we had lost our radios and thus had no contact with the squadron of Australian Typhoons that had been assigned to us by Patton and now circled overhead.

The squadron leader, whom you have also interviewed, described an apocalyptic scene in which an explosion traveled down the face of the Coudehard Ridge to the valley below like a massive Alpine avalanche divided into two channels by a vertical rock escarpment in the center of the ridge. The immense force of the blast concentrated in these two channels propelled earth, boulders, trees and every living thing on the face of the ridge down into the valley below.

Both channels cut a wide swath through the massed crowd of German soldiers and ordinance on the valley floor below creating two large, vacant strips paved with chopped up soldiers, horses and equipment, which were filled in minutes by more retreating Germans coming from the West. There was just nowhere else for the massing Germans trapped in the Falaise to go.

Our chaperones had been cleared to go on the attack once our time had expired, as it had, and we watched from the upper ridge as the Typhoons circled overhead to come in perpendicular to the line of the original blast rippling rockets and plastering the helpless Germans with cannon fire to cut a new swath that intersected the first.

The typhoons joined by other Allied squadrons hit the Germans again and again. With each pass, intersecting the one before, they turned the once bucolic valley into a lattice work of death and destruction, creating great heaps of vehicles, dead horses and dead men.  My thirst for German blood was at its peak then but never in my worst nightmares could I have imagined a more grotesque scene.

Eisenhower said it best, 'The battlefield at Falaise was unquestionably one of the greatest killing fields of any. Forty-eight hours after the closing of the gap, I was conducted through it on foot, to encounter scenes that could be described only by Dante. It was literally possible to walk for hundreds of yards at a time, stepping on nothing but dead and decaying flesh.'

Yes, it was a victory.  Clearly, the Battle of the Falaise Pocket ended the Battle of Normandy with a decisive German  defeat.

More than forty German divisions were destroyed during the Battle of Normandy with the loss of 450,000 men, of whom 240,000 were killed or wounded.

For our part, the victory came at a cost of 209,672 casualties amongst our ground forces, including 36,976 killed and 19,221 missing. The Allied air forces lost 16,714 airmen.

Yes, even had we not walked into Heydrich's trap in that clearing, Charley and Jane had concocted a plan within the plan. Our teams were there to attack the German encampment, using Charley and Jane as decoys and Jane's powers if required.

However, we were to be the decoys and they the tip of the spear. They would make the ultimate sacrifice -- no, scratch that -- they would laugh at that inflated term.

Let's call it the ultimate commitment like so many of our friends, who are now gone, have made to keeping History on some semblance of the proper trajectory. A damned victory, yes, but not one for which I will ever jump for joy.

# EPILOGUE

It was a brisk morning in December 1945, and Old Blood and Guts wore his two, pearl handled revolvers to the  interview with several reporters who kept pressing him on the Allies' failure to close the Falaise Gap. *The bilious bastards who write that stuff for the Saturday Evening Post don't know any more about real battle than they do about fucking,* he remarked later to one of his aides.

*The second-guessing sons of bitches in the war department,* he fumed, had just issued a report that let the British troglodyte Montgomery off the hook and put the blame squarely on his and Bradley's shoulders. He knew that he was in for it from Bradley or even Marshall for the way he had addressed the issue with the reporters because both detested his foul mouth, particularly that brown-noser, Bradley.

But Old Blood and Guts knew that when he wanted his men to remember something important, to really make it stick, he gave it to them *double dirty.* It may not sound nice to a bunch of little old ladies at an afternoon tea party, he thought, but it helped his soldiers to remember. He would often say, *you can't run an army without profanity, but it has to be eloquent profanity. An army without profanity couldn't fight its way out of a piss-soaked paper bag.*

He had wanted to make an impression on the press people, who looked like a bunch of New York dandies in their neatly pressed khakis. The grizzled war correspondents who had been in it with him from the start seemed to have all gone home.

He wanted these dandies to know that had Bradley given him the green light, he damn well could have made the turn north toward Trun and Chambois to close the Falaise Gap trapping virtually the entire German army in the west. Had he done so, there would have been no Battle of the Bulge, where too many good men had been lost, but just a few more months of mopping up the remnants of a devastated German army.

And he knew that if he said all those things that he would be a lying son of a bitch too. Those damn, brave fools had pulled it off on the Coudehard.

The idea that he could lose tens of thousands of men in one blast from the Nazi explosive device hidden in the Orne River Valley was a risk not worth taking, and he considered himself to be the greatest risk taker in modern warfare. In this instance, he possessed the singular advantage of having seen it before in another incarnation when the earth had been lit by a second sun and legions of men had been reduced to ash in an instant by a terrible force.

And so, it would be written that, having dispatched the sons of bitches from the Fourth Estate on this brisk December day when a fresh snow covered the ground like icing on white cake, Patton would set off at the insistence of Hobie Gay, his chief of staff, for a little grouse hunting to get his mind off matters. The hell if he hadn't asked for a command in the Pacific Theater of Operations, begging Marshall to bring him to that war in any way possible, only for Marshall to make asinine excuses for why that wasn't possible.

Instead he had been appointed military governor of Bavaria, where the damn Nazis got their start, to lead the Third Army in its denazification efforts. He had been particularly upset when he learned of the end of the war against Japan, writing in his diary, *yet another war has come to an end, and with it my usefulness to the world.*

They had not gone more than a few miles down the densely wooded hill in his command car when they rammed an Army truck from behind at low speed. Gay and his hunting companions escaped with bumps and bruises, but Old Blood and Guts smacked his head hard on the glass partition in the back seat. He bled from a gash to the head, complaining that he was paralyzed and having trouble breathing.

They rushed him to the hospital in Heidelberg where they discovered that he had suffered a compression fracture and dislocation of the cervical third and fourth vertebrae, resulting in a broken neck and cervical spinal cord injury that rendered him paralyzed from the neck down. They had to put him in spinal traction to decrease the pressure on his lungs.

It is also written that the Old Blood and Guts died in his sleep from pulmonary edema and congestive heart failure 12 days later. *Let them think what they want to think,* he would say to himself.

At 18:00 hours on December 21, 1945, the great General who had raced across Europe to save it, took his leave of this earthly plane to assume his next command on yet another with these words on his lips:

*From this day to the ending of the world,*

*But we in it shall be rememberèd—*

*We few, we happy few, we band of
brothers;*

*For he to-day that sheds his blood with me*

*Shall be my brother; be he ne'er so vile,*

*This day shall gentle his condition;*

*And gentlemen in England now a-bed*

*Shall think themselves accurs'd they
were not here.*

******

The daughter cut in the mold of her father, the former English rugby star and MI6 operative, met him at the  Map House on Beauchamp Place. Roddy was well known to the people there as he lived just around the corner and would come in from time to time to linger in the stacks among the historical engravings and the dog prints. He was a particular fan of Lucy Dawson who drew under the nom de plume, *Mac.*

When she arrived, he was admiring an engraving of the "Charge of the Light Brigade" bordered by Tennyson's poem of the same name. The proud father smiled broadly as he greeted the young woman, an MI6 agent herself not to say a former Penn track star, with a kiss to each cheek. As she looked on, he declaimed theatrically for her benefit:

*Cannon to right of them,*

*Cannon to left of them,*

*Cannon behind them*

*Volleyed and thundered;*

*Stormed at with shot and shell,*

*While horse and hero fell.*

*They that had fought so well*

*Came through the jaws of Death,*

*Back from the mouth of hell,*

*All that was left of them,*

*Left of six hundred.*

*When can their glory fade?*

*O the wild charge they made!*

*All the world wondered.*

*Honor the charge they made!*

*Honor the Light Brigade,*

*Noble six hundred!*

The true significance of the verse was not lost on either one of them. The curator of engravings at the Map House observed from a discrete distance as the two held each other's gaze before the striking girl with the black eye patch put her head on the man's broad chest. They stood there for what seemed an eternity. The emotion of the moment made the curator of the Map House, who collected dandruff on his lapels like the stacks collected dust, most uncomfortable.

Daughter and father eventually snapped back to form and made a beeline around the corner to their favorite pub, the Bunch 'o Grapes, to settle into their customary corner booth. They both ordered double Tanqueray and tonics but used barely a splash of tonic water.

He had promised to give her his decision today. The daughter had laid the proposition out plainly and persuasively.

The time dilation in Hyde Park that had been used by Franz Six to mount his attack on Archangel was one of the most unstable of the unstable bunch known to those who tracked these things. It was like a large worm in meta-space with two heads lacking eyes and any sense of direction, which flopped with an open mouth from one place and point in time to another. And like the two heads of Janus, one portal always faced back in time and the other forward.

Its near end had stayed largely in post Boer War Britain but for one period of several years when it took sanctuary at the Kirstal Abbey in what is today Leeds in approximately 1152. The contemplative and chronically inebriated Cistercian monks who built the abbey and practiced their own brand of Alchemy had unlocked the secrets of the time worm. The mischief they wrought on the history of the continent in the early Middle Ages was only just coming into focus.

The near end of the time dilation in question had now returned to present-day London to settle on the opposite side of Hyde Park from  its former position on Park Lane that terrible night at Archangel.  Access to the portal had been tracked to a point just northwest of Kensington Palace near Campden Hill Square.

The scientists who tracked these things had alerted Rory to the return of the prodigal time worm.  Its presence went largely unnoticed by the average person because after all it was invisible, but its energy field was immensely powerful and during the surges caused by especially large sunspots or the ascendance of a distant star called Capella in the constellation Auriga, it would wreak havoc with electronics in the palace and much of Kensington.

The scientists had also given her their triangulations of where the time dilation could potentially lead one. Therein lay the opportunity that she had put before her father.

Apart from its unexpected dalliance in the 12th century, the  mathematics associated with its touch points in other time periods, which were like large pores on the side of the time worm, had become reasonably predictable barring a solar storm.

Rory could not understand his resistance to the idea she had put forth.  *Papa, I have been, and it was wonderful to behold.* Roddy bore a striking physical resemblance to the Great Sphinx with his long unruly mane and massive head and shoulders, and he sat there as inscrutably as the original. *Do you remember the episode in Le Caprice with Lady Diana? Mama was carrying me, and she looked so radiant,* Rory asked.

*Indeed*, Roddy said, as in his mind's eye, he joined his daughter for that moment at Le Caprice. *One barely knew then that my slight ballet dancer was pregnant but for the red, chubby cheeks that assumed prominence on her face*, he added.

*I don't know where you were then, Papa, off to a rugby match I suppose, but Mama and Diana plus one or two others shared a table at Le Caprice after leaving the hospital they had visited that morning. They were lovely birds of a feather and managed over lunch by sheer force of their radiant personalities to shake off the sadness of that famous morning.*

Roddy's listened, his ruddy cheeks deepening in color. *At one point, both Mama and Diana started laughing boisterously as each noticed small bits of parsley stuck in the other's teeth. They had by then had much too much drink, which may explain my many defects. They behaved like children, drawing the attention of virtually everyone in the room to their lack of decorum.*

*I couldn't help laughing myself. It was such a warm, comical interlude*, Rory said.

*Where were you at the time, Rory my dear, as you played the 'Ghost of Christmas Yet to Come,'* Roddy asked. He wanted to hear more all the while trying to bring the pounding in his chest under control.

*I was at the bar where a not so young royal delighted in grabbing my arse. So much for nobility and for that matter the fingers on his right hand.*

Roddy let out a hoarse laugh and said, *do you mean to say that was you…hah! I thought his injury had been the result of a polo accident! You were dangerous even when you were technically still in the womb, cherie!*

Rory continued, *it was the day that Diana, Mama and a small entourage had been to Midmay Hospital, and their sheer silliness at lunch was a small antidote indeed for the sadness of that morning. Mama was there of course because more than a few of her fellow Royal Ballet dancers were coming down with the scourge of AIDS.*

*I remember the episode well,* Roddy said proudly. *As your mother told it, Lady Diana zeroed in on a 7-year-old boy with AIDS in blue pajamas standing with his nurse during her tour at Midmay. Elegant in a red wool suit with black velvet buttons on the sleeves, your mother never missed a fashion detail, Diana walked up to the boy. He looked up in awe at her shining blonde hair.*

*'Are you very heavy?' Diana asked, stopping. She bent down, picked up the child, and hugged*

*him. The 'Times' the next day aptly wrote that for two or three minutes, the worlds of poverty and plenty were united as the princess and the patient stood in the hallway, the little boy's head resting on Diana's shoulder, his arms around her neck. With a sad smile, the Lady Diana finally put him down.*

*This is why your mother and I admired and loved Diana so much. It was never about fashion or the notoriety of being a so-called Sloane Ranger. We basked in the glow of her humanity.*

*And this is why I hesitate, child, to take you up on your lovely offer. This confounding principle of which you speak gives me pause. That I could alter the trajectory of something so perfect as the time your mother and I had, or this moment between Ophelia and Diana, by reintroducing myself into it anew, is a risk not worth taking. Our life together, as it was, is a treasure that I will covet forever.*

*Roddy added, Rory, I am grateful to you for your exceedingly romantic notion of reuniting me with your mother. There is nothing that I would not give to touch her again or to share an intimate thought with my best friend.*

*But I would not change a thing, and there is no guarantee that the replay or redo or however your colleagues may wish to portray the experience could ever be as good as the original nor risk its ruin.*

Rory knew that this was tearing her father apart, and she conceded defeat. Roddy's decision would be final.

******

It had rained like hell on the drive down from Paris to Blois. The traveler in khaki had arrived in Paris the old-fashioned way this time by a modern airplane rather than by riding a time dilation like a bucking bronco and that was just fine with him.

His plan was to rejoin his compatriot in Normandy before week's end, but the traveler in khaki had one important stop to make first here in the Loire Valley, a rendezvous that he had neglected for too long.  He stayed the night he arrived in a trendy B&B near Blois in a village made for a picture postcard. They called the B&B *La Maison de l'Eglise*, and it bordered on a lush forest that spread to the west atop rolling hills.

He stumbled upon a middle-aged American couple and their two teenage children from Haddon Heights, New Jersey, who were holed-up at the same B&B on their wine tour of the Loire.  Matt Rosenberg was an insurance exec in Philadelphia, so the ever-gregarious traveler in khaki was happy to

446

accept the invitation to dinner from the Rosenbergs to catch up on his hometown.

It was after dinner when they all retired to their rooms in the small B&B that the traveler in khaki overheard Matt tell his wife that their dinner guest was a heck of a nice guy who looked like he had been cut from the same mold as G.I. Joe. The traveler in khaki chuckled and thought to himself, *fuck, if they only knew the half of it.*

Babe had indeed returned home after the war as post-war life in Philly assumed a pleasant rhythm of returning warriors, new marriages and a tidal wave of new bambinos, along with an awakening prosperity that his family and buddies in South Philly had never known before.

Mario had passed away, and he deeply regretted not having had the chance to say goodbye. He wanted to thank the man for making a tow-headed Irish bastard the unlikeliest member of the large and raucous Italian riot that they called the Caffo family. And, for better or worse, mostly better, he was the man he was because of Mario. He would miss going to Sunday mass with him.

His Bolshie brothers had taken over Mario's laundry business and were now captains of industry. No more union rabble rousing for them and just as well because he was not going to be there to pull their fat out of the fire every time a rumble started.

He had once been asked why he didn't want to leave the post-war world for the creature comforts of today's bright and shiny age of digital communications, faux-heroes and eco-everything. The thought had occurred to him. There was a lot to be said for forward time, especially the cool set of wheels he had driven down from Paris.

His resistance stemmed from his loyalty to his family and thus he was drawn to 22nd and Snyder like a homing pigeon to True North. But he was now on the fence because his compatriot in Normandy had been very persuasive and, perhaps, his Bolshie brothers did not need him quite as much as before. His compatriot had a mission to discuss and, because she was involved, he knew it would be a doozie.

A light drizzle set in as the traveler in khaki set off the next morning after wishing the Rosenbergs well as they too set out, but for them it would be a day of vineyard hopping and wine tastings. Babe drove into the forest on a small two-lane road until he turned south on the *Allee Catherine de Medici* which eventually took him to a large clearing.

His destination lay ahead on a low ridge. The white markers of this place of rest shone like candlelight in the gloom and stood out against the backdrop of the green-brown ridge with an honor guard of cultivated cherry trees on its crest.

The carefully groomed cemetery was a memorial to soldiers and civilians who had lost their lives on the retreat from Paris in the early days of the German invasion of 1940. There was a large collective grave dedicated to the unknown, the innocents who were casualties of the German onslaught in this region.

At the highest point of the ridge, there was an area surrounded on three sides by a trellised wood fence on which the locals had trained roses. There were budding white tea roses and huge, blood red roses in full bloom.

There were about a dozen headstones in this area, and in front of three of them were plaques in the ground to single out those who had been awarded the French Legion of

Honour. He wandered a bit before he found what he was looking  for.

The Irish orphan from South Philly dropped to both knees on the cold, damp turf and clasped his hands as he had been trained to do when he was an altar boy at St. Edmond's.  Babe first looked over to the memorial to the unknown where Freddy lay in eternal rest and then back to his sister's headstone and the plaque in front of him, which bore the outline of the Grand Croix, the highest order of the French Legion of Honour, which read:

*Honneur et Patrie*

Leftenant Marguerite Martragny

1920-1944

S.O.E.

*Pour Valoir Incomparable*

le Mont Ormel

21 Août 1944

*Vous le méritez bien*

Marguerite had returned to Mont Ormel with the 10th Dragoons after the episode on the Coudehard Ridge because they were depleted in officers. Among the remaining

French on the ridge supporting the Poles  was Vanessa, now a combat nurse, who had been with Marguerite and Freddy on their exodus from Paris in 1940.

Marguerite had ordered Babe and Rory to get the remnants of their squads back to base, and a direct order from Marguerite was an order indeed. Babe could not shake the memory of the moment that he let Marguerite go with the Poles. He knew he never would.

Of the twenty or so German infantry and armored divisions trapped in the Falaise Pocket, perhaps a dozen were still operating with any degree of combat effectiveness during their mass exodus from the Falaise.

As the German formations retreated eastward, they fought desperately to keep the Falaise Gap from closing, and German movement through the gap on the night of 19 August cut off the Polish battle groups on the Mont Ormel ridge that had been harassing the Germans with great effect.

The Poles controlled about two square kilometers of commanding terrain overlooking the German retreat and were inflicting heavy casualties. The exasperated commander of the German Seventh Army finally ordered the

Polish positions eliminated, launching a pitched two-day battle.

The Poles had hoped to see the Canadian 4th Armored Division come to their rescue by evening on August 20th. They were dangerously low on supplies and unable to evacuate their prisoners or the wounded of either side. Many of the wounded were still stranded in no man's land on the steep ridge and were wounded again and again by the unrelenting hail of German mortars.

There would be no Allied relief force that day. Lacking the means to interfere further, the exhausted Poles were forced to watch as the remnants of the XLVII Panzer Corps left the pocket. The commander of the Poles, himself wounded during the day's bloody fighting, struck a fatalistic note as he addressed his five remaining officers including Marguerite:

*All is lost. I do not think that the Canadians can come to our rescue. We have only about 110 able-bodied men left...Five shells per gun and 50 bullets per man. That's very little but fight all the same. Surrender to the SS is futile; you know that.*

*I thank you. You have fought well. Good luck! Tonight, we shall die for Poland, for France and for civilization! Each tank will fight independently and eventually each man for himself.*

Two hours later, shortly after midnight, Marguerite and Vanessa led a handful of Polish fighters down the ridge about 25 meters to retrieve several wounded men who had been cut off from the main force by a German ambush. They had managed to make it halfway back up the hill with the wounded when the Germans attacked again seemingly from all sides in the tangled woods below the main Polish position.

Marguerite ordered the group to keep going and, as she did, she was hit in the legs by German gun fire. She and two of her men proceeded to lay down covering fire against a force of at least 50 Germans who eventually overran their position to attack the main Polish force in a suicidal effort that ended in hand-to-hand combat and the annihilation of the attacking Germans.

The Polish position on Mont Ormel was finally relieved at 14:00 hours later that day. Vanessa and the wounded survived.

******

She was getting reacclimated but ever so slowly, her heart and mind in conflict, each veering away, one from the other, on different paths that would occasionally converge only to veer apart again. It was a dizzying roller coaster ride.

Her rational side embraced the task at hand as she power-walked with conviction on this late Indian Summer day down Locust Walk to Meyerson Hall for her honors seminar in *The Roots of Modern Zionism*. It would take her, she calculated, two years to gain her Ph.D., and her adviser had encouraged her to participate in this seminar to get her bearings. It had been her life's dream to achieve a Ph.D., in Jewish Studies, one her parents encouraged her to pursue when they were alive.

She urgently needed to talk to Kumar once she was done today to address the future of the portal. Kumar had been one of her best buddies during their respective master's programs at Penn. He was a love and nothing short of a genius, she thought, Nobel Prize material, to be sure. His area of specialization in the School of Engineering was the applied physics of time, motion and matter.

So much for her rational side. Her emotional side had resisted reacclimating to this time and place, the place where she had started her adventure on the weekend of the Dad Vails regatta on the first truly warm day of Spring last year.  As she approached her destination, her mind toggled back to catch a glimpse of the cute coxswain on the Penn rowing team she met that day last Spring, and she wondered whether she would ever see him again.

Her emotional side, which had always held a slight advantage over its rival, struggled with the question of whether this time and place was the time and place in which she could do something truly worthwhile with her life, to get her hands dirty rather than simply admire those committed souls who did.  The events of the past several months, at the same time fretful and exhilarating, made it clear that she urgently needed to answer this question before she was denied the opportunity to choose her right time and place.

Kumar had not believed her wild tale of Nazis and gun fights when they had downed a bottle of Stockvogler's together. He was too busy obsessing about the problems with the portal to open his mind to her incredible story. It had become apparent to Kumar that while one could move in both directions through the area of warped time and space between the portals, its dynamic instability raised the risks of never returning to one's starting point.

Kumar pondered the question of shutting it down. He viewed the whole thing as a personal failure, but Melody knew it was not. These time dilations were slippery buggers.

One solar flare at an inconvenient moment might destroy one's hopes of ever returning home. It would be his life's work, Kumar vowed, to harness this resource, but it was simply too dangerous now for all of the reasons they had discussed over schnapps to allow anyone to use it, especially his best friend, who had already bravely tested it for him.

Her emotional side yearned for the place where she truly belonged, where she was part of something larger than herself. And like Superman or Supergirl, where her origins in another world gave her certain powers beyond the imagination of her adopted world.

And then it happened in a flash. Her emotional and rational selves embraced just long enough to get her bearings. Melody Schwartz knew what she must do. She could not let Kumar close the portal before she used it one last time to return to the time and place from which she had just returned and where she knew she belonged.

******

It was her second time back in less than a week, and the crew bagging the afternoon delivery to Paris pretended to load oysters into their wire mesh sacks as they secretly admired the girl with the tousled bob in gray jeans and a short black leather jacket. She was long, lanky and beautiful like one of those fashion models on Rue St. Honore, but her most striking feature was the black patch over her left eye.

As she had earlier in the week, she bought three-dozen oysters and the counter people at *Marc Viviers, Ostreculture,* just steps from the French side of the English Channel, gazed in awe at the striking young woman as much for her prodigious appetite as her raw beauty. They had asked last time just to be polite whether the three-dozen oysters were for a family feast, and she had responded by saying, *Non, pour moi seulement, no for me only.*

Rory had a few hours before the scientific team would check in again.  In the meantime, she had a date with her platoon of plump #1 oysters and a bottle of Côtes du Rhône. It was a welcome respite from supervising the rebuilding of the cottage and barn sides of the sprawling country house in Manvieux tucked away in the Bocage, which the locals were convinced had been destroyed by a freak gasoline explosion.

The imperious and wall-eyed local magistrate, Madame Leroyer, whom she and her comrades had rescued during the fight with the *Hitler Jugend* had already summoned her to a hearing. Madame Leroyer did not remember Rory, although the memory of the battle with the *Hitler Jugend* had never faded. Now she only traveled between her home and office and then only in the company of two burly Gendarmes.

She interrogated Rory about the ownership of the house. Rory replied by saying that she was simply overseeing its renovation whilst Charley and Jane were away on a missionary trip to India.

Madame Leroyer challenged her, *you mean to say Monsieur et Madame Montgomery? Tous les deux, both?*

*Ça c'est juste, that is correct,* Rory replied. The eye that pointed East and directly at Rory seemed placated by this explanation. The other, which bent noticeably to the Southwest, appeared skeptical.

It was pouring rain when Rory finally sat down to her feast next to a roaring fire in the Godin stove on the cottage side of the sprawling house under the newly painted wood ceiling beams. Her temporary role as its caretaker and construction boss were just about the only things that could take her mind off the roiling inner dissonance of shouted commands, screams of agony, the staccato of firearms and the fury of explosions that were a constant in her life.

Bad business it was, but it was her business all the same, and she had come to a tenuous accommodation with her demons, compartmentalizing them as best she could. But those boundaries would dissolve all too quickly with the intake of alcohol.

The scientists at ICA were optimistic. They were like zookeepers when you got right down to it, and the time dilations were their menagerie of wild and woolly beasts to be studied, tamed and utilized for the good of Mankind. But Rory was skeptical because whenever Man got involved in something like this, it was likely to come to no good for Mankind.

Charley and Jane had been together to the last, and it was their bold maneuver on the Coudehard Ridge that turned the tide for the Allies in the Falaise by thwarting Heydrich's plan to set off a nucleic device that would crush the Allied breakout from Normandy.  It was confirmed that Heydrich had been in the German camp at the time of the explosion although the whereabouts of the slippery Fulcanelli had never been determined. It was rumored that he had slipped away during the exodus of Germans from the camp preceding the explosion.

The experiments presently being conducted by the scientific team had been successful at least in part. They called it a "Grab-n-Go," giggling like silly schoolboys at their play on words.  So far, they had managed to get it right on only one occasion, whilst the subjects of two other experiments were returned from the past to the present in a hideous physical state.

Surrounded by the ghosts and monsters that were her constant companions, Rory sucked the briny meat of a #1 oyster from its opalescent bed and washed it down with the lavish fruit and firm tannins of the red wine as she contemplated the mission she and Babe would soon lead. At the same time, she admired through the rain splattered window of the *salle à manger* the stalwart winter lime trees that lined the gravel driveway and flared a bright red like torches lighting the fall gloom.

******

The day all but done, Rory unfurled her sleeping bag. Charley's beloved black leather furniture had been destroyed in the conflagration with the Hitler Jugend, and the dungeon room was bare. Diamante kept watch on her from the inlaid bookshelf in the rough stone wall with her tail propped up on a stack of DVD's that had not been watched in years, as Maya occupied her customary post across the doorway that led from the *salle à manger* to the gravel driveway – guarding and waiting. Rory knew that dogs had a sixth sense about the return of a loved one.

Rory bunked in the dungeon room because she was more comfortable on the hard stone floor than in a comfortable bed. It was one of the many occupational hazards of her trade.

She listened to Mahler's 2nd Symphony on her iPad. The quirky, moody melody of

Mahler's 2nd skirmished with the sounds of the violent wind and rain buffeting the house. It ended with the famous chorus, *Die shall I in order to live.*

She could not, would not, forget the two lovers who committed themselves to this very idea on the Coudehard Ridge. She should be so lucky one day, Rory thought.

She looked forward to seeing Babe the next morning. He was an exceedingly competent operative and someone that she just liked being around.

The call had gone well with the scientific team. The science was at last falling into place. It might indeed be possible to preserve the outcome that Charley and Jane had paid for with their lives while employing a time dilation to retrieve them microseconds before they met their ultimate fate.

Charley had once told her that the darkness in this part of Normandy drew him in like a black hole whose gravitational pull had captured for all eternity the roar of the men who fought and died here over a half century ago. Rory could indeed hear Charley and Jane in the fusillade of wind and rain that battered the house that night.

God willing, there would be one more successful Jed mission, and she would see them both again in Time.

463